ANN GREYSON

Gotham Kitty

Written by Ann Greyson

First Edition: August 2021

ISBN 978-0-578-70506-4
LCCN 2021904312

Printed in the United States of America

Gotham Kitty

Prologue

THE BROZIANS are an insectoid species with strong exoskeletons that act as natural armor. With greenish-brown color skin, and six feet tall bodies resembling large insects, their two long antennae protruding from their skulls make them deadly in close combat. This nomadic race no sooner settles on a planet in this far far away spiral galaxy, than it wants to change for another planet, usually one that is a spaceport hub for smugglers, their primary line of work.

A cargo spaceship carries a crew of six, including the Captain. After dropping out of warp speed, a small cylindrical spacecraft nearly grazes the side of the cargo spaceship before entering the cloudy atmosphere of a planet around a nearby Sun-like star. This infuriates the Captain, who orders the ship to change course and proceed in the same direction of the small spacecraft.

Coming out of a forest on the planet Malterra is a petite, bipedal catlike being carrying a few colorful plants in her arms. All the while her furry, black tail wags to and fro contentedly. Startling is the combination of humanoid, with feline attributes adding to its structure and design. No sooner does she leave the shadows of the trees when she sees a Brozian firing a laser gun at the door of her small spacecraft. Dropping the plants on the ground, she gets down on all fours about to lumber away until she sees two Brozians surrounding her. After shaking her bushy hair about her shoulders, her sad eyes look up at the insectoid, whose threatening look makes her stubby whiskers twitch.

Despite her stocky, muscular physique, she is no match against the Brozians. When her eyes turn to the cargo spaceship with its entryway hatch open, she knows her reconnaissance mission is over.

While an insectoid secures a steel chain around her neck, two other insectoids ransack her small spacecraft for valuables. Unfearingly, the catlike creature tries to pull away from the door leading to the cargo-hold of the spaceship. By doing that, she manages to annoy the insectoid holding the other end of the chain.

"Settle down. There is no escape," the insectoid demands in a raspy voice.

The creature doesn't understand the Brozian language. She is angry and just glares at the insectoid. Then she hisses and adds a growl afterward for emphasis of her anger, to no effect unfortunately. Upon seeing the display, another

Brozian stares angrily at the creature hissing at her captor. This insectoid doesn't like this delay to their journey.

"Stop haggling with it. Our time is short. Bring the creature to the cell," the insectoid demands.

The cargo-bay doors close. There is a rumbling throughout the smuggler ship, which signals it is getting ready to liftoff from the planet's surface.

The catlike creature crawls slowly down the wide corridor, following her captor. Once inside the cell, two insectoids arrive carrying a large wooden storage box, which shows signs of wear and tear. After removing the chain from the catlike creature's neck, the insectoid tosses the chain to the floor. Then the two insectoids shove her into the box and close it up. Before leaving the room, the insectoids slide the door with steel bars shut and disappear down the dark corridor laughing and talking in their language.

In the dark, the catlike creature's eyes, peering through a narrow slot, begin to widen and change from chestnut brown to a bright green.

"Meow," she calls out in a moody tone of discontent and the fear is setting in.

After a bit of whimpering, her mind spins in useless circles, thinking that her clumsy ways are the reason for her capture. The creature lies down awkwardly in the narrow space and starts to purr.

In a bright corridor nearby, three insectoids are laughing, and joking about what to do about their captive.

"The course is set for the Vlar Station trading port. We will get a good price for her there. She will make an excellent servant."

"What a pathetic weakling this female Catusapien is. The male Catusapiens are fierce warriors by nature with a great deal of pride," says another insectoid to his companions.

In the midst of their conversation, they feel the gravitational pull and a tremor as the spaceship comes in contact with a powerful rotating magnetic field. Right after the alarm sounds, it appears to them that the spaceship is slowing down. This is something the Brozians do not expect.

On the bridge, the Captain at the helm scans his instruments, flicks a red switch, and then his fingers press various buttons on the control panel with diligence, but to no avail. The ship veers toward the edge of the wormhole but inevitably slips into it.

Meanwhile, the turbulence on the spaceship rattles the box holding the Catusapien. It slides across the floor and ends up crashing into the cell's wall. An inside latch breaks on impact falling near her head. She gets up on two legs with the intention to free herself. So, she hopes. With the full force of her body, she drives into a side of the box, sure that it will open. It does.

Quietly, she steps out of the box. Now what?

She studies the cell, searching for an escape route, maybe a ceiling panel she can pry loose, an air duct she can crawl through. But the ceiling and walls are solid steel, blank and black.

All of a sudden, the spaceship shakes a little. The Catusapien's body slides across the floor. Her teeth rattle from the outrageous turbulence. Then, to her good fortune, something clicks, and the steel-bar door slides open on its own. She gets down on all fours and crawls away, disappearing down a metallic hallway.

The spaceship spits out in the Milky Way Galaxy, thousands of lightyears from the Brozians world. In front of the Captain, the long window enables him to see a planet — Earth.

Standing by the window, the Captain's second-in-command says, "This planet looks good for fuel and supplies."

In another part of the spaceship, the Catusapien passes through octagonal doors that open and shut automatically, then carefully crawls down a tiny corridor that leads to the engineering area. The far side of the room leads into several alcoves, an access tube to the Captain's office, and an airlock to the outside. Her eyes fall upon an access ladder leading to the outer hull where she is sure there's a cluster of escape pods.

Before she can leave, she must disable the spaceship. She doesn't want the Brozians to follow her. The perfect revenge against her captors. The Catusapien rises to both feet, pulls open a small section of the dark paneling of the wall and yanks out a few wires. Something pops, the lights in the room start to flicker, and sparks and smoke billow from the circuitry.

She climbs down the ladder and looks straight ahead at the escape pod in front of her. Breaking the seal, the indicator light turns green, and she flips up the cover of the outer door of the small airlock that leads into the escape pod. After stepping inside, she closes the airlock and shuts the escape pod door. Once you know how to operate one ship, you can operate them all. She finds the evacuation button and pushes it. The safety locks disengage, the egg shape pod jettisons from the spaceship, accelerating toward Earth.

Elsewhere on the spaceship, an insectoid performs a random check on the cell, sees the door open and their prize Catusapien missing. "The creature is loose somewhere on the ship."

Minutes later, a search party of two begin to move throughout the ship.

Walking through a corridor, an insectoid says out loud, "Hiding is useless. We will find you."

Upon entering the engineering area, another insectoid sees blue bolts of electricity and a trail of gray smoke snaking from the circuit board on the far wall and suspects the Catusapien is the culprit of the damage.

Using the portable communicator on his wrist, he says to the Captain, "There is extensive damage to internal systems. The creature is responsible."

"Landing is our only option. We will make repairs. And find the creature," the Captain replies.

Chapter 1

THE SKIES OVER TANZANIA are partly cloudy, but every now and then, the sun peeks through the clouds. It is just past 10 A.M., and the temperature is a warm seventy-five degrees on this nineteenth day in December 2010.

In the northeast of Arusha National Park, flamingos wade in the shallow, alkaline water of the Momella Lakes. Everything seems in place in the Arusha region of Tanzania.

On a dirt road off a trail to Mount Meru Forest Reserve on the western border of the park, you can see an empty white Honda Odyssey minivan. Its owner, Allison Banes, is somewhere on the trail. She's far away from the United States of America, her homeland, here in Tanzania with shining optimism — despite arriving just after a bad break-up with a boyfriend. And for a good reason. She is here conducting her PhD dissertation research in behavioral ecology of black-and-white colobus monkeys and documenting the effect of high temperatures on their behavior and health.

Already she has a Bachelor of Science in Animal Science from Cornell University and a Master's in Science in Primate Behavior from Central Washington University in Ellensburg, Washington. Obtaining a Doctor of Philosophy degree in Zoology from Cornell University of Ithaca, New York is the last leg of her long journey of becoming a primatologist. Her interest in studying primates in their natural habitats goes back to age sixteen after taking a part-time summer job at The Buffalo Zoo in her hometown of Buffalo, New York.

Allison Banes is a pretty woman with brown-hair and eyes, slim, very independent, and idealistic. Enjoying the single life for a little over two years, she is doing quite well without her ex-boyfriend, and finds that she can survive without love in her life. It sounds terrible, but it's the truth. At the age of twenty-eight, she is making the most of her life, enjoying all that East Africa has to offer. She is quite fond of the animals, the history, culture, and the people. When her research is over, she's not even sure she will leave this place, she now loves so much.

Like most Sunday mornings, she is walking west of the park, her usual route to the Mount Meru Forest Reserve. Surprisingly, Allison doesn't see any tourists, but after turning to her right she catches a glimpse of a female park ranger wearing a similar floppy khaki safari hat to the one she is wearing. The tall African woman with a pair of round black sunglasses covering her eyes, wearing a khaki short-sleeve button-down shirt and matching pants, black boots, binoculars hanging from a strap around her neck, and her rifle hanging on her shoulder, is heading in her direction. At a closer distance now, Allison remembers seeing her on the route a couple of times before on her many visits to the park. The ranger nods a hello as she walks past her.

Allison settles into a suitable place to park herself for observations. She digs into her tan canvas satchel hanging diagonally across her upper body and pulls out her eighteen-megapixel Canon EOS 60D digital SLR camera. After placing her satchel on the ground near her feet, she takes pictures of a troop of black-and-white colobus monkeys high up in the canopy of the ancient cedar trees. The camera's wide-angle zoom lens vividly captures the white fur encircling their faces and half of their luxurious long tails. She can see their beautiful glossy black fur that is in strong contrast to the long white fringes of silky hair that runs down the full length of each side of their bodies.

The blatant dissimilarity between the black and white of the monkey's fur against the green foliage of the forest creates a powerful form of camouflage. Blending in with the occasional moments of sunlight that forms both the light and shadows in the forest, there is an illusion that the animal is not there despite its obvious presence.

A short while later, Allison is sitting on the ground, writing with a pen in a small field notebook. She takes notes of the monkeys' feeding and positional behavior along with any irregular behavior in the monkeys' interactions. Some of her observations are vital to the dissertation she is working on. She has many theories about the black-and-white colobus monkey species, and she can't wait to complete and turn in her dissertation to the administration of Cornell. She wholeheartedly believes that sharing her contributions from her dissertation research may open up new insight in the field of primatology.

It is the cutest thing to watch how the monkeys nag at each other, chase each other about, pet and caress each other, and so much more. It's quite amazing to her to see so many wild animals roaming freely in the forest. She enjoys the peace and tranquility she feels among God's creatures, so to say. This is just like East Africa, where one is close to the Earth, living and breathing with the Earth's rhythm.

She takes time out to get a cool drink. While reaching into her satchel for a bottle of water, her khaki safari hat falls down her back to hang from its string around her neck. Quickly she takes a few swigs of water from the bottle.

Briefly looking at the partially cloudy sky, she thinks it's a little disappointing. Just like that her focus returns to the rare primates when she hears a screeching sound coming from some of them. What's the commotion about?

Unpredictably, the black-and-white colobus monkeys are on the move. Some start to run one way, some another, while others swing from the tree's branches, the long white hair on their shoulders flying behind them like capes. Still sitting by itself on a branch, one monkey searches through its fur, delicately removes an insect and eats it, perhaps for the salty flavor which animals love, looks quickly about and up at the sky, then takes off fast. Watching their behavior, she wonders what is agitating them?

Something is causing a light wind to blow around in the distance. The stirring air seems out of place in the region. It is coming from above. Something is definitely behind the clouds, but she can't see exactly what it is from where she is sitting on the ground. Only that there is tension in the clouds. Whatever it is, it's coming her way. That she can tell by the motion of the clouds.

Chapter 2

THERE IS A HUMMING SOUND in the air as Allison Banes stands up from the ground. The noise is a physical thing, the sound of something mechanical, an engine of some kind in the sky above. After brushing off some dirt from her khaki three-quarter-length shorts, she takes a gander up at the sky. She recognizes right away the sound is a lot different than an airplane or helicopter.

This must be the reason the black-and-white colobus monkeys are in a state of panic. Animals are more sensitive to their surroundings than humans are and can easily pick-up vibrations from their environment. And judging by the noise, which is deafening now, it all makes sense to her.

Whatever is making the noise is closer to her and fast approaching.

To her surprise she sees something descending from the clouds that is so shocking. At first, she cannot make herself believe it. It looks like a spaceship. She has to adjust her tortoise-shell frame eyeglasses for a moment to see what she's looking at.

It is fully visible to her now. And its engines are making a loud distressing sound. Her jaw drops and she puts her hand over her mouth to stifle a gasp.

This can't be happening. The same sentence runs laps inside her head.

Lowering her hand from her mouth she asks herself aloud, "Is this real, or am I dreaming? Is it really a spaceship?"

One thing she knows for sure is that she is not on a movie set. There is no film crew around that she can see. And it isn't like her to fantasize or see things that aren't there. It just isn't in her nature to do that. She's always been a commonsensible woman with her feet on the ground.

There it is. An alien spaceship with strange symbolic markings on its sides flying overhead. The outer covering is like an alloy of titanium and beryllium, rather than steel, but she can't say for certain. Yes, her eyes are not deceiving her. She is slowly tucking her hair behind her ears, a tic of hers and something she does when she's nervous.

What Allison Banes fails to notice, or hear the roar of, is an escape pod descending no more than forty feet away. During the descent, a metallic, pyramid-shape parachute opens and gently lowers the pod, tearing into the upper branches of the forest and shearing through the canopy. After the pod lands safely on the African soil, a catlike being crawls out of it. The creature is struggling a little for breath, its hand clenches in a fist over its chest. It is having trouble adjusting to breathing the air on the Earth. Apparently nauseous and displaying an onset of weakness, it curls up on the ground and knocks out — and yet Allison sees none of it.

It dawns on Allison that she needs to call for assistance. Picking up her satchel from the ground, she begins searching for her cell phone inside of it. She is about to grab it. She hesitates. Who is she going to tell? What about the police? She doesn't think so. Still, she feels she needs to inform someone. But who? Not knowing many people in Tanzania, she just can't think of anyone capable of dealing with this. She'll wait and see how it all plays out. Though she doesn't see anyone in the vicinity, she is sure, eventually, someone is bound to notice, and word will get out to the proper authorities, whichever they may be.

As a soon-to-be primatologist, it is natural for her to wonder what kind of species are on board the spaceship. What planet does it come from? Is she about to make first contact with an alien civilization? Hopefully, the aliens inside aren't threatening or dangerous. She doesn't plan on dying today.

This is the time she thinks about taking pictures. Most unexpectantly, the spaceship makes loud mechanical noises that are unnerving and sound like some sort of malfunction. With a sonic crack the spaceship explodes midair right before Allison's eyes, and before she can pull out her digital camera from her satchel. The explosion breaks the vessel into tiny, burning fragments that fall to the ground. Despite her distance, she uses her hands to cover her face from debris and heat.

"There can't be anybody alive on that ship after that," she says in shock.

For the rest of the day her studies of primates are off the table. Instead, she will check out the alien spaceship crash site. Perhaps there are survivors. She can only hope.

Allison reaches into her satchel hanging diagonally across her chest, pulls out a surgical mask, and places it on her face. Not long after, she steps into the area with debris from the ship on the ground, some pieces still burning. There are wisps of smoke in the air, but not enough to attract much attention.

There isn't much left of the spaceship. To her disappointment, there are no signs of life anywhere around her, except for a lone blue monkey sitting on a branch in a nearby tree, watching her intently. The possibility of the ship being devoid of life and under control by a master computer crosses her mind. This makes sense as to why she can't find any life forms. What now? Is it worth her time to filter through the wreckage? She ponders this for a beat.

Just when she is about to throw in the towel and go about her merry way, she turns her head in another direction and sees something in the distance on the ground. Can it be? A survivor? Is it really an alien, or an animal hurt by the falling debris? She suspects her eyes are playing tricks on her but needs a closer look to know for certain.

As she walks onward, coincidentally in the direction of where her Honda minivan is, she regularly looks in all directions. Still, no one is around. Venturing closer, she thinks more and more that extraterrestrial life is a certainty after all. It looks like she will be making first contact.

Is she ready for the find of a lifetime? She isn't exactly sure what to do. Yet, she moves forward, if only from mere curiosity.

Chapter 3

WHATEVER IT IS, it's sleeping beside a tiny spaceship having an outer shell like an alloy of titanium and beryllium. This is what Allison Banes sees now that she is standing around ten feet away. It is definitely not some wild animal. A real alien! she thinks to herself. She has to pinch herself to make sure this isn't a dream. Sure enough, it is real. Butterflies flutter deep inside her, knowing that she is discovering a new species — and one from some other planet — most likely from some other solar system.

Still staring in disbelief, she slowly takes a few more steps closer, carefully in her brown hiking boots, not to disturb the alien. After stopping a foot from the creature, the first thing she does is visually examine it with her eyes for a moment. From what she can tell, it doesn't look hurt, because there are no visible injuries on its body. Looks like a cat with human qualities but it is from another planet, so it is not actually a cat. A hybrid, petite female with an athletic body, a bushy mane of brown hair, small furry ears atop her head and a long black tail. In Allison's eyes, she thinks it is rather cute to some degree.

Now, she has the intention to help the alien, but hesitates about what to do. Something in the back of her mind tells her to be on guard. She has no idea whether this alien may or may not be hostile. Is she willing to take such a risk? As she asks herself this very question, she knows the answer already. Yes, she is going to assist this alien. Whatever the reason, her gut tells her this is the right thing to do. In the strongest possible way, she feels the alien is harmless, so she convinces herself.

It seems so peaceful in a deep sleep. In such a vulnerable state, it is completely non-threatening. At least she tells herself that and hopes for the best as she starts to disentangle the cords of the parachute from around the alien's legs, using her bare hands. Pulling out a washcloth from her satchel, she gently wipes off some loose particles of dirt from the alien's body.

Now what is she going to do? Is it wise to wake up the alien? If she does, will it run away from her? So many questions like these permeate through her mind, while she stands over the alien, looking down at it.

Thinking fast, she glances over her shoulder. The area is quiet. There is no one around that she can see.

There is only one thing she can do. Take the catlike creature home with her. She smiles, suddenly giddy by this way of thinking. Yes, that's exactly what she will do. To her it is like a stray animal. Ever since she can remember, she's the kind of girl who is always ready to take in a stray animal that needs a home or medical treatment.

Rather nervously, she bends down carefully lifting the catlike creature up off the ground trying not to wake her. Once she has the alien in her arms, she stands and carries her off.

"You are one heavy extraterrestrial," Allison says to the sleeping alien.

She doesn't expect a response. But she speaks anyway, out of frustration in carrying the possibly ninety-pound alien. How thankful she is that the alien is not awake. For all she knows, it may be hostile. Though she keeps telling herself it isn't, especially at this moment.

Her arms and back hurt when she arrives at her Honda minivan. Somehow, she manages to pull the keys from inside her satchel, unlock and open the door, and lay the sleeping creature on the backseat. Still, the alien doesn't wake up.

As she closes the door softly, trying not to wake the catlike creature, she realizes the chance she is taking. She doesn't know what she's getting into and doesn't care either.

Taking a moment to brush off some dirt from her camouflage V-neck T-shirt, she thinks about the escape pod. Is it wise to leave it out in plain sight? It's too heavy for her to carry. A beat or two later, she smiles wide amusing about it. There is no other option for her but to leave it where it is.

"Let someone find it and wonder," she says and shrugs her shoulders like it's no big deal.

Allison Banes gets into the driver's seat and closes the door behind her, letting out a long sigh of relief. After she tosses her satchel and her floppy khaki safari hat onto the passenger seat, she removes her eyeglasses, rubbing the bridge of her nose between a thumb and forefinger. Her mind is spinning with excitement of the days' events. She can just imagine what will happen when people discover the wreckage of a spaceship and an intact escape pod. Will they believe there are aliens loose in Tanzania? It's possible. She can just imagine reporters from CNN talking about aliens landing in Tanzania.

Quickly, she looks at the alien in her rearview mirror. The creature is still asleep. After a little laugh to herself, she is ready to go. Shaking her head, she starts up the minivan and the song "A Piece, A Chord" by Bobby McFerrin comes pouring out at a low volume from the speakers in the vehicle on the radio station. She quickly reaches for the radio and turns the knob to the off position. Then she puts the minivan in drive and takes off.

After turning left onto Sanawari Road, she decides to take the longer route back to her house, driving the rest of the way on the empty dirt roads to avoid having other cars get in her way. Little does she know in that instant the alien's eyes suddenly blink a few times as it seems the creature is slipping out of consciousness. For a brief moment, the alien lifts her head up. Her eyes open a crack while her little, round, black button nose twitches as she sniffles a couple of times. The reflection of the white clouds sliding across the windshield mesmerizes the drowsy catlike creature. The heads of two giraffes near the road appear in the window of the slow-moving minivan. The animals catch a glimpse of the creature clinging to the corner of the backseat. Their image sends the alien into shock, her eyelids droop shut, and she falls into a deeper sleep.

Chapter 4

AT A LITTLE PAST TWO IN THE AFTERNOON, Allison Banes is home. Home is a small, white house on Kigongoni Road in the Arusha area of Tanzania. The spacious, one-story house has a living room, kitchen, two-bedrooms, one bathroom, a sitting room serving as an office, and a backyard that covers 200 square meters.

Allison is now wearing a white and blue-stripe V-neck T-shirt, loose-fitting ankle pants, and brown leather sandals. She stands nervously in the living room, looking as if she is pacing inside her head as she waits for the alien to wake up. After removing her glasses, she polishes them on her T-shirt, then perches them on the bridge of her nose. What an odd species, she thinks to herself as her eyes scrutinize the alien, body together like a ball, on her mauve fabric sofa cozily asleep. But for how long?

Is it sick? How can she know for certain? The only logical thing to do, she decides, is to give the catlike being an examination for any possible injuries and what have you. To Allison Banes, this alien is just like any other primate that she can observe and study. Thinking she has a spectacular discovery on her hands excites the aspiring primatologist. She can't wait to begin.

As she enters her office to grab the necessary items for her examination, she knows that most primatologists dream of this very opportunity. When she brings forth the alien, she will be the envy of them all. She is certain this is a step toward making scientific history.

After nervously putting on her white lab coat she pulls with a trembling hand off the back of the tan leather swivel chair at her heavy oak desk, her elbow knocks down a metal pencil holder spilling the pens and pencils all over the desk. Quickly she gathers them back into the holder before putting some items in both of her lab coat pockets. Then she leaves the room.

Back in the living room, she zeros in on the alien lying on her sofa. As far as she can tell, the alien is still sleeping. Allison proceeds as if she is, anyway. She watches the alien for signs to the contrary, but she sees none.

She pulls out a Panasonic microcassette tape recorder from her lab coat pocket, presses the Record button and says, "The specimen is asleep. Upon examination, the female adolescent is approximately seventeen years old in human years, a little over two years in cat years. She has human and feline anatomy."

After putting the tape recorder on pause, she lays it on a round maple end table by the sofa. Next, she takes out a stethoscope from her lab coat pocket and presses the cold metal disk to the skin of the alien's back. Surprisingly to her, the alien has a heart. And the heart sounds good. It is a normal sixty-four beats a minute.

Reaching into the pocket of her lab coat, she puts the stethoscope back and pulls out a six-inch mercury glass thermometer. After carefully placing the thermometer in the catlike creature's mouth, with its bulb under her tongue, Allison waits for two minutes before removing it and putting it back in the same place where she next pulls out a flexible tape measure. She measures the alien's body, finding that her legs are longer than her arms, and measures her long black tail.

Afterward, she picks up the tape recorder, speaks the results and ends with, "The tail is fifteen inches long."

Pause. That's when a bright idea comes to her: a testable theory about the alien that seems to make some sense in evolutionary terms. But it will require a blood sample to know for sure.

She runs a finger over the black tape recorder, presses Record again, and says, "I will take a blood sample for DNA analysis."

Allison leaves the living room and returns a moment later with a syringe. When she uncaps it, she carefully inserts the needle into a vein in the alien's arm and draws blood. As soon as it flows into the tube, she notices the alien's blood is a bluish-purple color and looks forward to further analysis. Once the tube is full, she removes the needle. Then she applies pressure to the site with gauze for about two minutes. And still the alien does not wake.

Back in her office, she places the vial of blood in a small, white refrigerator where she stores specimens of sorts and tosses the needle in a small, green metal garbage pail, with a black polyethylene bag as a liner, in the corner of the room.

Upon returning to the living room, she freezes in her tracks when she sees the creature is awake, eyes wide open, looking directly at her. This startles Allison, but she isn't afraid, and neither is the alien.

She pulls the tape recorder out of her lab coat's pocket, presses Record, and excitingly says, "The specimen is awake. She is curious and demonstrates no fear of me."

There is a slight hesitation as Allison doesn't know what else she's going to say. She looks the catlike creature in the eyes, smiles warmly, then opens her mouth to speak, and the words come spontaneously.

"Welcome. You are on the planet Earth. I am a human being. My name is Allison. Where do you come from?"

Not understanding, the creature responds confusingly with a soft meow as she slowly wiggles her body, changing her posture and position of her legs.

"This species uses feline communication such as body language, facial expressions, and vocal sounds," Allison states, pushes the Stop button on the tape recorder, then puts it back in a lab coat pocket.

Shaking her head sleepily, the catlike creature comes off the sofa and crawls around the room. Trying to focus her brown eyes, she seems to probe everything. Things are still a bit blurry. The light coming from the window attracts her attention. When she gets to the living room window, she cautiously peeks out and shudders a little bit before returning her gaze on Allison.

The alien proceeds to approach Allison but stops midway, twitches her black nose, and sniffs the air. Suddenly she lowers her head humbly, crawls back onto the sofa, and immediately falls asleep.

Allison grabs a patch-work quilt from the hall closet and tosses it over the extraterrestrial before returning to her office. Sitting in the chair behind her desk, she turns on the desktop computer. Afterward, she retrieves the vial of the alien's blood. More on a whim than anything else, she runs some DNA tests on the blood and discovers that chromosomes 3 and 7 of the alien are homoeologous to human chromosomes 1, 7, 19 and 22. Confoundingly alike, the alien's DNA appears to share the same protein-coding alphabet as humans. She enters her findings into her computer.

After turning off the computer, she grabs her notebook, takes a pen from the pencil holder, and quickly jots down a couple of notes regarding the reason she believes the alien is so sleepy. That it is suffering from something like jet lag. And her body needs time to adjust to the air on Earth. Allison also jots down notes about the spaceship and the escape pod from earlier that morning in Mount Meru Forest

Reserve. After that, she plays back the tape recorder, and starts to write everything down.

Four hours pass and there are ten pages in her notebook. And her head is still spinning, bursting with many theories about the alien. Abruptly, she looks at the digital clock on her desk. It is five after eight. She has to stop the images in her mind and eat something. She has to stop being a primatologist-in-training. After switching off the desk lamp, she leaves her office.

After a quick meal in the kitchen, her eagerness to research and record the data about the alien is gone from her mind. Now, in the bathroom washing up for bed, she successfully avoids thinking about the alien. But not really. How can she?

Still, she is sleepy now from a long and eventful day. Leaving the bathroom in her bedroom, she goes to peek in on the alien fast asleep on her living room sofa. She squints at it, yawning as she runs a hand through her hair.

"Good night, whoever you are. See you in the morning, little space alien," she says, then heads to her bedroom to change into pajamas and turn in early.

More analysis will continue tomorrow, she thinks to herself as she shuts the bedroom door, (just in case). After climbing into bed, she reaches over and turns off the large ceramic lamp on the glass bedside table. Smooth ivory, satin sheets coolly caress her bare legs as she climbs into her king-size bed for a night's rest. Briefly, she stares up at the mosquito canopy hanging from the ceiling over the bed, then drops into a dead sleep.

Chapter 5

IN THE DARK OF A SUNDAY NIGHT, a couple of small fires burning on the ground glow in the area surrounding Mount Meru. It's around nine o'clock, and the Wa-Chagga, or Chagga, Bantu-speaking indigenous Africans, happily congregate on the southwestern slope of Mount Meru. The Chagga are the third largest ethnic group in Tanzania, and you can find the bulk of them occupying the bountiful slopes of Mount Kilimanjaro, on the south side of the mountain where rainfall is high. On the southeastern half of Mount Meru is where you'll find the Meru, a Masai-like people due to their closeness with the Wa-Arusha, despite being a branch of the Chagga with strong linguistic and cultural affinities.

The drizzly sub-montane microclimate in the foothills nurtures the rich volcanic soil to agricultural extravagance. For many years, the Chagga, an agriculturist people, make use of the fertile soil to grow Arabica coffee, bananas, and medicinal herbs they sell at local markets in Arusha.

Around a campfire, are a hodgepodge of onlookers watching a shirtless and shoeless African man slicing off slabs of meat with a razor-sharp cleaver. When he pauses a moment to gaze fiercely into the fire, the multicolor bead necklaces around his neck catch the glimmer from the fire. After shoving the handle of his meat cleaver in the belt of his brown trousers, he starts roasting the meat over the fire in a cast-iron skillet.

A feast is in preparation to honor Ruwa, a god who lives in the sky. Regardless of the fact that many Chagga are predominantly Christian, they still worship Ruwa because he is their Supreme Ancestor and Supreme Parent. By tradition they believe that all men descend from Ruwa, their great protector, a liberator and provider of sustenance who they seek for power and assistance.

Shortly after dinner, the women and children stand in a cluster and sing a song in Kiswahili, the East African Bantu language. Behind the group of singers are two African men sitting on wooden stools, fiercely beating on round wooden drums with their hands. The two young men have on red kitenge shirts with orange patterns, dark trousers, and sandals. At times during the song the crowd sways from side to side, and some laugh and clap their hands.

Standing a little off to the side behind one of the women, is the Mangi Mkuu, or Paramount Chief, Anton Naruma, the tribe's administrative and spiritual leader who knows all the rituals. He scans the gathering, watching, and listening intently.

Chief Naruma smiles with his false teeth that are too white. It is clear he is enjoying his tenure as foremost chief. Standing at 5'5," wearing a black fabric kanga around the hips over a pair of long tan shorts, the slim man has white in his afro, genial features, and an exceptionally warm smile. He has a small goatee, is sixty-five, but with a short cut 'Afro' and thick round glasses he can pass for fifty-five, not that he gives a hoot about how old he looks. He shaves once a week when it starts to itch. When the weather is cool, which is most nights in Tanzania between June and September, he will grow a beard.

As soon as the song is over, the crowd disperses, and Rhoda Kisanga, a heavyset, buxom African woman of mature years with a wide silver ring through her nose, wooden necklace around her neck, wearing a bright peach and brown pattern head covering with matching kitenge wraparound skirt that reaches to her ankles, starts to gather all the children.

"Come my children," she says leading them to sit down.

The obedient children sit on the ground around a campfire. While some of the adults stand in the background, chatting together in low voices, others sit on flimsy looking wooden fold-up chairs.

It is around this time of year in December that the children hear the tale of Kwaad Skaduwee Takwimu, the Evil Shadowy Figure. The adults know this story all too well. Some of the older children know it too.

This is when Chief Naruma smoothly maneuvers right into the center of the gathering.

"Thank you, Rhoda," he says to her, as she takes a standing position in the back.

Twenty of the small children, some sitting Indian style, some lying full-out, chatter away. Chief Naruma sees this and doesn't like tomfoolery. Standing in front of them, he raises his arms to quiet them. They obey.

"Who understands the curse of the Evil Shadowy Figure?" Chief Naruma asks, but to no one in particular.

All heads lower as the kids are silent. No one volunteers. Chief Naruma's eyes move slowly and methodically around. He waits. Dead silence.

Most eyes follow Chief Naruma as he paces now, slowly in front of them, staring at them.

Eleven-year-old Laila Diwani lifts her hand slightly, and the kids around her breathe a collective sigh of relief.

"Please explain," he says.

Laila does not look at him. "The Mount Meru volcano erupts in the middle of a Chagga sacrificial ritual. A dozen or so innocent people die in fires in and around Chagga huts. That makes Ruwa angry — and so comes the curse of the Evil Shadowy Figure."

It is something you expect of her. Laila and her nine-year-old brother, Toby, sitting next to her, are direct descendants of one of the victims of the fires. Laila can recite the story of the Evil Shadowy Figure backwards and forwards, and in her sleep if necessary. Unlike his sister,

Toby doesn't care about curses or evil spirits. He's a rough-and-tumble boy, physically active and needs to play.

Chief Naruma walks up to a little boy who has his eyes in another direction, and says, "Pay attention, little one." He then turns to Laila and asks, "That's good. What else?"

"Be careful not to go too close to the fire. That's where the Evil Shadowy Figure dwells, controlling the souls of the victims of the long-ago fires. If you are bad, the Evil Shadowy Figure emerges from a dark portal in the flames, pulls you into the fire and takes your soul."

"You are right. A terrifying spirit, so scary, you can't look into its fiery black eyes!" he exclaims, holding his walking stick up high with his right hand.

The children sigh in unison. Chief Naruma has their complete attention. With his wooden walking stick and colorful personality, the children are in awe of him and listening to his every word. Even the adults lean in closer to listen and watch.

Chief Naruma continues his speech telling them the Chagga legend. During the great drought, over two hundred years ago, the paramount chief at the time declares it as a sign that Ruwa is angry. He convinces the tribe that a sacrifice will make everything alright. It is not uncommon for the Chagga to offer animal sacrifices to Ruwa and the spirits of their forefathers. A volcanic eruption ensues. But the ritual with a goat continues at the insistence of the Paramount Chief. Chagga huts catch fire and people die. Born from the burning ashes of those dead in the fires is the Evil Shadowy Figure, an evil spirit as a curse upon the

Chagga from Ruwa, angry at the Paramount Chief's selfish and irrational behavior, carrying on the ritual despite an impending volcano eruption.

Two African men take a seat on the wooden stools and begin to pound on the drums with their hands.

"Evil Shadowy Figure going to get you, going to get you," the women sing.

"Going to get you. Going to get you," the men sing.

"Evil Shadowy Figure going to get you, going to get you," the women sing again.

Now, close to eleven o'clock, the parents gather their children and begin to return to their homes.

Nobody notices something causing one of the fading campfires to pop, snap, and send clouds of dark smoke into the dark sky. Fiery black eyes peer from the flames. Slowly, the Evil Shadowy Figure materializes to its full form in the fire.

What causes the evil, restless spirit to appear is a mystery. It is apparent that there is a disturbance in the supernatural sphere, a clash between good and evil, a direct effect on the years-old curse on the Chagga. What is the disturbance? The Evil Shadowy Figure senses the alien's presence.

For a short while longer, the Evil Shadowy Figure lurks in the burning fire. As it begins to fade away, a cackling sound echoes loudly from the fire even after it vanishes from sight into the flames that dissipate thereafter.

Chapter 6

BY MIDNIGHT CHIEF NARUMA is back in his small wooden hut, a cabin-style house with one-bedroom, kitchen, and bathroom. Living there ten years now, it's a good distance away from, although originally part of, Saddle Hut, spacious rental huts with lockable doors, bunk beds, and kitchenette. The rental huts serve as a base camp for tourists to summit Mount Meru. The vicinity of the hut is aflame with pineapple plants and red-hot pokers, a plant that has unique flower spike stems jutting from grass-like foliage.

After putting away his walking stick in a closet in the hallway by the front door, he is anxious to get to bed. After stripping off his clothes and kicking off his sandals, he heads to the bathroom for a quick shower then dresses into a long African tunic, his sleepwear.

Twenty-five minutes later he is still in the bathroom conducting his nightly routine. He gets a little glass jar and a denture cleaning tablet from the cabinet. He removes his dentures and places them inside the jar. After filling the jar with warm water at the sink, he drops in the tablet which immediately dissolves and fizzes in the water. He places the jar on the counter, next to his toothbrush and then leaves the room.

After placing his eyeglasses on a small wooden table by his cot-size bed, he gets into a restful position on his back in the bed. Resting his head back against the large goose-down pillow, he pulls a rust-color blanket up to his chest, closes his eyes and drifts into a deep sleep.

That night Chief Naruma has a vivid dream that transports him to "long-ago Africa." In it, the Evil Shadowy Figure is present. He is not sure where he is or what is real. Tossing and turning in bed, he groans as images of burning huts and people screaming scatter through his mind. It is 1809. He is witness to how the curse of the Evil Shadowy Figure comes to be.

The next morning, he awakens abruptly from his sleep. This is the first time that he can remember ever having a vision of this story that passes on to every generation in the Chagga. He sits in bed for a long moment and tries to remember everything from his dream.

The first thing he remembers seeing is the Chagga Paramount Chief performing a ritual of animal sacrifice in the foothills of Mount Meru. Without warning, the ground shakes briefly like a small earthquake. The drums stop beating and the women stop swaying and singing. The large gathering of men and women anxiously stare at the Chief. The minutes pass and nothing happens. Not taking it seriously, the Chief, a tyrant in his own right, insists the ritual continue. For a while, everything seems perfectly normal: the women keep chanting and singing, the Chief prays to Ruwa and then slaughters a spotless male goat.

Then, the most horrible thing happens.

The plates shift beneath Mount Meru, magma pushes upward, pressure builds, and a minor eruption occurs. Small boulders scatter, and a series of rapidly moving lava flows make contact with the Chagga huts directly in its path. The bee-hive huts with banana-leaf roofs and woody vines that intertwine between the walls of flexible branches from trees and shrubs stand no chance against the lava stream. All panic breaks loose as men, women and children try to escape the area full of rolling smoke and poisonous gases. Many are able to escape, but about a dozen people aren't able to run fast enough and die in the rapidly spreading fires.

"Somebody, please help them," Chief Naruma protests.

No one sees him. No one listens to him. From the sidelines, pacing frantically, he simply watches it all unfold in a surreal dream state.

From nowhere, a young African woman comes stumbling out of a burning hut. As she walks forward, sulphureous vapors and smoke surrounds her and rises to the turbulent, cloudy sky.

"Can someone please help this woman?" Chief Naruma screams out.

The woman, wearing a multi-color kitenge wraparound dress that reaches to her knees, stops walking to look at him. There is a smudge of black soot across her face, and streaks of black soot on her arms, legs, and bare feet.

With a look of desperation on her face, she says, "Help me."

"How can I?" Chief Naruma asks her.

Tears stream through the black soot on her face, and drip off her chin. "The one you seek is here. You must find the one. It is the only way."

"Who is here?"

"He is jealous of it."

In that moment, a powerful vacuumlike force begins to pull her body backward into the smoke and darkness toward the fires burning in the background.

The last thing she says is, "Find the one before he does."

Her body flies into a raging fire and consumes all of her. The next thing Chief Naruma sees is a slowly developing image in one of the fires. Then he hears many voices at once. What is emerging from the flames?

With loud cackling, the Evil Shadowy Figure materializes before his eyes. He begins to approach him. The fear is obvious in Chief Naruma's eyes, but he manages not to flinch, wanting to see how this plays out.

How can anything occur that Ruwa does not want to occur? Something isn't right. In all his life, this is the first time the Evil Shadowy Figure appears in any of his dreams.

The Evil Shadowy Figure stops, just feet in front of him. He lets out a loud screech, waits a moment or two, and then lets out another one. He is angry. Why is he looking so complex, as if something is disturbing his sanctity?

He says something that sounds like a strange language to the Chief but actually it is a cacophony of voices speaking constructively together, speaking at different levels. Another loud screech before he pulls himself backward and magically vanishes into the flames in the background, and then everything goes to black and Chief Naruma falls into a deeper sleep.

Still sitting upright in bed, Chief Naruma blinks his eyes, and his foggy head clears. He comes to a shocking revelation. In that instant everything changes for him. He interprets the dream as a sign of the end of the curse of the Evil Shadowy Figure on the Chagga. That the alien is here in Tanzania, the one the Chagga are waiting for. It just has to be. He has come to that conclusion that it is the only explanation as to why the Evil Shadowy Figure is so furious.

Something else that comes into his mind is that he must familiarize himself with the ritual to end the curse. As Paramount Chief of the Chagga, he has no other choice. He has to perform the ritual that will also free the precious souls of the victims of the fires from the grasp of the Evil Shadowy Figure, plucking them from the burning fires and delivering them from torment of the underworld.

The Evil Shadowy Figure's banishment, by any means or method, will be a relief. No, it will be a glorious occasion. Chief Naruma likes this way of thinking.

Now he must act.

He springs out of bed in a hurry. Talking to himself while he dresses, he curses like mad until both sandals are on his feet. He wants to find the alien. But where is it? What does it look like?

In the meantime, he walks to the kitchen to make some Rooibos tea; his favorite herbal tea to calm his nerves.

Chapter 7

AT 7:45 that same morning, Geoffrey Mkama closes the front door of his small two-bedroom house on Tengeru Road in the Arusha region of Tanzania. Besides being tall and physically impressive with a short cut 'Afro,' his features are angular and there is a mole under his left eye. After locking up, he turns around to see his daughter Cassidy standing next to Laila Diwani waiting at the end of the road for the school bus to arrive. The girls carry themselves splendidly, looking immaculately proper and demure in their school uniforms of white oxford shirts under blue V-neck sweaters, blue-and-white plaid skirts, white socks, and black shoes, and clutching their backpacks. He aims a smile at his daughter halfway down the street, though she doesn't see it. He's in the mood to smile at almost anything this morning.

"See you later, sweetheart," he calls out to her and waves goodbye with his right hand.

Cassidy interrupts a conversation with her best friend, looks over her shoulder, and says, "Okay, Daddy."

She is the apple of his eye. Eleven, going on sixteen, she's a bit mature, what with losing her mother a few years back. St. Mary's Primary School, just off Lake Duluti Road, is slightly over a mile away and he wants to drive them, but the girls feel independent if they ride the bus, and it's good for them socially, too.

He enters his gray Land Rover Range Rover Sport SUV off to the side of the house. For a few minutes or so, he watches the school bus stop to pick up the girls, something he does every school-day morning.

After starting up the SUV, he takes off down the road in the same direction as the school bus toward his work.

Today, like any other workday, Geoffrey is wearing an olive-green khaki button-down shirt, matching khaki pants, and black boots. Work is at the office of Tanzania National Parks Authority, or TANAPA, where he is the Chief Ranger. He is a man who is very much in charge, and he has the respect of all the park rangers under him.

After making a left onto Momela Road from Usa River, he drives seven miles to Ngongongare Gate, an entrance gate in the southern boundary of Arusha National Park. Just north of Ngongongare Gate is Serengeti Ndogo, a small patch of open grassland that almost always has zebras grazing. And fourteen kilometers further on is Momella Gate, the TANAPA administrative checkpoint and park's headquarters, that is adjacent to a starting point for hikes up Mount Meru.

Not far from Ngongongare Gate, near the souvenir shop and café, is the parking lot where he leaves his Range Rover Sport SUV. The day being bright and sunny adds to his enthusiasm to come to work. At a little before nine, he is all smiles as he walks into his office.

For much of the time, he is in charge of the park's special details. At times out in the field, his job as a park ranger or rather he considers himself a conservation ranger, entails duties such as conducting patrols and guarding the park, serving as a guide on walking safaris. However, being a park ranger is not easy, as he regularly puts his life at risk to protect wildlife including elephants and rhinos. Still, it gives him satisfaction that he is giving back to the land he so loves. He loves his Tanzania and all the people and animals to go with it.

At the sink in the nearby bathroom, he fills water in the glass pot from the coffee maker. He needs caffeine. At the makeshift coffee station near the back of his office, a light goes on the coffee maker when the coffee is ready. After lifting a ceramic mug from his desk, he pours coffee from the glass pot into it. He mixes in sugar and cream and takes a quick gulp. When he hears birds cooing by the window to the left of the room, he puts the mug down on his desk. It annoys him.

"They need to do something about those Namaque doves in a nest under the ceiling board," he blabbers to himself.

After pinning the latest forecast next to a weather map on the cork bulletin board on the wall behind his desk, he goes to a black metal file cabinet in the corner, pulls open a drawer, searches through the file folders, selects one, opens it and grabs a form, which he places on his desk. After putting the folder back in place, he slides the drawer shut.

As soon as he sits down at his desk, the walkie-talkie on his desk crackles and interrupts the calm. Then comes a few screeches, as if a transmission is coming through. He looks at the walkie-talkie and waits.

Nothing comes through.

The Chief Ranger clears his throat self-consciously. He grabs the walkie-talkie, twists a knob on it, then puts it back down on his desk.

"Geoffrey are you in the office yet?" a woman's voice comes over the walkie-talkie.

Quickly, he grabs the walkie-talkie crackling in his hand, "Yes, I'm here. Paulina, what's going on?"

Paulina Mongella, one of his newest rangers, is his eyes and ears in the field, where she checks up on wildlife's well-being or conducts research. Mature with a strong character, she's someone he can depend on. Time and again she contacts him on his walkie-talkie or telephone to relay activities.

"I don't know how to describe what I'm seeing. There is something here you have to see for yourself."

"Paulina, this is not a good time. It's the beginning of the week. I have multiple reports to type and file. Can it wait till later this afternoon?"

With his free hand, he picks up the form from the desk and starts reading it. His mind is not in the conversation.

"Negative, sir. I'm standing in the middle of a crash site," she begins to explain.

Upon hearing that, he places the form back down on the desk. Then he puts his elbow on the desk and rests the full weight of his head under his hand before he answers her.

"What kind of crash are you talking about?"

"Like the wreckage of a UFO. I'm certain it's not an airplane."

He bolts out of his chair and asks, "Are you for real?"

"Yes, sir, I kid you not. You need to see it with your own eyes. It is truly unbelievable."

"Where, exactly, are you?"

"I'm in the Mount Meru Forest Reserve south of Sanawari Road."

He closes the conversation with, "Guess the paperwork will have to wait. I'll be right there shortly."

"This looks like it's going to be one of those mornings. I have a feeling this is going to be a long one," he says to himself as he empties his mug of coffee into the little brown waste basket by the metal file cabinet.

After clipping the walkie-talkie to the black leather belt around his waist under his shirt, he grabs his olive-green bush hat from the stool by the doorway and puts it on his head. *Is the wreckage from an alien spaceship?* he wonders as he reaches into his shirt pocket and pulls out a pair of sunglasses, slipping them on. Before walking out of his office, he grabs the black AK-47 hanging on the wall and slings it over his right shoulder.

Chapter 8

UNDER THE BRIGHT CORNFLOWER-BLUE SKIES at around nine thirty that morning in the vicinity of Allison Banes' home, the people are involving themselves with their routines and making the most of their lives. It's a friendly place, with people who frequently speak to each other and are willing to help anyone in need. So many are smiling and genuinely happy in the Arusha region as elsewhere in Tanzania. Her side of the city is often full of such behavior from people in the neighborhood.

Allison is waking up. On her bed is a copy of "Gorillas in the Mist" by Dian Fossey, which she keeps on the bed to remind her to finish reading it. She's already halfway through it. She's hoping it will give her inspiration and insight into another person's undying passion for the preservation and study of primates. This she can relate to. She pushes the book aside and focuses on her surroundings.

Everything from yesterday rushes back to her. Just as she's wondering what to do next regarding the stranger in her living room, the sound of a "meow" comes from the living room. The alien is awake! Immediately after comes the sound of something scraping against glass. It sounds like the catlike creature is fiddling with her Persian pottery vase of frangipani flowers on the round glass side table with chunky cluster bamboo legs.

Allison leaves the bed and walks to the living room, where the catlike creature is standing on two legs, holding the pottery vase in her hands to her mouth drinking the warm, slimy water in it. The bunch of delicate white frangipani flowers are on the floor by her feet. She is thirsty.

"That's not the healthiest thing for you to drink," Allison says, startling her.

The alien whips around and her hands shake so much that the vase slips from her fingers and clatters onto the floor, splitting into two pieces. The sudden crashing noise reverberates through the house. Looking at the pieces of the vase, Allison quietly gasps because she remembers it as a housewarming gift from her friend Azita Hussein.

"Meow," the creature softly responds.

Now that the creature is awake, she is obviously fearful. She doesn't recognize or remember Allison. So, Allison is going to have to refresh her memory or just reintroduce herself to the alien as pleasantly as possible.

"Good morning. My name is Allison. This is my house on the planet Earth."

Fearful and apprehensive, the creature begins to slowly step backward. It looks like she wants to take off. That she does.

In a heartbeat of a second, the alien lowers to all fours and scampers off to another room, the office, before Allison can say anything else.

She follows the alien to her office, who is now hiding under her oak desk with her wiggling tail sticking out. As if she's not going to see the creature. In her state of fear, she doesn't appear to know what to do other than hide. She stops in the middle of the room, bends over, hands on knees and looks directly at the alien.

"There's nothing to be afraid of," she says, too eager to make contact.

The creature responds with a loud hissing sound.

Allison's eyes roll in her head, and she says to herself, "This first contact is not going to be easy."

The alien is moving.

A glass elephant paperweight falls off the desk to the floor with a loud thud. This scares the creature more. Suddenly Allison hears a low sounding growl and then more hissing. Then the creature takes off again, flying past Allison at top speed.

She has to ask. "Where are you going?"

Frustratingly, she leaves her office without knowing where the alien is hiding now, until she hears a noise in the kitchen.

"Ah ha!" she says out loud, and heads in that direction.

When she steps into the room, her gaze goes directly to the alien, who is hiding under the rectangular black marble kitchen table. That's when an idea pops into her mind.

"How about something to eat? You must be hungry after your long journey from outer space?"

Still, no response.

In any case, she opens the door of the refrigerator and eyes the selections. She takes out two cans of tuna and a carton of milk and sets them on the counter. From the cupboard above the sink, she pulls out two blue ceramic bowls and pours milk into one of them. She opens the cans of tuna with the can opener she finds in a drawer and dumps the contents in a bowl. Lastly, she places the bowl of tuna and the bowl of milk on the floor and pushes them a little toward the table where the catlike creature is hiding.

"Hmm… smells good, doesn't it?"

Still, the alien doesn't budge.

"I'm just going to the bathroom. I won't be long," Allison says, before she leaves.

In fact, she does exactly that. She decides to leave the alien alone while she gets herself together in the bathroom. Maybe the catlike creature will be better after she eats something.

After stripping out of her pale pink satin pajama shorts and white tank top, she tells herself she'll take a shower later. She washes up at the sink, pulls her hair back into a ponytail, then dresses in an olive-green V-neck T-shirt and a pair of jeans. Looking at herself in the mirror above the sink, a smile creeps through as she thinks who's going to bother with makeup when there's nobody to see you but an alien from outer space.

Twenty minutes later, she steps out of the bathroom into the hallway. She quietly tiptoes around the corner in the direction of the kitchen. Upon entering the room, she sees that the bowls are empty, and the catlike creature is no longer there.

Where can she be now?

Chapter 9

IN ANOTHER PART of town, far from the carefree spirits of the rural suburbanites, things aren't so happy among the people.

In the busy GoHealth Walk-In Urgent Care on Simeon Road in Arusha that is serving the needs of the community is where you will find Dr. Azita Hussein. The bright, and frequently cranky internist is a long way from her hometown of Tehran, Iran.

Why? It is not uncommon that we are all running away from something, whether we know it or not.

Azita looks to be in her late twenties. Really, she is thirty-two as of three weeks ago, a Sagittarius, quite single, and, well, her life is threatening to pass her by. These days, she feels that she is a relic. In a dingy office, she sits in her swivel chair, behind her desk, recording medical data on the computer under bad fluorescent lighting.

Every day she throws herself into her work, and in this way, a year passes quickly at the clinic, where she sees everything. Most often, it feels like a crash course in febrile illnesses. She cleans wounds. She prescribes medications. All and all, she practices everyday medicine on the locals in what is her first-year post-residency.

Following a three-year internal medicine residency training at the Selian Lutheran Hospital in Tanzania, she ends up working at GoHealth Walk-In Urgent Care. All business, she rarely socializes with her coworkers, only when necessary, something that relates to work. With her black sense of humor, a darkness in her that drives her on, it's maybe why she stays. Tanzania is a far stretch from Iran but similar because it is also full of needy people. At times she misses her parents, who are busy with their own lives and sympathetic to her interests. Her father is a justice minister, and her mother is a professor at the Tehran University of Medical Sciences, where Azita has her medical degree.

Another thing — she doesn't dream of marrying, doesn't know the first thing about being a wife, or if that is something she will ever do. Which is fine with her.

The walk-in clinic barely gets by and the pay is something not for the mentioning. The clinic is always in need of medical supplies. Little things like cotton balls, gauze, bandages, saline solution, and even syringes are often down to the last bits. Today is no exception. Doing her best to make sure the steel cabinet in the examination room is full of supplies, she fills out an online order form.

Whatever else she purchases at a local pharmacy along with prescriptions for her clients, usually the first Monday of the month.

But there's no more time to worry about what little the clinic has to work with. Her clerical duties are few and far between, because she must treat patients during the majority of her shift. As of four days ago, she is the only doctor at the clinic. The other doctor quit abruptly. The clinic's administrator has faith in Azita's ability as a doctor to manage on her own for the remainder of the holiday season until he can hire a full-time doctor after the New Year. The clinic is open six days a week, so at least she gets one day off.

After logging off the computer, she stands up from her chair and walks out the door. As soon as she walks into the waiting room, Azita wipes her brow with the sleeve of her white lab coat then checks in with the African nurse at the reception desk. The nurse briefly peers at the three people sitting in various degrees of pain and discomfort among all the people in the waiting room.

"Is everything all right, Brenda?" Azita asks quietly.

"Just waiting for Neema to return."

Brenda Mann usually provides coverage while the receptionist is on break or at lunch. She's a petite twenty-five-year-old African woman, professional in her blue scrubs, but kind, and an extremely competent nurse.

Azita Hussein's Middle Eastern good looks of dark brown eyes, and shoulder-length hair set in a style so becoming, that two men sitting near the water fountain look at her twice already. A small Hindu girl with a bloody towel around her foot cries in her mother's lap. Trying to soothe the girl's nerves, the Persian beauty flashes her a quick smile as she turns, and for a second they forget all their pain. The men watch in admiration. They can just tell there is a fabulous body under that lab coat. But she's not one to flaunt it. She is a beautiful woman, and even wearing the typical physician's outfit of a button-up dress shirt and navy slacks under a lab coat, she looks out of place among the locals.

Azita charges on. Almost immediately, she is in an adjacent examination room giving an injection to a baby when she hears a woman speaking loudly in the waiting room. The distress in the woman's voice reveals another patient in need of care. Azita glances briefly toward the door, her face full of compassion, and tries her best to work faster.

"How much longer do I have to wait? My son needs medical attention," a woman asks, holding a boy of about seven years old in her arms.

Standing in the center of the waiting room, tears are in the eyes of the skinny, African woman wearing a batik wrap. She's quite frantic about her child. Now and again, she sways gently, rocking him in her arms as she whispers words of comfort.

The pretty, twentysomething African woman with short curly hair sitting behind the reception desk has an annoying look on her face that seems to center around her nose. Neema must realize she's not getting through to the frantic woman, as her words peter out. But it's her job to do that. Because being a receptionist at a medical facility is about being able to handle a demanding setting and being nice.

"You need to try to calm down. And speak slowly, okay? What's the medical emergency?" Neema asks, in a pleasant manner.

She cuddles the little boy in her arms, stroking his face as he watches her with curious eyes. "My baby's sick. He has been having diarrhea and abdominal pain. I think he has intestinal worms."

Neema sees the door of the examination room open and says reassuringly, "Please be patient. The Doctor is coming."

"Can you go and tell the doctor to hurry?" the woman pleads, still sobbing.

"Not long now. The doctor will be here any minute."

Coming into the waiting room, Azita hands the baby to an African man standing near the reception desk. The man thanks her before walking away.

Once the woman sees the doctor, she blinks the tears away and hollers out, "Can't you see this is an emergency? My boy has a parasitic infection."

Azita turns her head to look at the woman hollering. She gives her a quick once-over. No matter how many times she sees this, it still takes her by surprise. There is always someone entering the clinic screaming for assistance.

"Just another typical day in the office," Azita says to Neema, then says to the woman, "Please, come with me. I'm a doctor, it's all right. But you need to be calm now, so

I can help your son. His symptoms sound like he has Schistosomiasis, a waterborne disease, that is the second most common in Africa, behind malaria, and easily treatable with a Praziquantel pill. I'll know for certain after examining him. He's going to be fine if that's what he has."

Azita Hussein speaks to her politely, avoiding any condescension. The well-meaning doctor is good at keeping control.

Chapter 10

AS GEOFFREY MKAMA drives along the road, a herd of elephants come stampeding through the brush and begin to saunter across the road in front of him. He quickly stops the Land Rover. They sleekly skulk around as if they own the place, which they probably do. As he sits there, more elephants come out of the bush in single file to cross the road. One large male elephant stops at the side of the road as if he is a crossing guard. He turns toward Geoffrey, stomps his foot, flaps his ears, swings his trunk and roars, but realizing he is not a threat, the elephant turns and walks away with the others.

Moving onward, the Land Rover bounces along a road that is a little more than a set of tire grooves before reaching the forest. He pulls the SUV alongside a GMC pickup, Paulina's vehicle. After rolling out of the SUV, he anxiously begins to walk to the site.

When he catches a glimpse of Paulina Mongella foraging through the debris, he slides his sunglasses off and tucks them into his shirt pocket to get a better look. From a distance it looks as if it's pieces of some kind of aircraft. The effect of the sun's rays causes the many geometric shapes and black glass-like fragments to sparkle. Paulina is definitely a woman of her word. The adrenaline is really pumping now. Nothing like a UFO to get the juices flowing.

Paulina steps out from behind a tree and sees him just as he stops near the tree. The tall female conservation ranger is wearing a khaki short-sleeve button-down shirt and matching pants, black boots, and a floppy khaki safari hat on her head. She has a rifle hanging over one shoulder and sports a pair of black binoculars hanging from a strap around her neck.

"Paulina, I dare to ask? What do we have here?"

"Just like I'm telling you. It's something you have to see with your own eyes."

He quickly sifts through some of the strange metal objects lying on the ground.

"This is the remnants of an alien spaceship. I'm right, aren't I?" Paulina asks enthusiastically.

"I have to agree with you."

"And guess what else?"

"There's a survivor?"

"No, Geoffrey. Less than a quarter of a mile away, where I'm pointing, is a small spacecraft, in all probability an escape pod from the spaceship."

"Take me over there so I can inspect it."

She starts to walk him toward the small vessel on the ground. "From the looks of things, the escape pod is empty because the hatch is open."

"Oh, I can't wait to see it."

Upon arriving at the escape pod, Geoffrey crouches down and angles his head to look inside. There is nothing there. Marveling at its construction, it's frightening, but there's no denying the escape pod comes from another planet, or another dimension.

"What do we do now? Is there a procedure for this?"

Still in a crouching position, he takes a minute to absorb everything and reflect on how he's going to handle this.

"This is out of our jurisdiction. It's best not to disturb anything. I'll call this into the Commissioner at TANAPA," he says, rising to stand.

Two hours later, just after 12:00 p.m., a pair of TANAPA executives from the Law Enforcement and Strategic Security Section arrive at the crash site. They greet each other, shake hands, and receive a briefing by Geoffrey, who escorts them to the escape pod. The two men shake their heads in disbelief from seeing it.

"So, you think there's some sort of alien loose in Tanzania?" Geoffrey asks with a tone of humor in his voice.

The men have serious looks on their faces. None of them respond.

"Okay, I'm just making light of the circumstances."

For the next hour, the men carefully examine the escape pod. After sifting through the bits and pieces, taking a thorough look at the remains of the spaceship, they decide that this area of the park is to remain off limits to visitors indefinitely. One of the men makes a call on his cell phone. Then he takes some pictures of the crash site and the escape pod with a Nikon digital camera.

The investigative team informs Paulina to pack up the debris in plastic bags and leave them outside the TANAPA building by the Ngongongare Gate for pick up tomorrow morning. Without wasting another moment, they direct Paulina to begin right away as they want the area devoid of any debris that may harm the animals or pollute the area.

The men close the hatch of the escape pod, roll it over on its side, then push it onto a massive platform truck with wheels. As quickly as possible, Geoffrey and Paulina work hard to push and pull the massive platform truck, with the heavy escape pod, to the back of their white Hino 500 truck. The men will deliver the escape pod to a warehouse in the possession of the Tanzania National Parks Authority. There it will undergo tests. The small ship may provide clues to the home planet of the aliens. They will also analyze the spaceship debris there.

Before the men get into their Hino truck, they inform Geoffrey and Paulina that the matter is confidential and don't blab it to anyone. There is total silence for a moment as the pair stand next to each other watching the truck drive off.

"They sure are acting strange," Paulina comments.

"That's management for you. I dare not ask any questions."

"What do you think they're going to do?"

"They are going to keep it quiet. A cover-up most likely."

"Yes, but for how long? Can they keep it from coming out in the media?"

"They can and they will," he says with conviction.

"I feel you on that. And now I'm off. I have clean-up to do."

"And you know where to find me."

Thinking to himself as he climbs into his Land Rover, Geoffrey can't wait to tell his daughter about this. There's no harm in telling a child, he reassures himself. And he knows Cassidy will get a kick out of it. It's the stuff children love to hear about.

Chapter 11

AT AROUND THREE O'CLOCK, Cassidy Mkama gets off the school bus, along with Laila Diwani. Right away, the school bus trundles off noisily after dropping them off at the corner of Tengeru Road.

With a tap on her shoulder, Cassidy tells Laila as they part ways, "I'll see you tomorrow morning."

"Okay. Bye for now," Laila responds as she turns quickly and starts walking in the other direction.

Cassidy cheerfully approaches her house. After opening the front door, she walks through the living room and into her bedroom. She takes the two schoolbooks and notebooks out of her backpack and spreads them out onto her twin-size bed. After putting her backpack in the right place, she changes out of her school uniform and into grubby jeans, a pink T-shirt, and sandals.

Now she's off to the kitchen for a cool drink before getting to her chores. When she isn't in school, she is cleaning up around the house, as well as preparing dinner. The glass of apple juice soothes her. After gulping down a full glass, she goes to wash it up in the sink.

After leaving the kitchen, she walks to the hallway bathroom and leaves carrying a tin tub. She walks through the kitchen and through the back door. In the backyard, she stretches up to the long wire clothesline to take down the clothes. She unfastens them from the wooden pegs and tosses them in the tin tub. After taking down the last piece of clothing, she carries the tin tub into the house.

Ever since her mother's passing from West Nile virus, she is eager to help her father with tasks around the house. After two years of thinking about her mother, constantly seeing her face, day, and night, she is now beginning to forget, rather she is learning how. Still, every so often, she misses her mother but is coping better as the time goes by.

Subsequently losing her mother, her father Geoffrey, is raising her with the help of his mother, Dottie Mkama, a former school librarian of many years who lives three blocks away on Nyerere Road. Sometimes Cassidy thinks she gets most of her personality from her doting grandmother, who is an inspiration to her. Not too headstrong, but Cassidy can be stubborn on occasion so much like her grandmother, who is a headstrong character in more ways than one. People in the neighborhood are fond of her, some are afraid of her.

Cassidy's gentle features and round cheeks make her irresistible to her grandma, for her Lil Cassie, as she calls her, is special and can do no wrong in her eyes. Dottie Mkama, a devout Christian, has her Cassidy in church most Sundays. They worship at the Mulala Evangelical Lutheran Church, popular with parishioners for their fiery sermons and choir singing. And Cassidy accepts Christ as her savior since the age of seven at the time of her baptism in Lake Duluti.

When all the clothes are put away, it's around 5:00 p.m. and time to start the dinner. Cassidy walks into the kitchen and removes various items from the refrigerator. She reaches in the cabinet above the stove for a stainless-steel pot, places it on a burner and turns it on. Tonight's dinner will be meat stew, spinach, and rice. While the rice is cooking, she sets the small rectangular table with two stoneware plates, cloth napkins, glasses, and silverware.

Moving quickly around the kitchen, she generally has dinner ready at six o'clock, the time her father returns home from work, which is in about fifteen minutes. But on those rare occasions he works late, he may come at seven o'clock.

Soon the front door opens, and she hears her father's voice calling out.

"Something smells terrific."

Geoffrey Mkama bursts through the kitchen door, reaches out, his arms wide, and pulls Cassidy into a hug. He holds her for a long time.

"Hello, Daddy. Dinner is almost ready."

"Thanks, sweetheart. I can't wait to dig in," he says and breaks their embrace. "Before I forget, there's something I want to tell you."

She turns off the burner, swivels around and asks, "What is it Daddy?"

"This morning, in the Mount Meru Forest Reserve, Paulina stumbles across debris from a spaceship and a smaller spaceship, an escape pod, and contacts me. After driving over there, I spend half the day looking at it."

"A spaceship? A real one from outer space?"

"Yes, I know it's shocking."

"You're just joking around with me," she says laughingly.

"I'm not. I swear," he says and takes a seat at the table.

"Wow!" she says as she places a plate of food down in front of him.

"Wow is correct. The matter is now in the hands of my supervisors to investigate."

"That's exciting, Daddy."

"Now you can say for certain that there are aliens somewhere in outer space," he says while watching her load up her plate with food.

"Will you take me to see the crash site and escape pod?"

"No, baby, I can't."

"Why not, Daddy?" she asks before sitting down at the table with her plate.

"The escape pod is no longer there, along with the debris. The incident is under investigation. And the area is now off limits to visitors for some time."

"That's too bad."

"And one more thing…"

Standing up abruptly, she says, "I have to tell Laila. I'm going to call her."

"Wait, Cassidy. Never mind."

Cassidy leaves the kitchen and runs into the living room. She picks up the telephone on the side table by the sofa.

"My bosses don't want this getting around," he says quietly to himself.

He sulks for a moment as if unsure what to do.

"Don't be too long. You need to finish your dinner," he calls out to her.

"I won't, Daddy," she says as she starts to dial Laila's phone number.

So much for keeping a secret, Geoffrey's thinking. But how can he say no to her? Cassidy is a personality of sorts, a little woman in the making. Most of the time, she does as she pleases. It's just between friends, right? They're just children, he reminds himself. It's best to just focus on finishing up his meal.

Chapter 12

AROUND 6:45 P.M., darkness is all around Paulina Mongella in the Mount Meru Forest Reserve as she dumps the last of the spaceship debris into a large green garbage bag. After she drops off the nine bags outside the front door of the TANAPA building by the Ngongongare Gate, she can go home. She feels she needs to rest after the long eventful day.

After taking the small flashlight from her belt, she points it around the crash site. From what she can see, there is no more debris to salvage. The only evidence of a spaceship crash-landing are some large trees and thick branches on the ground. Lastly, she drives wooden stakes into the ground with yellow barrier tape between them to cordon off the crash site. This is what her bosses want, and she is happy to accommodate. All part of the business, she thinks to herself.

Carrying a bag, Paulina starts walking toward her white GMC Sierra pickup. At the truck, she opens the tailgate and lifts the bag onto the pickup truck bed.

A screech follows the sound of soft padding footfalls, as three black-and-white colobus monkeys suddenly run past her and dash away into the night. After a tense pause, she hurries her steps to get another bag. Looking up, she sees a flock of birds circling the trees and even hears the rustling of their wings. When a gust of wind propels the birds skyward, she notices the gloomy, turbulent sky, with masses of dark clouds appearing so suddenly. My, how strange the weather is around here, she thinks.

Approaching the cluster of eight full bags, next to them is a young African woman standing with her back to her. What is she doing there?

Paulina slowly walks forward, stopping five feet away, trying to get a better look at this woman wearing a multi-color kitenge wraparound dress that reaches to her knees.

"Miss, I have to ask you to leave. This area is off-limits."

There is no response from the woman.

At that, Paulina puts a hand on her rifle. She quickly looks around to see if anyone else is around. You can't blame her for doing that in these parts where poachers lurk. And to top it off, after a hard day's work, she's in no mood for foul play.

"Miss, I'm a park ranger. I'm asking you to leave the premises."

The woman's shoulders move, and soon her whole body starts to sway like a tree in the wind, backward and forward, and with each move from left to right it looks like she is shapeshifting. Is this woman real? Paulina wonders if she is an apparition.

Finally, the woman says something odd to Paulina. "Please help me."

"If you need medical attention, I need to know that."

The woman turns her head around and looks at Paulina seriously. There is a smudge of black soot across the woman's face.

"He is looking for it. He knows it is here."

"Miss, I don't know what you are talking about."

Turning her body around to face Paulina, there are streaks of black soot on the woman's arms, legs, and bare feet.

"He is jealous of it."

Paulina is at a loss for words. Instead, she can feel the darkness creeping over her. She can't explain it, but it seems like something is preventing her from moving or speaking.

"Going to get you. Going to get you," the woman starts chanting with a look of desperation on her face.

A powerful vacuumlike force pulls the woman's body backward, disappearing into the darkness. In that instant, one of the bags of debris ignites, burning spontaneously without any apparent cause. In disbelief from seeing this happen, Paulina looks around for the woman. Where on

Earth is she? She can't vanish into thin air. Or can she? People do though, don't they? Vanish.

As the bag burns, Paulina is unable to move as she sees a shadowy figure emerging out of the flames and hears many voices at once. The air for the next minute or two is noisy with loud voices. As the outline of a deep black shadow materializes before her eyes, a strange, cackling noise assails her ears.

Finally, forcing herself out of the trance, if that's what it is, she runs over to her pickup. She opens the door to the backseat as fast as possible. Then she dismounts and grabs a fire extinguisher from behind the seat.

Churning clouds above swirl into a menacing dark gray and the rushing wind roars around her. When she approaches the bag on fire, the wind pushes the flames toward her. Though she doesn't notice it at the time, the fiery flames brush against her left hand, burning a hole right through her glove.

With a bit of luck, she is able to extinguish the fire before it gets out of control, preventing the other bags from catching fire, too. What a relief, she thinks.

"Oh, thank God."

The cackling sounds and deep voices no longer ring in the air. But the fear is still in her eyes. Is she a witness to an apparition? she asks herself. She frowns, for she is suddenly thinking about the folklore of the Chagga, whose numerous tales and superstitions even about Mount Meru are of unusual interest to her. She knows this because her Aunt Rhoda Kisanga is a member of the Chagga.

Thinking further on the matter, she just doesn't want to believe it.

The fear in her is dissipating now. She feels pain in her left hand. After removing the white work glove, she looks at it. There is painful blistering and swelling, and fluid seeping from the skin.

After taking some breaths to calm the turmoil inside her, she returns to her pickup and lays the fire extinguisher in the back. After opening the passenger's door, she fishes out a red rag from the glove compartment and wraps it around her hand. The look on her face is one of frustration because she will have to get medical treatment for her hand.

After loading the remaining eight bags onto the truck, she shuts the tailgate then climbs into the driver's seat. She sits there quiet for a long time. She thinks about how she's going to explain this to Geoffrey Mkama. Maybe it's best not to say anything. Is this something she needs to report? Unfortunately, yes. Her company's health insurance plan will pay for her medical treatment. A garbage bag just catches fire at once. It may sound a bit wild, but it doesn't sound like fiction after looking the situation over closely. Perhaps the spaceship material is flammable. She'll think about it later this evening.

Paulina pulls a Samsung Galaxy cell phone from the beige knapsack on the passenger seat and dials her husband's cell.

After two rings, a man's voice comes on the line. "Yes?"

"Hello, Joaquim. I'm going to be home a little later tonight," she says in a tense voice.

"What's the problem, sweetheart?"

Paulina regretfully tells him, "I hurt my hand while handling some debris in the park. I'm going to a medical clinic."

"Oh, my. Is it serious? Do you want me to meet you there?"

"No, it's not necessary, honey. It's just a mild burn. I don't expect to be there long."

"Call me before you leave the clinic so I can have dinner ready for you."

"I will. You are a dear."

"I'll see you soon, baby."

"I love you, bye," she tells him and ends the call.

"Can't wait for this day to end," she mutters to herself as she starts the ignition.

Trying very hard to relax herself, she turns the knob on the radio. The song "Oh Africa" by Akon is already in progress. She doesn't change the station when she drives away.

After dropping the bags in front of the door of the building where Geoffrey Mkama works, she feels a sense of relief that the men from TANAPA's Law Enforcement and Strategic Security Section will pick them up the following morning. Walking to her GMC pickup in the parking lot close to the Ngongongare Gate, she clutches her painful hand to her chest and no longer worries about apparitions. She'll go to the clinic and then straight home.

Chapter 13

AT FIFTEEN MINUTES BEFORE NINE, Azita Hussein is ready to leave the clinic. Today, like most days, she is the last one to leave. And she is bone-weary at the end of a long day's work. After dinner at home, she can't wait to cozy up on the sofa and watch a little television.

She hears pounding on the front door as she walks down the hall from her office. Then comes a woman's thick, painful voice — quite clear.

"Hello? Is anyone in there?"

"It always happens when you least expect it," Azita says to herself.

At first, Azita ignores the woman, thinking she'll move on to another clinic, sooner rather than later. GoHealth Walk-In Urgent Care is not the only clinic in the area, but on nights like this, it feels like it is. A sign on the door reads *"CLINIC OPENS 8:00 A.M. CLOSES 8:00 P.M."* The woman is obviously ignoring it because she knocks on the door again and again.

"I really need assistance rather urgently," comes the voice again.

At this point, Azita finally gives in. "Coming. I'll be right there."

When she emerges from the hallway, she makes her way through the waiting room to the front door and blurts out, "As of forty-five minutes ago, the clinic is not open. What's the medical emergency? I'm a physician. I can refer you to a nearby hospital."

"Pardon my intrusion, but with the lights on, I figure that someone is inside. My hand needs medical attention," she says, takes off the rag around her hand, holds her hand up for Azita to see, and lets out a groan of pain from deep within her chest. "It hurts really bad."

Standing by the door, Azita caves in. A second later, she reaches into her lab coat pocket and pulls out a set of keys.

"Oh. That does look serious. Come on in," Azita says as she unlocks and opens the door.

She tucks the rag into her front pants pocket, walks in and says, "Name's Paulina Mongella, by the way."

"Dr. Azita Hussein. So nice to make your acquaintance. After, there will be some paperwork to fill out," she says, giving a sideways glance at her tense expression.

"I know how it works. After I pay, I'll need a copy of the bill for my employer, Tanzania National Parks Authority, to reimburse me."

After locking the door, Azita escorts Paulina through the waiting-room and down the hallway to an examination room. After washing her hands at the sink, Azita puts on latex gloves. She asks Paulina to sit on an examination bed and looks at her hand.

"Th-thank you for seeing me, Doctor. I'm not up for driving to another medical clinic," she says, stumbling over her words because of the pain.

"I understand that. May I ask how —"

"this ends up happening to me? Can you believe from trying to put out a burning bag of debris while at work?"

"You have a second-degree burn, Ms. Mongella."

"And that's what it feels like. It's really stinging now."

Azita leads her to the sink and turns on the cold water. For the next ten minutes, Paulina holds her hand under the running water.

"Is the pain subsiding?"

"Oh yes, this is really helping," Paulina says, her whole face seeming to relax.

Azita takes a bottle of antiseptic from a cabinet and sets it on the counter by the sink, along with a white washcloth. "Keep your hand under the water. I'm going to cleanse that wound with an antiseptic to prevent infection. It may sting a little."

"Oww. Yes, it stings," Paulina explodes in a painful wail, which she quickly cuts short when she sinks her teeth hard into her lower lip.

After turning off the faucet, Azita asks her to sit on the examination bed. As she stares at Paulina's face, a memory flashes in her mind.

"Are you a park ranger?"

"Yes. This month marks my one-year anniversary on the job."

"Do you work with Geoffrey Mkama?"

"I sure do. He's my boss. If you don't mind me asking…how do you know Geoffrey?"

"Sadly enough, I'm the doctor responsible for treating his late wife Tess at Selian Lutheran Hospital, my former employer."

"Geoffrey doesn't talk about his late wife. He seems to be holding up well, considering."

"I'm glad to hear that."

She gets a tube of Bacitracin from the cabinet, applies the ointment to Paulina's hand, then bandages it up.

"Thank you, Doctor. My hand feels much better."

"Burns like this take time to heal. You may be wearing bandages for several weeks. Here are two bandages you can use later."

Paulina stands up to leave while Azita strips off her gloves and tosses them in the trash can in the corner of the room. She watches Azita washing her hands in the sink, then steps out of the examination room before Azita turns off the light and closes the door. Paulina follows her down the hallway to the reception desk where Azita picks up a clipboard, and hands it to her.

Paulina picks up a pen, starts writing and jokingly says, "Lucky for me I'm a righty."

After Paulina pays the bill, Azita sets the credit card receipt and clipboard on the chair at the receptionist desk. They say their goodbyes as Azita closes and locks the door behind them. Then they part ways in the parking lot.

On the way to her truck, Paulina pulls out her cell phone from her knapsack. Before climbing into her truck, she speed dials her husband.

As soon as he answers, she says, "Joaquim, I'm on my way home now."

"Excellent!"

Chapter 14

IN HER ROOM, Cassidy Mkama is sitting against the headboard of her bed, dutifully finishing her homework. After shifting a little, this way and that, she pauses to tap her pencil on the notebook as she tries to figure out the last math problem on a worksheet. After writing it down, she heaves a huge sigh, and her eyes roll around in her head before she starts chugging her way through it. Calculating it in her mind, she sees the solution to the problem, and solves it correctly, with a beaming smile.

She closes the textbook with a slap and lays it down on the bed, thinking about her phone call with Laila. Why doesn't Laila share her enthusiasm about the UFO crash site? Laila's utter silence on the matter is at odds with her personality. Her strange mood still baffles Cassidy. Just on her feelings Cassidy senses something wrong. But there is no point in dwelling on it any longer. The only way she'll know what's eating at Laila is to ask her tomorrow at the bus stop or in school.

The clock on her small wooden dresser tells her it's nine forty-five. It's rather late, way past the time she normally goes to bed. She gets up from the bed and stuffs her math and science textbooks and notebooks into her backpack, which is navy with white piping, then puts the backpack on top of the dresser.

Entering the living room, she discovers her father asleep in his comfy leather recliner with the television on. Trying to keep quiet, not to disturb him, she flips off the TV switch and softly kisses her father's cheek.

"Good night, Daddy," she says in a whisper before she walks away.

Still, for some reason he startles awake. "Where are you going, princess?"

Surprising her with his tender tone, she turns around and says, "I'm off to bed. You know I have to be up early for school."

"That's right, you do. Don't forget to brush your teeth."

"I won't, Daddy. But thanks for reminding me."

"Sleep well, and I'll see you in the morning."

With his eyes half open, he watches her turn and walk out of the room. He allows his shoulders to sink deeper into the chair and extends his legs more comfortably in front of him. No reason to turn the television set on again. Because he falls back asleep.

Cassidy heads down the hallway toward the bathroom in her bedroom to wash up and brush her teeth, while it's fresh on her mind and before she forgets. It doesn't take her long and soon she's back in her bedroom where she yawns a rumbly yawn and fidgets her way to pulling off her T-shirt and jeans. She tosses them in the wicker hamper in the corner of the room and puts on her pink pajamas.

Once she sits down on her bed, she picks up a doll she likes to sleep with, kisses it, rocks it, then lays it beside the pillow. A pretty little doll with soft blond hair and a white satin dress, it's soft cloth face resembles a real girl. Like all little girls, she even has a name for it, Mollie.

"It's sleepy time now," she says to the doll.

At last, she lies down on the bed and yanks a light yellow blanket up to her waist. Her eyes fall on the window opposite the foot of the bed. The waxing gibbous Moon's yellow-white glow shines through the thin curtains and the bright stars piercing through the darkness in the room is like having a streetlight shining in the window.

The news about the discovery of a spaceship in the forest of Arusha National Park is still on her mind. Her eyes start to close as she starts to think of other possible worlds, wondering about aliens and life elsewhere in the universe, somewhere out there, and maybe aliens somewhere around Tanzania. The idea seems to amuse her. She giggles as she floats off to sleep.

In the living room, Geoffrey Mkama is in a rhythm and dead to the world when the telephone starts ringing. He's a heavy sleeper. It rings three times before he hears it.

Rising slowly out of his chair, he walks to the side table, stares at the black cordless telephone, picks it up on the fourth ring, and stares at the clock. Ten-thirty p.m.

Geoffrey Mkama listens to a woman's voice say, "The top of the evening to you, my son."

He is in no mood to talk to his mother, but carries along with the conversation, "And a very good evening to you, too. To what do I owe this pleasure?"

"You two are coming over for Christmas dinner, right?" she asks in an unsure voice.

"Of course, we are. Your home is the only place I want to be for Christmas," he tells her reassuringly.

"Well, hearing you say that makes me very happy. How is my Lil Cassie?"

"She's her usual self. And fast asleep at this late hour," he says, cramming the words together like it will speed the conversation along.

"Please give her a hug for me and remind her to wear that pretty white dress with the yellow sash on Christmas. She'll look so pretty in it."

"I'll tell her that first thing tomorrow morning. I'm sure she'll be glad to oblige you by wearing it."

Barely listening to their exchange, he stands there hoping the conversation doesn't drag out any longer.

"It's always a pleasure talking with you. I'll say good night now, son."

"And a good night to you, as well," he says, mentally sighing in relief.

After hanging up the phone, he sinks back into his chair. Shortly after, he's asleep again.

Chapter 15

AT NOON, TUESDAY, Cassidy, and Laila are at lunch. They sit across from each other at a circular oak table near the entrance of the St. Mary's Primary School cafeteria. Laila pops a straw into her milk carton while Cassidy pulls off a piece of her blueberry muffin and stuffs it in her mouth.

"Why are you so quiet today? You're barely talking to me this morning. Is there something wrong?" Cassidy asks, leaning forward.

Laila looks at her, then across at the teacher standing in the corner by the entrance, then back at her. She remembers last night's telephone conversation. It's percolating in the back of her mind.

"Let me ask you something. Are you certain that debris in the forest is from a spaceship?"

Cassidy looks around to see if anyone is listening. Her eyes fall on a boy sitting at a table on the other side of the cafeteria. He's chatting and laughing with the boys sitting next to him. Her expression changes to apprehension. Then she glances at the teacher patrolling the lunchroom before turning back to her friend.

"Shhh, keep it down. I don't want Jason or his friends to hear this," Cassidy snaps.

"I have to know for sure. You're not pulling my leg, are you?" Laila pleads in a quiet voice.

"It's true. My dad says that TANAPA is investigating the incident. And get this. The crash site area in Arusha National Park is off limits to visitors."

"Do you think they're looking for the aliens from that spaceship?" Laila asks in a low voice.

"Yes. Can you believe it?" Cassidy asks and starts to swing her feet under the table.

Laila's quiet again for a while. She shakes her head, still processing it all. Can it really be true that the alien is here? A Chagga prophecy tells that the curse of the Evil Shadowy Figure will be transient. There will come a day when the one who can end the curse will come from the sky. A being from another world will help bring peace to the Chagga. She never let herself really and truly believe it until now.

Throwing Cassidy off guard, she declares, "Do you know what this means? The Chagga prophecy is true. This alien will end the curse of the Evil Shadowy Figure."

"I don't remember you ever telling me that part of the story of the curse on the Chagga."

Laila pauses for a second, then replies, "It's not something I usually share with anyone outside the tribe. And for a long time, I don't really believe in the curse. You know how adults can be. It's just something to tell children so they'll behave. That's what I think. But not anymore. I can't wait to tell them about the alien spacecraft crash-landing in the park."

Laila takes a mouthful of macaroni and cheese and chews.

Cassidy heaves a sigh and pops the last bite of her peanut butter and jelly sandwich in her mouth. She looks around the room, again. Her eyes stop on Jason. At that particular moment, he happens to glance at her. For a second or two, he squints his eyes at her. His face has a fiendish expression. She immediately looks away and sets her eyes on Laila.

"This is our secret. You can't tell anyone about this."

"But I just have to tell. I feel it's my duty as a tribal member," Laila says, then eats the remainder of her macaroni and cheese.

"But this morning my father tells me not to tell anyone else. They're going to ask how you know about this. If you mention my father, he may get into trouble with his superiors."

"Truthfully, I'm only going to tell Chief Naruma. He makes decisions for the tribe. He may tell members of the Chagga Council. And if he does, they'll keep it to themselves. The Chief will want everyone to quietly search for the alien. They'll be careful not to arouse suspicion."

"What if they don't find the alien?"

"They'll be upset. And I guess things will go back to normal again."

"I hope you're right about that," Cassidy says and finishes her carton of apple juice.

Cassidy tries to reassure herself. It's just the Chagga, a tribal society. She can't imagine anything bad happening.

Just then, Jason, walking ahead of two other boys, starts to pass by their table. Laila sees them stop and turn to look at Cassidy. She thinks she knows what's coming next. Something that happens a lot with Jason.

"I see you looking at me Cassidy. What do you want with me?" Jason asks with a laugh.

Jason waits for an answer while his friends look at Cassidy with silly grins on their faces.

Cassidy answers without turning to look at him, "I'm not looking at you. So, move on."

"Whatever you say," Jason says squeakily and then shrugs his shoulders.

The boys laugh again. When Jason sees the teacher approaching, he turns, and the boys quickly return to their seats.

"Jason Farquar don't get out of your seat again," the teacher scolds him.

The room goes silent, and you can feel the tension in the air. Literally everyone turns to look. The teacher glares at all of them. Jason sinks into his seat. Then the teacher glares at Jason over the heads of his classmates, who are holding in their laughter. Another moment passes until the teacher turns his attention to something else. And slowly, the chatter in the room returns to near normal.

What a little twerp, Cassidy thinks. Looking at her from a distance, running around whispering to his buddies, pestering her about looking at him, then running back to his table whispering to his buddies again. He enjoys goofing around with other boys, the more noisily, the better.

"He is so weird. Only God knows why my brother is friends with him," Laila says.

"Tell me something I don't already know," Cassidy answers and they laugh.

Chapter 16

CHIEF ANTON NARUMA is behind the wheel of his blue Jeep Wrangler, driving on Waterfall Road, heading to the grocery store. For the time being, his mind is somewhere else. But no doubt his dream from Sunday is looming heavily in the back of his mind.

Turning onto Sokoine Road, he pulls into a Gapco service station. After filling the tank, he drives into the parking lot of Shoppers Supermarket next door.

At around 1:30 p.m., his mood is carefree when he selects a shopping cart inside the supermarket. It isn't more than five minutes, when in steps Dottie Mkama. The dark eyes behind his glasses latch on to her. He can't help but notice how the overhead light accentuates the silver streaks in her hair set just right. She looks about forty-five, he thinks. After a few moments, she turns and pushes her cart down the aisle toward him. Since meeting her through her son, Geoffrey Mkama, many years ago, he has a habit of bumping into her at the oddest moments. Like now. She casually looks in his direction and greets him with a warm smile. His heart sinks. Something in her face, something in the way she looks and moves, is serious, and is affecting him.

"Chief Naruma. What a nice surprise finding you here," she says kindly.

"Hello, Dottie. And you may call me Anton. You don't need to be so formal. What brings you here?" he asks, stopping his cart next to hers.

There's no doubt that she feels confident about her appearance, wearing an elaborate dress of yellows and browns just below her knees and raffia sandals. Her figure stands out in this attire, this Chief Naruma notices without making it obvious he is looking.

"Well, Anton, I'm shopping for my special Christmas dinner. And you?"

"Just picking up a few things."

Dottie Mkama, a widower of some years, and owner of a two-bedroom house, is roughly his age.

"It's just a small gathering. My son, granddaughter Cassidy, and her friend Laila Diwani. Certainly, there's room for one more," she says suggestively.

"Oh, right, the park ranger. And how is Geoffrey these days?"

"Chief Ranger," she says, correcting him. "He's fine. Thanks for asking."

He grabs her cart and pushes it past his to allow another shopper to get by.

"Your Christmas dinner sounds pretty wonderful, but this year, like every year before, I will be celebrating with the Chagga."

"Of course. I expect you to."

There is something meaningful underneath their chatter. But it doesn't last. Another five minutes pass, the words fade away and they part ways.

Grandmother Mkama steers the cart into another aisle, slowing to look at the items on the shelves. She reaches for a couple of cans of fruit cocktail and places them in her cart. Shortly thereafter, she finds herself twisting left and right, looking around. For Chief Naruma no doubt. She's half expecting to see him, but he is nowhere in her view. In that brief moment, her eyes are soft with concern. But then she turns toward the vegetable aisle. She counts out eight ripe tomatoes and flings them into her cart.

Chief Naruma stands holding the freezer door open in front of the shelves of ice cream. He turns back from the freezer, looks up and down the aisle, thinking of Dottie Mkama. Not seeing her anywhere, Chief Naruma feels a disappointment that he can't explain. After tossing several frozen dinners and a quart of blueberry ice cream into the cart, he shuts the freezer door. Then he pushes the cart to the front of the store and parks it next to the register.

Dottie rolls the cart up the aisle and peeks around the corner. She spots Chief Naruma whipping out some cash and paying for his groceries as the lady at the register punches at the keys. She doesn't say anything, but as he swivels his head in her direction, she smiles to him. He smiles back at her and walks out of the store with his bags of groceries. For some reason, it's important to see him smile back. To have him look her in the eye. He can make her blush. And she likes that about him.

The grandmother wheels her cart to the front of the store and stares out the window. She watches him load the back of his Jeep Wrangler and walk around to the driver's side. A small smile creeps up on her face as she watches him drive away.

So much for distractions. Grandmother Mkama turns all her attention to her shopping list. She has to prepare a Christmas meal. Does she need to remind herself?

Dottie hums, pushing her shopping cart down the frozen food aisle. She opens the freezer door, letting the cold air kiss her cheek as she picks up several packages of frozen corn and throws them into her cart. Just before leaving the aisle, she narrows her eyes, studying her list carefully, making sure that she has everything she needs.

Confidently, she is ready to check out. She pushes her full cart to the front of the store and takes her place in one of the checkout lines. After paying for the items, the clerk offers to carry the bags to her car for her.

"Thank you," she says with a smile.

The clerk follows her to her black Volkswagen Touareg and sets the bags carefully inside before closing the trunk. After another thank-you and goodbye to the clerk, she walks around to the driver's side and slides behind the wheel. She is in an especially good mood since encountering Chief Naruma at the supermarket. She drives onto Sokoine Road and loops her vehicle around the corner and disappears from sight.

Chapter 17

AT APPROXIMATELY FOUR O'CLOCK, Chief Naruma is busying himself in his house with rearranging the sandals in his bedroom closet, because he has so much energy lately. The telephone in the kitchen rings and, with a sigh, he goes to answer it. Much to his surprise it's Esther Diwani, who, after saying a few words to him, hands the phone over to her daughter Laila. He learns from her that a section of the forest in Arusha National Park is off-limits to people because of a spaceship crashing there. A classmate of hers, whose name she won't say, is certain of it.

In more ways than one, it seems the news comes as a bit of a shock. After hanging up, he stands there for a minute thinking, trying to process it all. Knowing Laila is a friend of Cassidy Mkama, the daughter of the Chief Ranger of Arusha National Park, he suspects that Cassidy is the classmate whose name she won't say. Still, it doesn't really matter. He must investigate Laila's claims while there is still light in the sky. Especially now, ever since that dream, he senses that the extraterrestrial, the one from the prophecy, is here.

Before leaving the house, he hurries to the bathroom, peels his lips back and checks his teeth in the mirror.

Roughly an hour later, the Chief sees a ring of yellow barrier tape around an area in the Mount Meru Forest Reserve. It's something he can't miss. As he nears, he can see some thick branches on the ground inside the perimeter. Looking around, one has to speculate that only a large aircraft can tear through the trees like that. More than likely, this is the site of the spaceship crash.

To his misfortune, Paulina Mongella turns up. He takes cover behind a thick tree. Peeping out from behind the tree, his eyes fall on her as she ducks under the barrier tape. She takes a couple of large branches from the ground, slips under the barrier tape, and walks toward her truck. She doesn't know he's there, at least that's what he thinks. How can she know? She has no reason to think anyone is watching her and for what reason?

But he has a reason.

While Paulina is away, he wonders if the alien is hostile. What if the prophecy is false? This question burns through him.

Still, he is content with what his eyes see. There's nothing more he can do here. It's time to leave the area.

After one more peek, he moves quietly behind another tree and turns in another direction. Out of nowhere comes two black-and-white colobus monkeys running, almost colliding into him. Approximately four feet away from him, one monkey stops in its tracks and looks at him. It lets out a screech, then runs after the other monkey off in the distance. He stares dumbfoundedly as his walking stick slips from his hand and falls to the ground. After picking up his walking stick and adjusting his glasses, he can only suspect that this commotion will alert Paulina to his presence if she is around.

While gathering his composure, he hears footsteps approaching, knows who it is but is going to pretend like he doesn't.

"Who do we have here?" Paulina asks him before he can turn around.

Feigning surprise and planning to show it, he slowly turns around nonchalantly but with a look of surprise at seeing her. A little distance away, she stands there with her hands on her hips and sporting a suspicious look on her face.

The only thing Chief Naruma thinks to say is, "Hello, Paulina. It's so nice to see you."

"What are you doing snooping around here?" she asks immediately.

The Chief forces a smile as his brain works feverishly, trying to come up with an explanation. He thinks it's best to keep things simple.

"On my nature walk. Something I do habitually," he says slowly, like he's thinking as he goes.

"So, you say. Do you see anything of interest to you?"

"Is there something I am missing?" he asks, a surprising hint of playful distrust coloring his voice.

That's an odd coincidence, Paulina thinks, that the Paramount Chief of the Chagga is here. Her arms drop to her sides as she takes a step closer to him.

"You look at me as if you know something I don't."

"I'm simply an old tribal man enjoying my walk through this quiet, pleasant forest. What is it you think I know?"

Barely able to contain her annoyance, she says, "I'm losing my patience, Chief Naruma. It's after five o'clock. I'll be going home soon —"

At that very second, she stops talking because she sees him looking at her left hand with the bandage. Quickly, she slides her hand behind her back. An uneasy tension grows between them as they stare at each other oddly for a moment.

"I think it's the other way around. There's something you're not telling me," he says, rubbing his goatee, staring, unblinking, into her eyes.

He's right in saying that. And Paulina wants to tell him about last night. Maybe seeing a ghost. And that maybe it has something to do with the Chagga. But something inside her won't let her. Not now. Maybe not ever. It's her secret to keep.

"You're right. This place is off limits."

"May I ask why?"

"You can ask, but I won't tell you."

"From the look of things, I think it's the crash site of a large aircraft."

"I am under strict orders from TANAPA not to discuss any of that. Sorry, it's confidential."

"You don't have to tell me anything if you don't want to. But if I'm right, I hope there are some survivors," he says and looks at her with a question in his eyes.

She hesitates before answering him. Why does he want to know that? Is that why he's here? These questions run through her mind.

"I have no knowledge of any survivors."

It slips out before she can think it through; a major error on her part. Too late. As it is, she's already feeling tense. Well, thinks Paulina, she'll just have to grin and bear it and put an end to the conversation before anything else slips out.

"I'm sorry to hear that," he says, with a look of disappointment.

"I have duties to tend to. Enjoy the rest of your walk," she says, turns around and starts walking away.

He calls out to her, "I'll be sure to tell your Aunt Rhoda what a great job you're doing."

"Goodbye, Chief Naruma, and thank you," Paulina hollers from the distance.

"There's a survivor — and deep down inside I know it," he says under his breath.

Moving with a purpose, he is setting a fast pace for a man of his age. A smile graces his face and a feeling of content washes over him as if every step he takes brings him closer to ending the curse of the Evil Shadowy Figure.

Still, he must find the alien. But how? That's the hard part. He's still working that out. There is nothing to go on — no description. Still, he remains optimistic. Following his gut instinct, fate will lead him where he has to go.

Chapter 18

A LITTLE AFTER SEVEN THAT EVENING, Allison Banes, opens the back door and holds the screen door open to let the alien out. By exploring the outdoors, she feels the alien will gain independence familiarizing herself with her new environment. When the creature hesitates, Allison puts a reassuring smile on her face.

"Just don't let anyone see you. I want you to follow that map in your bag. Otherwise, you won't be able to find your way back," Allison says, pointing to the alien's crossbody bag.

Another hesitation and then the extraterrestrial can't help taking a few tentative steps out into the darkness. Her eyes are green and full of curiosity. She sniffs the air and swivels her head in every direction, blinking her eyes.

"I'll see you later. Don't stay out longer than two hours, Kitty. And don't lose that map," she calls out to the alien.

Kitty, what Allison calls her now, looks back at her for reassurance, and Allison nods encouragement. She reaches inside the tiny black crossbody bag across her chest and pulls out a handwritten map of the route from Allison's house to the forest around Lake Duluti, looks at it quickly, and puts it back. She has about a thirty-five-minute walk ahead of her, but she doesn't know that.

Allison turns the back porch light on and watches her disappear into the darkness. For Allison it is an emotional moment just thinking of how far they have come and the hurdles they have overcome. As of a few hours ago, the extraterrestrial is warming up to her. Not only that, but the alien seems to trust her and understand some of the things she says, despite the language barrier. Allison steps inside the house, feeling very well indeed.

The gentle night sounds and scents gather around Kitty. She feels the temperature dropping with every step as the Earth's shadow falls on and covers the full Moon. It is deeply puzzling yet cast such a heavy spell over her that she can't turn her eyes away. Mesmerizing to the point of hypnotic, she watches the spectacular but disturbing lunar eclipse, during which the filtering and refraction of light from the Earth's atmosphere creates stunning color effects that range from dark brown to red, orange, and yellow. As she looks at the bloodred color Moon, some of her wariness about this unusual planet, that she knows is in another dimension, diminishes.

Kitty glances toward the thick forest surrounding Lake Duluti. Still in a bipedal position, she takes a few steps onto the Duluti Circuit Trail. In a state of wonder, she turns her head from side to side, listening to the chirps and warbles from the many different birds. As she moves further into the darkness, she sees this terrestrial planet as a mix-up of sights and sounds that do not fit together in her mind.

Somewhere in the forest a rather large, brown owl flies silently overhead and notices Kitty. The owl lands on a tree branch nearby then moves to a branch closer into the pine tree trunk for a better look at the alien. The bird is in a state of confusion, not knowing what to make of Kitty. Is she an animal or a human being?

Before long, the owl hoots and Kitty catches it staring at her with its large round yellow eyes. Kitty purrs and trills, giving the impression that she is trying to communicate with it. The owl nearly falls off the branch in fright. She walks over to the tree and waits for a response. The owl's gaze shifts away, refusing to meet Kitty's probing stare. After shaking its feathers, the owl leaps off the branch into the air, stretches its wings, soars above the trees into the sky and disappears.

Gazing at the red Moon through the trees, a shooting star streaks through the sky beside it making Kitty think of the planets in her solar system. Slowly, she looks down to the ground. She blinks and murmurs a soft meow as she thinks about her family and how she misses them. She has so many memories to cherish. Are they looking for her? They have to be looking for her.

They won't find her: this she knows for certain. She is too far away from her planet. The more she thinks about it, the more she is able to visualize every detail of her planet until a tear falls from her eye.

Around nine o'clock, Allison Banes is in the kitchen preparing a meal for Kitty as if it is the most natural thing to do in the world. Like Kitty's a pet, like a dog or a cat. After opening a can of sardines, she digs out a white ceramic bowl from an overhead cabinet and empties the can of sardines into it.

She places the bowl on the floor, opens the back door and calls through the screen door, "Here Kitty, here Kitty, Kitty."

Allison smiles to herself, applauding herself silently for making the wise decision to call her Kitty. If anyone hears her, they'll just think she has a pet cat.

A minute or so later, nothing comes back.

She takes off her glasses and breathes on them. She wipes the lenses with her white V-neck T-shirt and puts the glasses back on her face. When she peers through the screen door all she can see is darkness. There is no movement in sight.

Another minute goes by.

Nervously, she tucks her T-shirt into her brown three-quarter-length cord trousers and then tucks a strand of hair behind her ear.

"Kitty. It's time for dinner," she says, with a touch of worry in her voice.

Still there is nothing.

At around ten-thirty, Kitty approaches Allison's house and pins her gaze on the porch light glowing beside the door.

In the next moment, Allison comes to the screen door and looks out. There she is. Fifteen feet away. Allison looks at her with an expression of worry in her eyes.

She crosses her arms in front of her chest and makes a tsking sound. "Your dinner is getting cold."

In a humble manner, Kitty drops to all fours, crawls up the steps and onto the porch, and squints up at her. The screen door creaks when Allison pushes it open. She follows Kitty into the kitchen.

"There is something I feel I must emphasize, Kitty. You're an hour late. You know that you can't stay out very long," Allison says, with a touch of disappointment.

Kitty meows softly.

Allison has no choice but to stand there with her hands on her hips emphasizing the importance of the matter. Realizing she's overreacting because the alien has no sense of time, she drops her arms to her sides, and thinks about what she's going to say next.

She clears her throat, her voice coming out in a pathetic croak. "I'm just looking out for you, trying to protect you. I care about your well-being."

Kitty can hear the sincerity in her words and meows again using a different tone.

"Now go have your dinner."

With her back against the counter, Allison watches her eat the sardines and appearing to enjoy it. She is growing fond of this affable alien.

Chapter 19

IT IS ANOTHER DAY IN PARADISE for Azita Hussein, the general practitioner who specializes in internal medicine at the GoHealth Walk-In Urgent Care. Outside the sun is shining on the low-rise colonial-era brick building set in the midst of flowering shrubs and trees that flourish in Arusha's rich volcanic soil. Most prominent is a large tulip tree that shades the clinic.

It's eight thirty in the morning and the first patient of the day is an elderly African man in poor health. After an examination, Azita makes a devastating prognosis: He has severe hypertension. Currently, in the last stage, he needs emergency care and will not get better on his own. She recommends that he check into the emergency department of the nearest hospital.

But right now, the elderly man seems too weak to get there on his own. That's the thing that worries her. She stuffs a stethoscope into the pocket of her lab coat and turns to see his condition is worsening. Additional to the dark circles under his eyes that keep darting every which way, he is sweating heavily, breathing fast through his nose, a raspy sound, and she can see signs of trembling and weakness.

Believing he is about to experience a heart attack, he says to her, "I don't quite know how to say this, but it feels like I have an elephant sitting on my chest."

Seeing that he's dizzy and out of breath, she tells him to lie down on the examination bed and wait while she calls a taxi to drive him to Arusha Lutheran Medical Centre on Makao Mapya Road.

She comes out of the examination room shaking her head. Brenda Mann passes within two feet of her on her way to the reception desk.

Azita stops and asks, "Can you stay with the patient in the exam room until I return?"

"I'll head right there," her trusty nurse says and hurries into the room.

As soon as she picks up the phone at the reception desk, she hears Brenda say in a penetrating tone, "Wait a second there, Doctor."

Moments after, she hangs up and turns away from the reception desk only to see Brenda standing inside the doorway of the examination room with a grim expression. Sensing bad news coming, Azita's face is solemn as she walks down the hallway toward the room.

There's a pause before she asks, "How's my patient?"

Visibly upset, all Brenda can say is, "Mr. Lyanga looks rather bad."

As soon as Azita enters the room, the elderly man on the examination bed arches his back, gasping for air. The heart monitor shows erratic rhythm, at one moment beating fast, and then falling, falling so quickly. The man suddenly loses consciousness. This pushes her to the limits of her endurance. No matter how many times she sees this kind of thing, it never gets easier.

"Mr. Lyanga is going into cardiac arrest," Azita yells. "Blood pressure's down, heart rate's up."

Brenda whips her head around from the doorway and enters the room. "His vitals are deteriorating."

There are moments in a doctor's life when actions become automatic. Azita tries to stop the wild heartbeat by massaging his chest while Brenda slaps a wet towel onto the man's face. Nothing happens, just a flat line and a continuous long tone from the heart monitor.

Several minutes later Azita sighs with exasperation and confusion mars her brow. There is still no pulse, but she continues the external cardiac massage. Even if she knows it is hopeless.

A few more minutes pass and she is still trying to resuscitate the man until Brenda pulls her away from the body and says, "Jesus, Azita, you can't save everyone."

"I'm doing all that I can," Azita says calmly, despite the turmoil inside her.

"It happens sometimes, you know," Brenda says, in a soft voice.

A small sigh escapes Azita as she looks at her and nods.

Brenda takes one of his stiff hands in hers, closes her eyes, and says a sincere prayer.

Sighing with disappointment, Azita records the time of death in the patient's chart. "Death from cardio-respiratory failure due to natural causes."

Azita then covers the man with a white sheet. As she tosses her gloves in the trash, she watches Brenda leave the room. Regarding the dead man on the examination bed, she can't be more upset.

Azita comes out of the examination room with the patient's chart in her hand. She has no time to mourn the loss. There is too much to do in the present. She, naturally, has to quickly write up a report. Then all she needs to do is call the morgue to come pick up the body, before going about the rest of her day.

At one-thirty Brenda Mann returns from having lunch at the exact moment when two morgue attendants come into the clinic. They place Mr. Lyanga's dead body on a stretcher, push it out to their vehicle and drive back to the morgue in downtown Dar es Salaam.

Neema gets up from the reception desk, goes across the empty waiting room, and stares out the window with a blank face. Azita skids to a stop at the reception desk, stuffs her hands in her lab coat pockets, and casts a worrisome glance at Neema, who turns around and sees Azita standing there.

"Dr. Hussein, you have a patient waiting in examination room two," she says with an easy smile.

In a cool, but pleasant enough voice, Azita says, "Thank you, Neema. I'm going right there."

Like most clinics, GoHealth Walk-In Urgent Care is short on funds, short of staff and under enormous pressure to treat and discharge patients quickly.

Chapter 20

AFTER LUNCH, Kitty follows Allison Banes to her office. When Allison gives her a Harper's Bazaar magazine, the October issue with Drew Barrymore on the cover, she plops herself down into a round wicker chair by the window in the corner of the room. It only seems logical for Allison to think, looking through magazines is a good way for the alien to learn about the culture on this planet. Allison sees that with each page she turns, her eyes go wide with excitement too.

Allison drops into the chair behind her desk. She turns on the desktop computer, taps on certain keys, and compares the pattern of the alien's DNA on the screen. She notes that, while humans have 23 pairs of chromosomes, the alien's DNA structure is complex. Every body cell of the alien has 83 pairs of chromosomes.

The complete DNA sequence reveals the genes the organism possesses include both human and feline DNA. It is the evolution of two species from a common ancestor: human. Having come to her conclusion that the stuff from which life develops has many common qualities, there are more similarities than differences among most species, and that the development of humans along similar lines is something to expect, rather than question, thus the alien is in fact a genetic mutation. Allison jots it all down in her field notebook.

Kitty lets the Harper's Bazaar magazine fall to the floor with a plunk that startles Allison, distracting her from her research. Now, looking out the tall window with sheer curtains and streaming sunlight, Kitty needs something else to occupy her time.

"I know just the thing!" Allison says, her face pink with excitement.

Staring vacantly into the distance, Kitty doesn't pay her any mind.

Allison leaves the room briefly and returns with a silver iPod in her hand. "How about some music?"

Kitty turns from the window, angles her head, and looks at her oddly. A meow comes out as a quick high-pitch squeak. When Kitty returns to her chair, Allison slips the earbuds into Kitty's ears and hits Play on the iPod.

At first, the music scares her. Her body jerks, and she almost falls out of her chair. Her head moves from side to side. She wants to get rid of the earbuds, shake them out of her ears.

Trying to calm her, Allison gently, softly, caresses her cheek, petting her like a cat. "Kitty. Calm down. It's okay."

Kitty settles herself in the chair, closes her eyes and listens. Just a minute later, she moves her head up and down, and purrs like a motor car. Her soul is stirring.

As far as Allison can tell, the song "Empire State of Mind (Part II) Broken Down" by Alicia Keys is playing. Fortunately for her there are many more songs on the iPod to entertain Kitty for an hour or two.

Allison sits back in her chair. For an hour after that, she scribbles into her notebook at high speed, keen not to leave out anything important. She even has a theory about the origins of humanity. And that the alien is a close evolutionary cousin to humans. In a manner of speaking, that's exactly what Kitty is.

Her analysis of the alien is complete, for the most part. Allison turns her eyes to Kitty — her prize specimen. She walks over to her, watching her sleep and purr softly. Then, she pulls out the earbuds, takes the iPod out of her hands and turns it off.

After putting the iPod on the desk, she sits down at her computer. It is Wednesday afternoon, four in Tanzania and nine in Buffalo, New York.

"Where does the time go?" she asks herself.

She decides to check her e-mail. There's a message from her mother. She pulls it up on the screen.

Allison,

Christmas is around the corner. I only want to say I'm thinking of you today.

When are you coming for a visit? So, write
back as soon as you can. I'll be looking for
your e-mail.

Love from your mother

Allison hits Reply and types a reply: "Dear Mom. Of course, I want to visit, and of course I'm missing you and Buffalo. I can't say for sure when I'll be home. I'm working hard on my PhD dissertation. I'm passionately studying a new species which I will tell you about another time. I know you understand this. Wishing you a happy holiday season." She sends it and hits Exit. It will have to do.

Thinking about it some more, she feels as though she and her parents are living in different worlds. She has a habit lately of falling behind with her e-mails to her mother and father. Just days before Christmas, the alien consumes her every waking hour. She doesn't have time for anything else — like family. An actual alien, she has to remind herself. It's surreal, seeing Kitty sleeping there in the chair.

While she still has the momentum, she sends an e-mail to her PhD advisor at Cornell University about her progress on her doctoral thesis before shutting the computer down.

Allison Banes sits forward in her chair, puts her hands together and makes a little steeple on which she rests her chin. She begins to think hypothetically. What will happen if people see Kitty? How will people react? This is her chief concern. This leads, of course, to poaching, a major concern throughout much of East Africa. Will poachers try to kill her? After all she is in Tanzania, and poaching animals, especially the slaughter of elephants for their ivory due to an upsurge in ivory demand from Asia, remains a problem. She must consider the possibility.

She can't keep Kitty a secret much longer. One day she'll leave here. And, naturally, there's no way she can take Kitty to New York. She has a serious problem and needs some advice. There must be someone in East Africa she can confide in.

Allison is at odds with herself about what to do. Still, she must do something.

A soft meow interrupts her thinking. She sits back in her chair, looks over at Kitty and smiles. Kitty is awake and looking at her with much curiosity.

"Let's find something fun to do," she says, with a big smile on her face.

Chapter 21

A LITTLE BEFORE SEVEN O'CLOCK, Kitty is standing at the living room window watching the sun bleed into the horizon, then disappear from view. She wants to go outside. Just as the night closes in outside, Allison comes into the room.

Soon after, Kitty slides the strap of the crossbody with the handwritten map inside it over her head. Allison tells her to be careful and to be back before ten as she opens the back door for her.

At twenty to nine Allison sits on the sofa in the living room, pondering what to do. Finally, she comes to a decision, her eyes fix on her Apple iPhone lying on the round maple end table by the sofa. She wants to call Azita Hussein. Azita may have some advice for her. She hesitates, then sighs.

The fact is, she doesn't know how to tell Azita. It isn't the kind of news she wants to share over the phone. Better not to tell her everything. It's her best bet. And somehow, she is going to have to find a way to convince Azita to come over to her house.

Curving herself into the sofa's comfortable depths, she reaches over, grabs her iPhone and dials Azita's number.

After three rings, she answers. "Hello?"

"Hi Azita, how are you doing tonight?"

"I've been better. So, I guess you'll be staying in Tanzania for the holidays?"

"Yeah, I'll be here. I'm very busy with my research, and the prospect of spending Christmas with my parents in Buffalo ends up at the bottom of my priority list."

"What can I do for you this evening, Allison?"

Judging by the sound of her voice, Azita is not in the best of moods and is forcing herself to carry on with small talk.

"Tough day at work?"

"Yeah. Another death at the clinic. I'm watching the news on television, trying to forget it all," she says, gathering her emotions.

Allison shifts around, trying to get comfortable before saying, "I'm really sorry to hear that. But need I remind you. Once in a while, patients will die. Kinda goes with the job."

"You're so right about that. Besides, I have the weekend off to recover from the ordeal. I don't mind company, either. If you don't have plans for Christmas, you're welcome to come over to my place. I'll serve you a wonderful lunch — Persian cuisine, of course. And we can catch up on things."

"That's kind of the reason I'm calling you, Azita. I actually want you to come over here. Tomorrow? Before you go to work?" she asks, mentally crossing her fingers, hoping for a yes from her.

A long, rather suspicious pause before she speaks. "So why tomorrow, Allison?"

"I must show you something."

"Allison, whatever it is, can't it wait till this Saturday?"

Allison's voice is soft, yet insistent. "It's really urgent, quite urgent. I'm, well, sitting on something big here. Really big. She is part-human and part-feline. So, I call her Kitty. Azita, you're the only one I can trust with this. If these backwoods, Chagga tribal people know about Kitty, I am afraid to think what may happen to her. You may not know this, but after some digging around in my spare time, to satisfy my own curiosity, I come to find out that they're so superstitious and believe in some curse. They can be just as scary as the poachers."

Allison can't help but mention the dominant tribe in Tanzania. She frowns on the idea of a supernatural curse hovering over the Chagga. It sounds like mumbo-jumbo to her ears.

"Don't get ahead of yourself, worrying about things that may not happen. I have to give you credit, Allison, you know more about the people around here than anybody else. If you say they're backwoods, I'll take your word for it.

About this Kitty, now. I want to make sure I understand what you're telling me. You're researching a strange species and keeping it in your house."

"Yes, something like that."

"Okay. I'll visit tomorrow morning. Seven sharp."

Allison feels a sense of relief sweep over her. "That's so great. I'll explain everything tomorrow."

"Oh, well, see you then. Bye."

After ending the call, Allison places the iPhone on the sofa. For reasons she doesn't understand, she feels weak all over and doesn't have the strength to put the phone on the end table. She takes off her glasses, lays them on her lap, and rubs her temples with her thumb and middle finger, trying to ease away the tension in her head. Something's not right inside her. It isn't very hot, but it's like she's suffering from dehydration and exhaustion.

Pushing up from the sofa, she steadies herself with a hand on the armrest before walking to the kitchen. She opens the refrigerator, grabs a bottle of water, takes a couple of gulps, then puts it back.

"Hopefully, this will do the trick," she says aloud.

She opens the back door and looks out the screen door into the darkness, wondering how Kitty's doing. Maybe she thinks she sees something, out there on the lawn. She rubs a finger under her eyes and adjusts her glasses. Allison can see clearly now — an African woman, standing with her back to her, wearing a multi-color kitenge wraparound dress that reaches to her knees. Who is she?

She bites the inside of her lip as if she wants to say something but decides not to.

All of a sudden, the woman turns her head around and looks at Allison. The porch light reveals the smudge of black soot across the woman's face.

"He knows you're protecting the one," the woman says in a deathly tone.

Allison can't believe she's talking to her and is trying to remain calm. Even she has no idea what the woman is talking about. Within seconds she is about to say something when a powerful vacuumlike force pulls the woman's body backward, disappearing into the darkness.

She's not there anymore! How on Earth is that possible? Is she hallucinating?

Allison glances around, then up at the sky. Clouds gather and swirl with unnatural speed so that soon they form a heaving mass, casting an eerie gloom over the landscape. Is there a storm coming?

Still wondering about that woman, she does a double take before turning away, just a fraction too slowly to hide her fear. Expecting Kitty to return at any moment, she leaves the door open.

Chapter 22

AFTER A FEW SHALLOW BREATHS, she walks out of the kitchen, heading toward the living room. Feeling a bit out of sorts, she is going to sit on the sofa for a while and maybe take a nap.

Why does she feel this way?

Unfathomable to Allison, the Evil Shadowy Figure is lurking outside the window. Nor does she expect him to be creeping around her house.

Leering hideously at her through the glass, the evil entity wonders where she's hiding the one. He wants the alien. That is why he is here.

Quickly realizing that the alien isn't in the house, he flies into an angry rage, muttering words of vengeance and scowling at Allison, who hears and sees nothing. Now the evil spirit turns his anger on her for protecting the alien, peering at her with treacherous, fiery black eyes. In view of the fact that he can't have the alien tonight, she will do just as well, for his need.

In that very instant all the lights in the house go out at once. The electricity is out. *Why is that?* Allison wonders as she maneuvers herself off the sofa.

And not a moment sooner, the Evil Shadowy Figure materializes behind her.

She feels a cold anger invading her. Standing by the sofa, she's completely alert, but she can't move or call out, and she feels there's an evil presence in the room holding her down — a spirit, a demon, a ghost. She can feel something behind her, approaching, and she knows it's not Kitty. She looks over her shoulder, squints her eyes, but can't make out anything in the pitch-black house. Eerie.

Snarling, the Evil Shadowy Figure blows a stream of sulfurous yellow smoke toward her. Smoke surrounds her. And yet she doesn't see it. But she feels it.

An unfamiliar heat is coursing through her body. Out of the blue, she feels a sharp stabbing sensation in her heart. In her mind, she wants to grab the iPhone from the sofa and call for help. Not going to happen. The pain in her chest is preventing her from taking a step forward. She can't do anything other than just stand there.

The Evil Shadowy Figure shifts his head, slowly, as he moves closer to her. She still doesn't see him. But he sees her, and he's seething. His eyes are on her with a revenge deeper than anything she can comprehend. Standing merely a foot away, he swipes a creepy hand with long, thin, claw-like fingers across her face.

Once again, the pain is swirling around her. It is too much. Struggling to breathe, she can only cough, and she does so over and over again. When the coughing fit is over, she gasps out loud, loses her footing and falls on her knees on the leopard-skin area rug beside the sofa. She places her hand over her heart and tumbles over on her side, eyes rolling and glassy.

All the while, the Evil Shadowy Figure watches in delight and lets out a screeching cackle.

Suddenly, over the pain and somehow above it, she hears the screech. Then comes the sound of a discord of voices speaking in perfect unison. Twitching around, she manages to roll onto her back. She looks up for a moment, feeling the tension in the room. Then, to her amazement, she sees a shadowy figure. Even amidst her pain, she sees it clearly through her glasses. She knows what it is. It fits the description exactly. And it seems so unbelievable. But this is 100 percent real!

"Evil Shadowy Figure?" she whispers out loud.

The voices stop.

The curse is real! Right before her very eyes, the Evil Shadowy Figure cackles at her. It's the first time she's seeing him and he's giving her the stink eye.

Why is he doing this to me? she asks herself over and over.

She squints and tries to move her head away from his claw-like feet. But she can't move. It is difficult to breathe. Still, she swallows hard against the rising nausea, laying there, unable to do anything except suffer.

After a brief interval, she is able to move her head an inch or two so that she can stare at the Evil Shadowy Figure for a long second. He has the shape of a broad man, looking like an Egyptian god in what looks like a dark gray toga with many slits that stops above his knees. What a hideous sight he is. Besides, with a head in the shape of a lion's mane, he looks like he has long, thick hair.

Now, his catlike shape head makes her think of Kitty, further upsetting her. Will he kill her, too? She won't ever know.

The deep-set reddish black eyes have a life, a light like a burning fire, an inconceivable evil. She looks him in the eyes and fear explodes inside her chest like the burst of a firework.

She tries to get up, but the pain is intense. Her head spins, darkness clouds her vision. Lying on her back, she has no control over her body. Her heart is beating fast and hard — it's making her feel breathless. Is she having a heart attack? Is she dying?

As tears fall from her eyes, hot panic washes over her. She doesn't want to die. Not yet. It is inflaming her, squeezing her guts.

Her heartbeat is erratic. Barely able to breathe, she has an odd, waxy complexion as she starts to pant like a dog. Images flash through her head of her parents. In her frenzy, she reaches for the gold cross necklace around her neck. In the back of her mind, she recites a prayer to Jesus Christ, with the certainty that she is dying. What else can she do?

She closes her eyes and says, "Thank you for my life."

Her faith is strong. When her body dies, her soul will be with Christ. This, she believes.

The pain is immense as she embraces unconsciousness, and a wave of weakness shakes her limbs, dragging her to oblivion. As the last breath softly sighs past her lips, her eyes slowly open.

Allison Banes is dead.

Staring at her dead body, the Evil Shadowy Figure bursts into a maniacal laugh. Then he looks around, angrily. Where is that alien? Frustratingly, he will search elsewhere. A sadistic grin crawls across his face as a number of discordant voices talking at the same time echo through the room, spilling out of his mouth in an incomprehensible stream. Just before he vanishes in a puff of smoke, he lets out a long glass-shattering wail.

Chapter 23

ABOVE THE FOREST around Lake Duluti there are dark clouds banking up. Staring at the sky, Kitty looks at the cluster of geometric shadows beneath a waning gibbous Moon. The night is spooky. The wind whistles through the branches of the tree she stands beside with a melancholy sound.

In an uppity mood, now she's ready for one last stroll on the Duluti Circuit Trail. Under the moonlight, she takes off fast, dodges the trees, concentrating all her energy on making the most of the time she has. The muscles in her arms bunching and flexing as she takes a cartwheel and then turns a pretty backflip onto the ground, landing in a split. It is just in her nature to be physical. Having acrobatic skills is a trait of her species.

Kitty doesn't want to exercise anymore. She's really hungry and ready for her dinner. She decides it is time to head back to the house. It's ten after ten. The human that cares for her will be wondering where she is, too.

Kitty rises to her feet and turns to make her way back to the house.

A little less than thirty minutes later, Kitty approaches Allison's house. The porch light is off and the back door is wide open. There is no movement in the kitchen. That seems odd to her.

Something is out of place.

As she gets closer, she has an eerie feeling. Ghostly clouds move slowly over her head from behind the house brushing past the Moon. Then she has an ominous feeling, as if something unpleasant is about to happen when she steps onto the porch.

One step inside, and she knows something is wrong. In the depths of her heart, she knows. In the kitchen, she meows out. There is no response. Allison isn't there to greet her with a warm smile.

She lowers herself to all fours and crawls toward the living room only to find Allison Banes on the floor, lying there in her gingham blouse and tan Bermuda shorts.

Kitty freezes in horror, unable to move forward, instead staring at her and waiting for her to breathe. She knows Allison is dead, but she waits anyway, hoping for some sign of life. When there is none, she rises to her feet.

She may be an alien, but she understands the meaning of death. That much is clear from the look on her face. A tear slides down her cheek as she sets the crossbody, with the handwritten map inside it, on the round end table by the sofa. Despite only knowing Allison for a short time, it feels like losing a friend.

Slowly and mournfully, she speaks the little English she knows from hearing Allison talk and reading her magazines. "I'll see you later, Allison."

Her eyes sadly say good-bye as she slowly steps backward, then flees through the kitchen and out the back door. The back-screen door slams against the house. She whimpers and walks away into the darkness.

Not ten yards away, she looks back at the house one last time. From the distance, her eyes stare sadly, and she starts to shiver. Who can she trust now? she asks herself. Now more than ever she feels like an alien, alone on a strange planet.

Kitty finds her way back to the forest around Lake Duluti. Where else is she going to go?

The sounds of the night birds and the crackling of twigs underfoot are all as one. The nighttime noises move differently through the trees and echo louder in her ears. Fear tingles all around her — the blackness of trees and bushes, the unfamiliar sounds coming from animals she can't see.

Kitty sees some birds fly overhead. They pass by her without giving her so much as a glance. The animals seem to fear her or don't pay any attention to her. This puzzles her and she squints around, suspicious.

Tall trees cast dark shadows across her path and the Moon spills pale light around her. She is seeking shelter. But where?

Kitty is overcome by a wave of loneliness. Smells press against her. Everything seems to be closing in on her. Now she misses her home planet of Corsettia, her people, even the atmosphere. She wants to go back. But how? She is on a planet in another galaxy. She needs a spaceship that is capable of interstellar flight in order to travel through space at speeds greater than the speed of light.

This isn't possible. This planet doesn't have such technology from what she knows already. The revelation doesn't sit well with her.

She keeps going back to her planet. Images of her friends and the family she loves very much flash through her mind in random order and vivid color. But the fact is, there is no way to return to her homeworld. If only she can find a device to open portals across space and time. If there is a way, and that's a big if.

After moping around for far too long and now, walking along the edge of Lake Duluti, she's thirsty and hungry too. After drinking water from the lake, she wanders through the forest and soon finds some large-leaf plum trees. She walks over to the trees, stands on the tips of her toes, and plucks a ripe plum from the nearest branch. It tastes slightly bitter, but her face doesn't show it. After eating it, she lifts up on her toes and plucks another plum and then another.

Towering trees block much of the moonlight, and she doesn't see the swirling clouds. The sky opens up, dropping rain on her, catching her by complete surprise. Then she sinks to the ground, and huddles closer to the trunk of the tree, moving away from the slashing rain.

Kitty is wet, sleepy and her emotions are running wild. After a big yawn, she sobs and sobs about being so far away from her people and the loss of Allison Banes as the rain falls all around her. Pretty soon the sobbing subsides into quiet weeping, and she falls to sleep eventually.

Chapter 24

ON THURSDAY MORNING, two days before Christmas, a black Audi A6 brakes behind the Honda Odyssey minivan in front of the house of Allison Banes. Azita Hussein turns off the car and stares at the house, momentarily. It is seven o'clock.

Azita pulls off her sunglasses and places them in her pink raffia handbag on the passenger's seat. She picks up the thermos from the holder on the dashboard and downs the last of her chai tea. After placing the empty thermos back into the dashboard cup holder, she tosses her handbag over her right shoulder, opens her door, and steps out of the sedan. Wearing a pair of tan corduroy jeans matching her button-down, three-quarter sleeve blouse, and brown leather, open-toe sandals, she is perfectly comfortable in the seventy-degree weather.

Reflecting back to her last conversation with Allison, her only hope is that Allison isn't harboring a half-breed animal with a viral disease. Something she worries about. Crossing her fingers before stepping up to the front door, she also hopes this strange species is not dangerous.

She gives a one-two-three rap on the door. A beat of silence follows. She rings the doorbell, but Allison doesn't come. A beat later, she fans herself with her hand as a wave of heat washes across her as she stands directly in the path of the sun's rays. Unable to get a response, she rings again. No answer, so she thinks Allison is in another part of the house or perhaps in the bathroom. The next thing she does is knock loudly on the door. Still no response.

Almost five minutes later, she calls out loudly, "Hello, Allison? It's Azita, are you there?"

There's still no answer. Is Allison all right? Maybe she's still sleeping.

She pulls her HTC smartphone out of her handbag and dials Allison's number. The phone rings and rings, no answer. She hangs up and puts her smartphone back in her handbag.

Azita decides to walk around the house and peek in a window. She wanders around the side of the house and looks through the closest window and she sees Allison lying — on the floor.

She bangs on the window frame and yells, "Allison! Allison! Are you okay?"

No response.

Crying and frantic, she walks around the house. The back door's wide open. She pulls open the screen door and heads into the house.

Much to her disappointment, she examines Allison's body for signs of life and finds none. The death doesn't look suspicious, possibly a heart attack, but she just can't understand why she's dead because Allison has no history of heart problems. She looks into Allison's dead eyes and feels real fear. She pulls her smartphone out of her handbag, dials 112 — emergency services — and explains the situation to the woman at the other end. Then she calls the clinic and tells Brenda Mann that her friend is dead and will be arriving late in the afternoon.

Nervous, she is waiting outside for the police to appear. She heaves a sigh and leans back against the doorframe. This hurts Azita. To lose one of her only friends. She sniffles, fumbles in her handbag, pulls out a tissue and uses it to wipe away her tears.

In the next fifteen minutes, she spends most of the time crying. Splashes of memory are filling her head. She is remembering how nearly two years ago, Renee Sternberger, a recent graduate of Weill Medical College of Cornell University in the residency training with her at Selian Lutheran Hospital, tells her about Allison Banes. And that, Allison's moving to Tanzania to work on her PhD, according to an administrator at Cornell University who thinks they can connect unaware at the time Renee is planning to leave Tanzania. As an alternative, Renee asks her if she can give her cell-phone number to Allison for the purpose of showing her around Tanzania and helping her to settle in. If she's willing to do that? Azita agrees and gives Renee her number. Ten days after, Allison calls her and over a period of time they become friends.

Two policemen arrive on the scene. They hurry into the house. One of them starts to check Allison's vitals while Azita fills them in.

The police assume it's a heart attack — exactly what it looks like — and Azita doesn't agree.

"That just isn't possible. She doesn't have a heart condition!" she says, rather loudly.

At that very moment, two mortuary attendants walk into the living room, stop, and look at her. There's a pause as she looks around. Looking at the stretcher, more tears fall down her face. The breath escapes from her lungs in a long sigh. She turns away and takes a deep breath. Her heart is breaking in more ways than one can imagine.

"It just doesn't add up," Azita chokes a little, but fights it off.

Azita may crack up if she doesn't stop talking. During all the chaos to lift Allison's body from the floor, she starts to nose around the house. Everything feels unreal. In a flash she remembers. Where is that strange species? Nowhere that she can see.

She stumbles into Allison's office. The first thing she sees is her housewarming gift, the Persian pottery vase in pieces in the trash can by the door. Another disappointment. She pulls her hand through her hair, coming away with strands that she has to shake off her fingers.

Now she walks over to a desk with a small field notebook on top of it. Just on a whim, she opens the notebook and reads a page. There is a description of a half-feline, half-human hybrid. An alien from another planet. Is this true? Thinking about it, she knows Allison is not crazy.

Before she can read any more, the door flies open and an officer rushes into the room. She drops the notebook to the floor and shoves it under the desk with her foot. When he looks at her and nods, she realizes that the officer is talking on a cell phone and not really paying attention to what is happening. She waits.

Not a moment too soon. The officer turns his back to her to talk more privately. Seizing the moment, she bends down and grabs Allison's field notebook. After that, she quickly stuffs the notebook in the back of her pants and steps out of the room.

Upon entering the living room, she watches as the two mortuary attendants in white jackets swing Allison's body onto the stretcher, covering it with a white sheet. A wave of nausea sweeps over her and she is suddenly sweating. She endures it, waits for it to pass.

One of the officers approaches her with calmness, speaks to her in a low voice telling her that when a U.S. citizen dies abroad, he has to contact the U.S. embassy in Tanzania and make arrangements to send the body back to the United States for burial. The officer then writes down her name, address, and other statistics.

"I will contact you if there are any further questions," the officer says, without looking up from his notepad.

The attendants pick up the stretcher and the officer moves aside to let them pass. At that point, the officer gently removes her from the house.

In a zombielike state, she drops into the driver's seat of her Audi A6, reaches around her back and grabs Allison's field notebook from the back of her pants. After placing the notebook in her handbag, she drops her handbag onto the passenger seat. After shifting around to get comfortable, she turns on the engine and gets the air conditioning going. She closes her eyes briefly. Obsessing. Thinking. She opens her eyes and thinks, if only she can blot everything out, just for an hour, just for five minutes.

As she watches the hearse with Allison Banes' body inside drive away, she feels as though she's in a horror movie. The pictures go in, but there's no way to grasp it and make it real. Real tragedy! Her heart is in her throat now. She shakes her head as the tears begin to stream from her eyes. She lets herself cry, deep sobbing tears that make her nose run.

Chapter 25

A DISTRAUGHT AZITA, pulls her car into the parking lot of the GoHealth Walk-In Urgent Care and turns it off. It's just after one o'clock, but she isn't looking at the watch on her wrist. For a moment she sits in the driver's seat and fights the impulse to cry, knowing her eyes are already red enough for somebody to mistake her for a vampire.

As she walks into the clinic, Brenda Mann greets her with a hug. Brenda just holds her, patting her back and whispering soothing words to her. How everything is going to be okay and that she understands.

They break their embrace.

Standing there in her pale pink scrubs and white clogs, Brenda says sympathetically, "I'm very sorry about your friend. I know she's in a better place."

"Thank you." Azita's voice is thick and unsteady. "Thank you, Brenda. I still can't believe she is dead. After talking with her on the phone last night."

As the fresh images of Allison's death course through her like a tsunami, overwhelm her and leave her gasping for meaning that just isn't there, Azita looks away, sadly.

"There, there, dear. I totally get it. A bad day yesterday, losing a patient. Two deaths in two days. All of this, it's too much to bear."

"I hope the clinic is managing despite my earlier absence."

"Don't you worry about that. There aren't many patients today, with Christmas coming and all."

"That explains why the waiting room is empty."

"You have any lunch yet?"

"No, I haven't, and…" Azita's voice trails off.

"I'm just heading out now. Why don't you join me?"

"Oh, I don't know," Azita answers with a slight shake of her head.

"Come on, Doctor. A good meal is exactly what you need. You have to try this restaurant down the road. Spices & Herbs serves up the best Ethiopian food. You'll love it. Let's get something in your stomach and talk a little."

"What about the clinic?"

"It'll just be for an hour. Neema can handle everything while we're away," Brenda says, then asks Neema, "You can do that, can't you?"

Neema comes out of her chair behind the reception desk. "You remember, Doctor, I'm taking part-time classes at the Kilimanjaro Christian Medical University College. I'm going to be a nurse one day. I have everything under control. You ladies enjoy your lunch."

Neema casts a look at Azita, shrugs, and plops into her chair.

"We'll go in my car. Does that sound agreeable to you?" Brenda asks.

"Yeah, sure. Let's go." Azita's voice is hollow and distant.

The herby spicy smell of meat and peppers, and the aroma of coffee roasting, overtakes them the second they step into Spices & Herbs. Exotic music plays over the speakers: drums, bells, and horns. The place is mostly empty because it's already the middle of the afternoon, and it's days before Christmas. They take a seat at a square dark-wood table.

Even though Azita tries to hide it, sipping from a glass of water, she is just sitting there in a haze of misery. The day's unfortunate events trouble her more than she cares to admit or allows others to see.

After the waitress leaves with their orders, Brenda feels it's a good time for a chat.

"How are you holding up over there?"

"I'm getting through it."

"It's not easy confronting the death of someone close to you. It takes a long time to understand what a person means to you, what purpose they play in your life."

But there's more to it than that, Azita thinks to herself. But she can't just blurt out the truth. Even supposing she wants so badly to tell Brenda about the alien in Allison's possession before her death. Even she has trouble believing herself. Still, she thinks the alien may have something to do with Allison' death. On that note, her eyebrow goes up in Brenda's direction, but she doesn't say anything, and it's eating her alive.

Brenda can tell she is thinking about her response. Before saying anything, Azita sighs and leans back in her chair as the waitress arrives and places their orders on the table.

Just as Brenda's about to take a bite into her kitfo, an Ethiopian-style steak tartare, Azita begins to tell her, in some detail, how she does not like the circumstances surrounding Allison's death.

"It looks like a heart attack. That's what the police believe." Azita shakes her head. "Allison Banes doesn't have heart problems."

"Death never makes sense," Brenda says after she takes a sip of her ginger ale.

Azita pours a bottle of Kilimanjaro spring water into her empty glass and takes a swallow. After a moment's hesitation, she launches into a flowery obituary for Allison Banes. She has the deepest respect for Allison's tireless devotion to wildlife preservation. It's a strain, but she manages to keep a straight face, despite the fact that she feels melancholy.

"Allison's strong spirit of goodness, and her bubbly personality. I suppose that's what I miss the most about her," Azita says, still not eating and staring at her plate of thyme swordfish and prawns.

Brenda puts down her fork and wipes her mouth. "Will there be a funeral?"

Azita cuts her swordfish into bites, not one makes its way to her mouth.

"It's not going to be here. The funeral will probably be in a few days in the United States. New York, to be precise."

"Just relax and eat your swordfish."

"I'm just about to take a bite."

"You know, this is the first time we are having lunch together."

"Yes, I believe you are right," Azita says, more than a touch of surprise in her voice.

"Hopefully, next time we can get together under better circumstances."

"Brenda, this place is really nice," Azita says after a few bites.

For the rest of their lunch, they slip into making occasional small talk. They finish and leave the restaurant.

Upon walking into the clinic, Brenda says, "If you want to take the day off, I can handle things around here."

The waiting room is still empty, the only sound is the hum of the PC and the soft voice of Neema talking on the phone.

"No, thanks. I want to be here and stay busy," Azita says, and turns to walk down the hallway.

Brenda follows her down the hallway. "I really do understand how you feel. If you want to talk again, at any time, you know where I am."

Immediately after sighing, Azita manages to say, "Thank you again."

Like sprinting away from the conversation, Azita is walking faster now, getting farther ahead of her. Brenda tries to say something but can't. She watches Azita until she disappears around the corner toward her office.

Chapter 26

IT'S THE DAY BEFORE CHRISTMAS, and Cassidy and Laila are walking the trail to Lake Duluti, at a little after two o'clock in the afternoon. They move carefully with plastic buckets on their heads. There's no school today and they are going spearfishing.

"I can't wait to taste your grandmother's cooking."

Cassidy looks at her funny and says, "I know how much you like her cooking. I'm just glad your parents are letting you come over."

"Considering they are Chagga? Is that what you are implying?"

Cassidy carefully considers her answer. "Yeah, maybe."

"You forget, I'm also a Chagga."

"And aren't you leaving the life of a Chagga? Five years from now, your plan is to become an American citizen, audition for the *American Idol* TV singing competition series, be a contestant, win, and become a famous pop singer," Cassidy reminds her.

"You have that right."

The girls share a laugh.

For the next four hours they wade in the shallow part near the shore of the small crater lake and spear a few fish with their sharp sticks. It's after six and the daylight is fading very quickly. Watching the shadows fall across the lake, Laila wants to leave before it gets dark.

On the other hand, Cassidy isn't in any rush. Taking her own sweet time, she scoops water into her hands and pours it into her white bucket. Then she places the bucket at the edge of the lake and starts playing with the dying fish inside it, stroking the two-black bass with her hand. It's more that she treats them like they're pets in an aquarium.

To her surprise, Cassidy hears a rustling sound. She has the impression that someone is watching them. Looking around briefly, she doesn't see anything out of the ordinary. She suspects her mind is playing tricks on her and turns her attention back to her bucket.

In the coming darkness, Kitty is on her knees beside a tree. As she watches Cassidy and Laila, her eyes are changing color, but neither of them notices her. After two days alone in the forest surrounding Lake Duluti, Kitty's curiosity overcomes her caution, and she leans forward to see Cassidy better. Remaining in the shadows, she watches her awhile longer, then creeps off into the trees.

Growing anxious, Laila walks over and nudges Cassidy with her elbow. "I can't wait any longer. We need to go now. The snakes come out at night, remember."

Cassidy reaches into her African-print ankle-length skirt pocket and pulls out a peppermint candy. The sound of the cellophane paper crackling as she unwraps it causes Laila's mouth to twitch.

Sucking on the candy Cassidy says, "They don't try to hurt you if you leave them be."

"This is no time to joke, Cassidy. I only have a short time before I have to get ready to go to the Chagga gathering tonight."

"Fine. Then go. I'll be along in a minute or two," Cassidy mutters.

Laila stomps off in a way that is so Laila, Cassidy can't stop herself from smiling, then Laila walks to her white bucket of fish and places it on her head. Cassidy watches her walk away with the darkness slowly creeping over her.

Cassidy starts ringing the water from her skirt. Just then, three birds fly across her line of vision and skim across the surface of the lake before disappearing into the shadows of the trees. Her focus returns to her skirt. She slips a hand in the pocket, pulls out and unwraps a piece of candy and pops it in her mouth as she looks around.

A minute later, she hoists her bucket toward her head about to walk off. But she stops midway when she hears noises coming from the nearby bushes, although no one appears to be around. Deciding to check it out, she lowers the bucket back down.

She pushes through the bushes, then freezes when she hears a noise. What can it be? She stands still, trying to make out the noise. Then nothing. She steps behind a tree.

A moment or two later she sneaks a peek and sees a catlike creature, just under five feet tall, tumble across the ground. Whatever it is, it looks strange to her. She clamps her hands over her mouth, eyes wide. A girl with feline features? Is she delusional?

Cassidy never hallucinates. But she supposes that's what it is — a hallucination. Yet, she is still there, in front of Cassidy's eyes.

Blinking her eyes in wonderment, Cassidy watches as she curls her body into a ball. Pretty soon it dawns on Cassidy that she must be the alien from the escape pod, certain that it's not an animal.

"Jeez, Louise!" Cassidy whispers to herself.

Slowly inching herself closer, Cassidy steps on a twig and it crackles. Cassidy is shaking as she watches the alien rise from the ground, dropping her arms gracefully to her sides. Cassidy and Kitty are motionless, their eyes on each other. It's a stalemate. Cassidy grins playfully, staring hard into her eyes that show no fear. And Cassidy sees a hint of a smile blooming on her face, though she stops herself.

Cool beans, Cassidy thinks.

Cassidy stutters out a couple of incomprehensible words, unsure of what to say, as she steps in a little closer, peering at her. Almost instantaneously, Kitty feels overcome with panic and shrieks backward, moving back toward the trees, frantically swishing her tail. Her big, green eyes taking in everything around her, as if someone is going to pop out of a corner.

"Don't go away. I won't hurt you," Cassidy says in a kind voice.

Kitty looks at her apprehensively. She stares at Cassidy curiously and doesn't move.

Cassidy takes a breath before she talks again. "My name is Cassidy. What's your name?"

The friendliness of her voice registers somewhere in the depths of Kitty's mind. But a moment or so later, she lowers herself to all fours and takes off in a hurry.

"Oh, darn it," Cassidy exclaims to herself.

She wants to tell Laila. Now. She must tell Laila before telling her father.

Overcome with excitement, she stumbles, and pushes her way through the bushes, her peach T-shirt tearing on a branch. She sees that there is a tiny hole in the sleeve, but she doesn't mind.

It's dark now and a Moon is rising. At the edge of the lake, she stoops to retrieve her bucket of fish. Less than thirty seconds later, she sets the bucket on her head.

From a distance, Kitty hides in the bushes, in the shadows, where it is darker, where she can watch Cassidy walk away. There is a sadness in Kitty's eyes. And she feels so very alone.

A waning gibbous Moon appears and floods Lake Duluti with its brilliance. The lake, which lays within an extinct volcanic crater whose formation links to that of Mount Meru, looks like a pool of silver. The reflection of the Moon shimmering on the water catches Kitty's attention. She thinks it's beautiful.

After briefly looking up at the Moon, she lowers her head and retreats deeper into the forest.

Chapter 27

AT ABOUT HALF AFTER SEVEN, Cassidy walks into her house, and hurries to the kitchen where she sets the bucket of fish on the floor. In less than half a minute, she covers the two-black bass with plastic wrap and places them in the refrigerator. Thereafter, she empties the bucket in the sink, rinses it out, and puts it in the cabinet under the sink. Now she must go. She has to see Laila. She must tell her about her encounter with the alien in the forest. And it can't wait till tomorrow.

Thankfully, her father is busy watching a television program in the living room. Most likely the news. This means he doesn't care if she's away as he is content to relax a while.

Just as she's running for the front door, she stops herself. She can't just leave like that because it's wrong to run off without telling her father. Standing near the door, she tries to think of something to say in this moment, something that will sound convincing.

Bingo. She knows exactly what to say.

"I'll see you later, Daddy. I have to go help Laila," an out-of-breath Cassidy says after running into the living room.

"Just hold your horses a minute. Let me turn down the television," he says and uses the television remote to mute the sound of the television.

"Come on, I'm in a hurry. She'll be leaving soon for a Chagga gathering."

Geoffrey Mkama turns his head a few degrees to his right and wrinkles his brow. "Tell me again why you're going to Laila's house at this time of night?"

She is still trying to catch her breath. Her mouth curves into a smile of pure happiness. She is so confident of her story, looking innocent and honest with her rust-color eyes.

"Laila needs help carrying another bucket of fish to her house."

"I'm not crazy about you being outside at night."

"It's not going to take long. I'll be back in less than an hour, I promise."

When Cassidy wants something from you, she'll talk you into submission, if she has to. Her father knows this all too well.

"Give me a hug before you go," he says approvingly.

"Thank you, Daddy," she says, and she wraps her arms around him.

"No more than one hour. I'm going to hold you to it."

"Sure, Daddy."

There is no more time to spare. After giving him a kiss on the forehead, she tears herself from their embrace, runs from the living room and out the door.

She and Laila live on the same road. In practically no time, she walks the short distance from her house to Laila's house. Luckily for her she's arriving just in the nick of time as she finds Laila in the driveway, her hand reaching for the door handle of a gold Peugeot 3008. Her parents and younger brother, Toby, are sitting in the small SUV, waiting.

"Laila, come quick, you have to see her," she yells to her.

Laila whips around and asks, "Why are you here?"

"She's the alien you're looking for."

"You better not be joking around now, Cassidy."

"It's the truth. She's no animal. She's a cat person, both human and feline," says Cassidy, now standing next to her friend.

"I'll tell the Chief tonight."

"You have to go right now, before she disappears!" Cassidy says, too loudly.

Hearing the commotion, Laila's mother climbs out of the passenger's seat, stumbling forward with effort, almost tripping over her black and gold silk kitenge wraparound skirt that reaches her ankles. But she is able to right herself before she falls. Judging by the expression on her face, she's not happy with what she sees.

"Laila! Get in the car this instant, young lady!" her mother says, scoldingly.

In the window of the backseat Toby grimaces at Laila. Then he sticks out his tongue and wiggles his fingers in his ears.

Cassidy bites her lip but can't stop herself from blurting out, "But you have to see the cat person in the forest around Lake Duluti. She's the most magical creature of all."

"A cat person? What an imagination you have," says Mrs. Diwani, grinning.

With growing impatience, the father honks the horn and rolls down the window. "You are holding us up here, Cassidy Mkama."

"Just a minute, Karl," Mrs. Diwani hollers back.

Cassidy says, at the top of her voice, "The cat person is real. I am not making it up."

That sends Toby into hysterics. He bursts out laughing. Like it's the funniest thing in the world. Unable to control himself, he tumbles onto the backseat.

Mrs. Diwani looks at Cassidy as if she's crazy. "We have no time for this foolishness, little girl! Off with you, go home. This minute!"

Karl Diwani edges out of the driver's door and creeps around the car. "Come on, Esther. We're going to be late."

"But I'm telling you the truth," Cassidy says with conviction, placing a palm on her heart. "I swear on my mother's grave!"

Cassidy shoots a quick glance at Mr. Diwani, who is scratching his chin and hiding a grin. The intense look in

Cassidy's eyes seems to implore him to agree with her, as if his approval is important. Much to her surprise, he nods as if he believes her.

Mrs. Diwani says to Cassidy, "No more of this. Go now."

"Good night, Cassidy. I'll see you tomorrow," Laila says as she disgruntledly climbs into the backseat.

Cassidy watches Laila slam the door, then turns to walk off toward her house.

Sitting in the backseat, Toby sidles in closer so he's right next to Laila, and he pokes her in the arm to get her attention.

"Just wait till Jason Farquar hears about Cassidy's cat person," Toby says, looking at her mischievously.

"You better not say a word to him," Laila demands.

"Who's going to stop me?"

"Hush up, you two. Your mother is making a phone call," their father says, reprimanding.

Rolling his eyes, Toby scoots back over, thinking of something to say to appease his father.

"I'm sorry, Daddy," Toby says with a boyish grin.

"It's all right son," Mr. Diwani says, as he pulls away from the driveway.

Laila folds her arms across her chest, then thinks better of it and unfolds them, shoving her fists into the pockets of her long, red, and gold kitenge wrap skirt and turning her head to look out the window.

To make matters worse, Esther Diwani is on the cell phone talking to Geoffrey Mkama. Now Laila is really upset.

Chapter 28

SOMETIME LATER, Cassidy walks through the front door of the house to find a distraught father. No doubt in that. She carefully closes the door behind her without seeing him around. But, to her surprise, at that moment he steps into the living room and is peering at her. Her eyes widen as she turns around and sees her father standing there.

"Young lady, you have some explaining to do," he says, right off the bat.

She can't imagine what it is. "What about?"

"How come Esther Diwani is calling me?"

She frowns in a shrugging way, and says, "Oh, that."

"Yes, that. Is that all you're going to say?" he asks, wrinkling his nose.

That is the sort of thing she expects her father to say, she thinks to herself. She shrugs a "not right now" letting him know she doesn't want to get into it now.

That isn't going to work. And there's a whiff of tension in the air.

"I'm waiting," he says, looking at her expectantly.

"Mrs. Diwani is being unfair to me. It's because I'm a kid. She doesn't take anything I say seriously."

"How can I take you seriously? Instead of helping Laila carry a bucket of fish, you're telling tales about a cat person."

She presses a hand to her cheek, not quite sure how to say it. "It's true that Laila is going to a Chagga gathering. If you must know the whole truth. She needs to know about the cat person, I mean the alien, hiding in the forest surrounding Lake Duluti, so she can tell the Chief about it. I'm starving."

There's an alien in the forest? he thinks to himself. His brows pinch together like there's more he wants to say. Before he can say another word, she turns, and begins to walk toward the kitchen. He follows her as she enters the kitchen and quietly watches her.

Cassidy roots through the refrigerator, pulls out the jar of peanut butter and the jar of strawberry jam. She lays them down on the orange Formica counter and reaches for the cabinet. After grabbing the bread, she starts making a sandwich.

She slices her sandwich in half and lays it on a plate. Then she takes a glass from the overhead cabinet and pours tea from a pitcher in the refrigerator just before sitting at the table.

Now her father is ready to talk.

Standing beside the table, he asks, "When are you going to tell me more about this alien?"

Cassidy eats with a kind of passive guzzle while he watches her. She takes another bite of her sandwich. Before answering him, she puts it back down on the plate.

"See, Daddy, it's like this," she says, chewing, "I don't know exactly what it is. She is the most magical creature I ever put my eyes on. I have no choice but to believe it's the alien from the escape pod."

"Fat chance that it's an alien. Most likely a wildcat. Maybe it's a," he is unable to continue the sentence.

"It's not a wildcat. It's the alien," she can't help but interrupt.

Cassidy raises the glass to her lips and takes a long sip.

"Why does the Chief of the Chagga need to know?"

After putting the glass down, she says, "There's a curse on the Chagga. The only chance the Chagga has is for the alien to stop the curse."

His brow wrinkles as he puzzles over the situation. "Is that a fact?"

"Yes, it's true. The Chagga believe that extraterrestrials exist. Laila takes it very seriously."

"That's news to my ears. They say that the Chagga can be really superstitious."

"I guess they are."

He thinks carefully about what he is going to say. "But next time tell me the truth from the beginning. If you see this alien again, you need to tell me first. Despite the curse on the Chagga. My duty as Chief Ranger is to protect all living creatures, even if they come from another planet."

"If there is a next time. I will make sure to."

"That's my girl. Now hurry up and finish your dinner. It's almost eight. Normally you go to bed around this time of night. If you want presents tomorrow, you surely don't want to upset Santa."

"I know there's no Santa Claus, Daddy," she tells him, speaking with great authority.

"But you believe in aliens?"

"That's different."

"Whatever you say, my dear," he says and kisses her on the forehead.

"Good night, Daddy."

As he leaves the kitchen, he pauses in the doorframe, looks back, sees that she is giggling and quickly turns his eyes forward and leaves the room.

Not much later, Cassidy lies in bed in her pajamas. Staring at the Moon's glow through the window, she fantasizes about the alien. The only other person besides her father who believes her is Laila. Well, she thinks they do. Maybe the Chagga Chief believes her. She'll find out tomorrow. She wants to prove it's the alien, if only to herself. She has to.

Being Christmas Eve and all, she sits up on the bed to make a wish to Santa Claus.

"If you're listening, Santa, all I want for Christmas is to find the cat person. That's what I'm calling her until I can think of something better. Please let me find her and let her be safe. Good night and thank you so much."

That's all she wants from Santa Claus, even if she doesn't believe in him, but figures there's no harm in trying.

She slides back into a sleeping position.

Not tomorrow, but some day very soon, she will set out to find the alien. She'll have plenty of time after school next week. She will keep it to herself for now. This is last thing on her mind.

"Yes," she mumbles, before falling into a deep sleep.

Chapter 29

CHRISTMAS EVE is a festive time for the Chagga. For the small gathering on the southwestern slope of Mount Meru, it's an evening of song, dance, and traditional stories from elders about Chagga values. It is during this time that a fair number of Christian migrant Chagga return home to commemorate their ancestors. Many Christian Chagga don't see a faith in God and spirit beliefs to be in contradiction, but rather as equally relevant aspects of their theory of the origin and development of the universe.

In the darkness, the dust in the still air transforms into violet haze, through which the red glow of the campfires of the Chagga seem distant and unreal. The panorama is complete by the magnificent outline of the volcanic cone of Mount Meru, which rises from the surrounding plain like an ancient pyramid.

The festivities are about to begin. Chief Naruma makes a speech and leads the gathering in prayer. Right after he raises his goblet and takes a sip of mbege, a banana beer the Chagga brew from millets, bananas, and quinine for bittering, three African men in red kitenge shirts with black patterns, dark trousers, and sandals, sitting on wooden stools, begin beating on cowhide drums with their hands. A row of women standing behind the drummers sway to the frenetic rhythm filling the air like exotic perfume. Then, in an elaborate performance, the women sing in Kiswahili; a song honoring their ancestors. After the song, the women give their shrill shouts of joy and the men and children clap their hands.

Once the feast begins, Laila Diwani seizes the opportunity to talk to Chief Naruma. When she finds him, she reaches out and taps him on the leg.

He glances down at her. "What is it, my child?"

"I know where the alien is," she says in a whispering voice.

"And you know this how?"

"My friend Cassidy Mkama. It looks like a cat and a human and it's hiding in the forest surrounding Lake Duluti. You have to believe it because it's true."

Why, he wonders, does the alien appear to Cassidy Mkama who isn't Chagga? Still, this is the only lead he has for finding the alien. In a strange way he senses she is right.

"Thank you for sharing this with me, Laila. I will look into it. But I'm sure you're right, just like you are about the spaceship crashing in the forest of Arusha National Park."

"I am? I mean, of course I am. The reason I'm not a witness to the alien, is because after spearfishing at Lake Duluti, I end up leaving Cassidy behind to come here, so I miss out seeing the alien too."

Is Laila the child of the prophecy? The child the Chagga need for the ritual? The alien comes, but she's not there. Somehow, they miss each other. The Chief can't help but wonder.

"Your parents must be proud of you."

"In truth, they don't believe that the cat person exists."

"They will soon believe. I have a feeling they will."

"Thank you, Chief Naruma."

"No, thanks to you. Go and enjoy the festivities."

Chief Naruma must talk with the elders of the Chagga Council.

"Rhoda dear, please come over here right away," he calls out, waving a hand at her.

Rhoda Kisanga hurries over to him. She is wearing a caftan of violet-and-silver. A tall kitenge cloth headdress of similar colors hides the contours of her hair and head.

"What is it, your Eminence?" she asks respectfully.

"I want you to gather the council members. Later this evening, after everyone leaves, we're going to have a meeting."

At the end of the evening, most of the Chagga are no longer present. Rhoda Kisanga and four other men stand in a circle, listening to Chief Naruma talk.

"I must tell you all about a spaceship crashing in Arusha National Park five days ago. The extraterrestrial is here. The prophecy is correct. The gotham being descends from the sky."

Oohs from the men and ahh from Rhoda follow. All of their eyes are wide and almost bulging, no one dares to speak, not just yet.

"The alien resembles a cat and a human. You have to search for the alien in the utmost secrecy. Once we have the alien, then we will inform everyone and prepare for the ritual."

"What about the child of the prophecy? The alien can protect the child from the supernatural power of the Evil Shadowy Figure," Rhoda asks anxiously.

"I have my suspicions, but I still don't know for sure. We will know when the time is right," the Chief reassures her.

Chief Naruma speaks to her, but Rhoda Kisanga doesn't hear what he says. Her gaze zeroes in on a burning campfire approximately fifteen feet away. Something is causing the fire to pop and snap. As she watches intently, she sees a shape in the flames. And before long, she sees thick plumes of smoke begin to rise into the sky, which is filling with dark clouds. She's in a trance, unable to take her eyes away from the fire as if looking into another dimension.

What Rhoda doesn't realize is that the fire serves as a portal to no other than the Evil Shadowy Figure. Fiery black eyes appear in the flames. By chance Chief Naruma turns and looks toward the campfire. Slowly, the Evil Shadowy

Figure materializes before them along with the sound of horribly deafening screeching.

Chief Naruma doesn't look away but meets the Evil Shadowy Figure's eyes head-on. The evil spirit peers at the Chief as if he wants to pull his spirit out of his body and send it through the fire to join the other spirits of the dead in his possession. Which he's very capable of doing.

A male elder leaves and soon returns with a metal bucket of water, dousing the flames. Angrily the Evil Shadowy Figure turns around to face him, opens his mouth wide and lets out a blood-chilling scream. A rush of energy — like a powerful wind — lifts his body off the ground, tossing it ten feet through the air like a rag doll.

"No! Oh no, Thobias," Chief Naruma screams.

Lying on the ground, Thobias Miranda has some minor injuries, but at least he's still alive. There is soot on his face and clothes. In the foggy haze that comes just before blacking out, he grunts and mumbles something. And then the blackness begins to creep into his head. He tries to will it away, to keep himself conscious, but it's no use.

The other elders watch in awe and fear. It's not till now that Rhoda realizes she is shaking all over. Slowly she becomes aware of the uproar around her.

The Evil Shadowy Figure turns his attention back to Chief Naruma. But the flames are fading. Many voices talking in unison escape through his mouth, all the while glaring at the Chief furiously. The evil entity lets out a glass-shattering wail before he descends into the last remnants of the campfire, releasing a puff of smoke. The cacophony of sound ceases as abruptly as the Evil Shadowy Figure vanishes from sight.

Chief Naruma approaches the campfire. He stabs his walking stick into it, and a little puff of dust rises into the air. After poking it with his walking stick a little more, he determines that the Evil Shadowy Figure is no longer present. All that remains is an eerie feeling around him.

The Chief looks at the elders and says: "You're going to have to find the alien before the Evil Shadowy Figure does."

Chapter 30

CHRISTMAS is a day to celebrate with family and friends and the Mkama family is no different than any other. Dottie Mkama is up early this morning, like every morning. She's probably the first person up in Tanzania. Most mornings, you'll find her in the kitchen eating breakfast or cooking it on her stove. More often than not, she has the same breakfast. Two eggs sunny side up, or oatmeal, two pieces of toast with butter and jam, and chai tea with milk and double sugar.

Later on, she goes out to her porch, where she sits in her rocking chair, hands clasping the sides of her teacup, and waits with anticipation for the first glimpse of the orange glow rising on the horizon. Once the sun is up, she heads back into the kitchen for the preparations for the holiday feast.

Later in the morning, she often works on the flower beds on the east side of the house. But today there isn't any time for that.

Just before four o'clock Geoffrey Mkama's Land Rover is outside Grandmother Mkama's house. It's a gorgeous Saturday afternoon. The sun is so bright, almost blinding as it peeks through the treetops and bounces off the windows of the houses in Tanzania.

"This place looks festive," Geoffrey says, coming through the front door, wearing his best black suit and a blue tie, and seeing the Christmas tree in the corner of the living room.

"Lovely to see you, Geoffrey," Dottie says, holding the door open. "Welcome and Happy Christmas."

Dottie releases the door, steps back a little and takes in Cassidy, so much like her father with her high cheekbones that stand out whenever she smiles and Laila, whose real beauty shines from within, lighting up her soft brown eyes.

"You two look lovely in those dresses."

"Happy Christmas, Ms. Mkama!" Laila says, and performs a little curtsy with her red dress with daisies polka dotting it.

"A Happy Christmas to you as well," the grandmother replies.

"A present for you, from my mother," Laila says as she hands her a gift in gold wrapping.

"Tell your mother, Esther, thank you for me."

Laila smiles sheepishly in return.

Geoffrey hands his mother a bag of gifts for her. Dottie places Laila's gift in the bag and drops the bag beside the tree.

Ms. Mkama raises her arms, a huge grin on her face. "Lil Cassie, come over here and let me give you a big hug, you precious, precious thing."

"Yes, ma'am," Cassidy shuts the door behind her and hurries to embrace her grandmother.

Cassidy feels a surge of warmth in her embrace. It feels good. She kisses her grandmother on the cheek.

"Lil Cassie, you can be Santa Claus this year and give out the presents from under the tree," the grandmother tells her after breaking their embrace.

"I'll be happy to."

"Is there anything under that tree for me?" Geoffrey asks, winking at his mother.

"Why of course son," Dottie tells him, with a smile.

Dottie Mkama excuses herself to check on the preparations in the kitchen, while Cassidy gets the presents from under the tree.

"Why don't I help you," Geoffrey says, following behind her.

Upon walking into the kitchen, the aroma of spicy food and bread overwhelms him. As Dottie takes the apple pie out of the oven, it is clearly the moment to ask her about the Chagga. It just so happens; she knows a thing or two about them.

"I can't believe I'm asking this, but do you know anything about ending the curse on the Chagga?"

After setting the pie on the counter to cool, she asks, "What do you mean, the curse of the Evil Shadowy Figure?"

"The very one," he says, utterly serious.

"Why the sudden interest? You've been talking to Laila?"

"Yes, in the car on the way here. Laila's been telling me quite a lot about the curse. First time I'm hearing this. It sounds rather superstitious. Just out of curiosity, I want to hear what you know."

"I'm afraid superstition is difficult to avoid in these parts. According to Chief Naruma, undoubtedly, there are rumors connecting suspicious deaths with the Evil Shadowy Figure for a little over two hundred years. It's such a shame. If there is a way to end the curse, I don't know what the Chagga must do."

"Thanks for sharing what you know with me."

After picking up a basket of Indian Chapati bread, she says, "Follow me to the backyard."

Geoffrey follows her outside as she exits through the screen door. She sets the basket on the wooden picnic table with matching benches on each side. There is a dark green linen tablecloth, silver cutlery, napkins, glasses, and a pine cone centerpiece with silver candles on the table.

Presently in the living room, Laila is standing next to the sofa trying to persuade Cassidy, who is sitting on the floor near the tree, to head out to the backyard. In honor of the occasion, Cassidy is wearing her best dress, cut to her knees, which is white, with a yellow sash around the waist and doesn't feel very comfortable wearing it. Her posture is slouchy — it's like trying to dress a hunchback.

"Let's go. I'm hungry."

"She'll call us when it's time for us to come out."

"She usually puts bowls of snack food out on the table while she gets the food ready."

"Now just a minute there, Laila. Answer me this. Honestly. Your Chief really believes me about the alien?" Cassidy asks again.

"Yes. I keep telling you. But what's really cool is that your Dad seems to believe it too. Hopefully Chief Naruma will find the alien real soon."

Not if I find her first, Cassidy smugly thinks. Only what Laila doesn't know is that she plans to go searching for the alien. She's the one who's going to find it because she's the only one who knows what it looks like. She just wants to see it again, to know it's okay.

"Time to eat," the grandmother yells from the kitchen.

"Okay, let's go," Cassidy says, stands up, and starts walking toward the kitchen.

"Praise the Lord. Straighten that dress, Cassidy, your shoulders are showing," Grandma Mkama says when they walk into the kitchen.

"Yes, grandmother," Cassidy says then, quickly adjusts her dress, and smiles.

The Christmas meal comes and goes and there's still food on the table. It's no surprise Geoffrey ends up with a plate to take home. After hugs and kisses and more hugs and kisses, Geoffrey, Cassidy, and Laila leave just before seven o'clock. On the way to drop Laila at her house, sitting in the backseat of the SUV, the girls are enjoying their favorite pastime, staring out the window and daydreaming. And, of course, Cassidy is thinking of the alien. Lately, the alien seems to be the only thing on her mind.

Chapter 31

THERE are plenty of tourists to spot in Tanzania even after Christmas. Most tourists come to visit the parks on a game-viewing safari. They don't call Arusha the safari capital of Tanzania for nothing. Practically everything in Arusha revolves around the safari industry, which generates large amounts of foreign currency for the country. Therefore, there is no shortage of guides to chaperone visitors seeking to pigeonhole the 'Real Africa.' One of the most popular tour guides operating his own high-end safari company in Arusha goes by the name of Kwami Amutullah. He is also popular for another reason. Poaching. On the down-low, of course. People like Paulina Mongella think him unpopular for that reason, too.

The life of a park ranger isn't easy for Paulina, who is responsible for protecting wildlife. Africa is home to many unique animals, and she wants to protect them. Whenever she finds a dead animal, most often, it's the result of hunting by poachers. On days like that, she wonders if the work she does matters. Though she knows how unaware most people are about modern-day African hunting.

Arusha National Park is a frequent destination for tourists who want to see free-roaming wildlife, such as giraffes, zebras, and Cape buffalo. It keeps Paulina busy all year round. Standing near Momella Gate at the start of the trail up Mount Meru, she picks at the edge of the bandage on her left hand while waiting for Kwami Amutullah. She will oversee the first stage of his tour to ensure their safety without disrupting their peaceful trek.

Despite how she feels about Kwami, she manages a smile as he drives up in a tan Toyota Land Cruiser, with the logo of Africa Quest on the doors, the name of his safari company. Putting on her best game face, smiling at the tourists sitting in the back clinging at their armrests, a communal expression of hope and wonder on their faces. She understands their reaction, the first time they set foot in Africa. Their eager excitement about the animals they are about to see. That's what keeps people coming back.

The driver's side opens, and out steps Kwami Amutullah wearing khaki cargo pants, a white Abercrombie & Fitch polo shirt, and running shoes. Half a dozen feet away, she can smell his cologne: grapefruit and leather and pepper, exceptionally spicy.

Eager for the day to end, Paulina clenches her teeth and whispers, "I don't like having to be here the day after Christmas, but it's even worse seeing him."

Without wasting a moment, she greets him with her usual cordial welcome. "Welcome, Kwami. I'm so glad to see you again. I'm looking forward to supervising your tour of Arusha National Park."

"Why thank you kindly, Paulina. My guests have come here all the way from Bilbao, Spain, for a two-week sojourn during their Christmas and New Year's break from the Universidad del País Vasco. They are more apt to have fun and anxious to glimpse the exotic wildlife which Africa is famous for," he says to her and then turns to the tourists coming out of the SUV. "Isn't that, right?"

"We all can't wait," one of the girls says in a Spanish accent.

Paulina watches him smiling at her all the while she's talking. On her right is a girl with dark brown hair and bangs, and on her left is a short, skinny young man with dark, bushy hair and fierce, staring eyes. That's Kwami for you, automatically flirting with every woman he meets, Paulina thinks as she rolls her eyes to the back of her head.

Kwami is five-nine, thirty, has a short 'Afro' haircut, and has a baby face. He's growing a mustache to make him look older. Sometimes he flirts with Paulina, but she reminds him that she's happy with her husband. She doesn't care for him in the least. It's just, knowing that he's participating in the capture, and killing of game animals for sport is enough to turn her off to his charms. She can't prove it, though. It's difficult to prosecute seeing as there's no evidence of any kind against him.

The last to exit the safari vehicle is Edwin Joseph, a former military officer of the Tanzania People's Defence Force, Kwami's right-hand man, and a poacher on the side. He's two inches shorter than Kwami, thirty-four, with a broad nose, thick lips, a scar on his chin, a bushy 'Afro' haircut and weighs less than a hundred and fifty pounds, with no fat. Additionally, he's a divorcee, father of a teenage boy, an intermittent heavy drinker, and lives alone in a house not far from Kwami's. He is wearing khaki cargo pants, a blue nylon backpack, and a tight-fitting white T-shirt with an Africa Quest logo across the front.

Edwin's looking at Paulina. He smiles a lazy smile and seems to nod before he looks away. If she notices the look, he gives her, she doesn't show it. Even if he makes her feel uneasy.

Paulina fumbles with the bandage on her hand as she pulls out a map of Arusha National Park from the back pocket of her khaki pants.

When he sees the bandage on her hand, he asks, "You hurt yourself?"

Before handing the map to him, she points to a spot on the map. "Never mind about my hand. This area is off limits to visitors. You know what that means. Don't go there, Kwami."

He looks at her with a smirk on his face. "Very well, Paulina, I will do exactly as you wish. I am more than happy to comply."

"I am so glad to hear you say that."

"May I start the tour, Paulina?" he asks, tucking the map inside his pants pocket.

Up close, his voice is low and sounds throaty. Hearing it makes her skin tingle.

"So soon? What's the hurry, Kwami?" she asks, with a trace of amusement.

If nothing else, he can always count on Paulina to keep his ego in check. He doesn't say a word, doesn't even nod his head. Heat fills his cheeks as frustration gets the best of him. Still, he just looks at her with wide eyes.

"Need I show you the way. You know the Momella Route well," she says, pointing to a dirt path.

"Let's get this show on the road," he tells Edwin excitedly.

Eagerly Kwami starts walking toward the trail with his entourage. Walking at a distance behind them, Paulina hangs back, watching. She adjusts the rifle riding between her shoulder blades. It's obvious she is in Ranger mode.

Chapter 32

FOUR HOURS LATER, Kwami Amutullah and his entourage arrive at the Miriakamba Hut campsite. After placing their belongings inside a lodge, where they will spend the night in a dormitory-style room, the three tourists from Spain meet Kwami and Edwin for lunch in the common dining area.

At one-thirty, Kwami and Edwin come walking out of the dining room. Not a second too soon. Rhoda Kisanga comes out of relatively nowhere, smiling in her usual carefree fashion, walking around the site. The very instant she sees Kwami, she waves to him and says something. When he starts walking toward her something inside her melts, while Edwin stops and waits for the Spanish tourists. Granting that Kwami is rather thin, his broad shoulders give a fine balance to his height. At least, Rhoda, a recent divorcee, thinks so.

Nobody knows the northern game-viewing circuit better than Kwami. If there's an alien in these parts, Kwami will surely spot it. She doesn't know where else to turn. Chief Naruma expects the impossible from her. She doesn't have any experience tracking animals, much less tracking extraterrestrials. That's what she's thinking as she describes in detail the cat person, peering over her shoulder to make sure no one else can hear.

"I'm telling you in confidence. It's an exotic species from the Amazon jungle. Chief Naruma smuggles rare animals into Tanzania every year. The Chagga use them as ritual animals for a ceremony on New Year's Eve. Only now it's missing. If it's alive, chances are it's hiding in the forest around Lake Duluti. Can you capture and return it to the Chief?"

Rhoda has to tell him something believable. She can't exactly tell him the truth, can she? That it's an alien, even if that's what it is.

"Will there be a reward, Rhoda?"

"A small reward because the Chagga are simple religious people."

"It is not a very tempting offer," Kwami says with disappointment.

Is she naïve to think of him as an exotic animal lover or a hunter par excellence? There is something a little too smug about the look in his eyes. From the strange way he's looking at her, it's easy to tell he has something other than returning the alien to the Chagga on his mind. She wonders if the rumors are true. That perhaps he really is a low-level poacher. Looking as if he is about to say something more, something about money, she's almost starting to regret telling him about the alien.

A smile breaks across his face. "You need not worry anymore. If it's out there, I'll find it."

When he says that it restores her faith in him. "I'm so glad I can count on you, Kwami."

After a short lunch break, Paulina comes out of the ranger's office. That's when she sees her. She narrows her eyes suspiciously at her Aunt Rhoda conversing with Kwami. As if they are friends. What is she doing here? Her mind spins around and around like a top. She can't even guess what they are talking about.

Rhoda glances at her niece out of the corner of her eye. That's not good, she thinks. She has to wrap up the conversation.

"I want you to call Chief Naruma at this number, if somehow you find it."

With a sly smile, he takes the slip of paper with the Chief's number from her. Quickly, touching her fingers with his own, and he knows right then that she fancies him. It doesn't take any special gift to sense that in a woman; he only has to look in her eyes.

"I promise that he'll be the first person I call."

Kwami's not sure why they evoke each other, except that he finds plump women attractive. Even when she walks away from him, he can't stop from looking. The bright red and orange pattern kitenge dress hugs her curves in all the right places before flaring out ever so slightly below her knees. There's something in the way the older woman walks that strikes his fancy, a kind of recklessness and looseness in her stride.

And for a quick second Rhoda looks back at him with a gleeful twinkle in her eyes, "That is what I'm counting on."

Paulina has the same look on her face as she walks over to her aunt, the same suspicious look from before. "Auntie, what brings you around here?"

She gives her a quick hug before answering. "Well, hello, my darling Paulina. Just passing through. If truth be told, I'm on my way to visit Chief Naruma, who you know lives an hour's walk northwest from here."

In all actuality, she and other Chagga elders are searching for the alien, per the Chief's instructions, thereby exhausting the resources available to her. There's no way she's going to tell Paulina.

"Of course! That explains everything."

"How is your hubby? What a kind man Joaquim is! Still working as a chef at a hotel restaurant?"

"Joaquim is fine and is cooking his heart out day in and day out. To be specific, he's working at Saba Saba inside the Gran Melia Arusha."

"That's just terrific. Well, I must be going. It's been a pleasure seeing you, Paulina. Give your Auntie Rhoda a kiss."

The moment she walks away Paulina turns her mind to business. But before she has time to turn around, Kwami appears at her side, completely catching her off guard. His lips curve into a smug smile, raising his eyebrows, taunting her. Her face goes blank, so overcome with annoyance that she doesn't register that the smile is bigger on one side than the other.

He takes a quick gander at Edwin, who is smiling and conversing with the Spanish tourists, before asking Paulina, "You ready to hit the trail again?"

"I'm ready to proceed. You have a nice talk about me with my aunt?" she asks with an air of suspicion.

Kwami does a funny sort of laugh. "Why on earth do you think that?"

"You keep looking at me like you know something."

"I often see Rhoda around Mount Meru. Sometimes we chat a little. All innocent, I assure you."

He says all this easily, but there's something more to it. She suspects as much, but she doesn't have time for any further delays.

"Guess I'll take your word for it. Shall we move on now?"

He turns on his heel, goes back to Edwin and taps him on the shoulder. "Let's get back on the trail!"

Edwin rubs the back of his neck and doesn't look at Paulina. One of the Spanish girls bends over to load her water bottle into her backpack, while the Spanish man approaches Kwami with a curious expression and stands silently.

Ten minutes later, as Paulina walks the path steeply up through the glades toward Topela Mbogo, a buffalo swamp, she wants to turn around and go back to the Miriakamba Hut campsite. Already, she's looking forward to hitching a ride from one of the porters to Momella Gate, climbing into her pickup truck and driving home. Too bad that's not going to happen for another two hours. The Spanish tourists plan to walk to Mgongo Wa Tembo, elephant ridge, for a view down into the Meru crater.

Chapter 33

ON A BRIGHT AND EARLY TUESDAY MORNING, Azita
Hussein is at Kilimanjaro International Airport in the Hai
District of Tanzania. Gazing out the airport window at the
hearse carrying the coffin of Allison Banes drive out to the
KLM Airlines plane, where a freight elevator lifts the coffin
into the baggage compartment. Too soon, she watches the
ground crew wheel the plane around, watches as it taxis out
onto the runway, watches it gather speed and climb. The
flight is on its way to New York.

But why? she asks herself.

Weeping softly, she can't come up with an answer. Not
so far, anyway.

Overcome with sadness, she sucks in her breath, leans
against the wall, puts her hands over her face and cries some
more, but only for a short spell. Whirling around, she
lowers her hands and looks around. She sees lots of tourists

walking around with eager expressions on their faces thanks to daily KLM flights that link Europe to the airport. Nobody seems to notice how she looks: heartsick.

After visiting the bathroom, she feels hungry and thinks about food. Well, why not? she asks herself. She makes her way to the coffee shop for a light meal before she goes to work.

The trip from the airport to GoHealth Walk-In Urgent Care is approximately forty-five minutes to one hour. In the clinic's parking lot, she stays in the driver's seat of her car, thinking that she doesn't want to go inside the clinic. Her stomach's not doing well. Her head is in worse shape. The rest of her is cold. She is remembering different things about Allison. She is just in such a haze and feeling so bad inside.

Looking into the rearview, she pulls her hair into a ponytail at the top of her head, while telling herself to move forward. Maybe a hard day as a doctor will take her mind off Allison Banes. She will work the rest of the day, and tomorrow, and by late Thursday she will feel better. Over and over again during difficult times, her work is her refuge.

Thinking this way "works." She pushes herself out of her car.

About a quarter after one, Azita steps inside her office. After placing her raffia handbag on a hook behind the door, she hears a scream, a girl's scream. There is a long silence, and then the sound of crying. She knows the sound of pain.

She takes two steps into the hallway to see Brenda Mann hurrying toward the reception desk and follows after her.

When Azita gets to the waiting room, she finds an African girl, around nine, in her father's arms. His hand is awkwardly patting her back like he's trying to comfort her. The girl is having muscle spasms because her upper arm bone is out of the shallow socket of the shoulder blade.

"Dislocation," Azita says swiftly to Brenda.

Neema is standing behind the reception desk looking tense, not sure what to do next.

"Good afternoon. I am Dr. Azita Hussein. I'm going to help you feel better. What's your name, dear?" she asks the girl.

"Ayana," she says through the tears.

"What a pretty name," she replies, then turns to Brenda. "Bring her into the examination room."

"Yes, Doctor," Brenda says, rushes to Ayana, and takes the girl into her arms.

"You, sir, if you don't mind, please stay in the waiting room. Once the procedure is complete, the nurse will bring your daughter back," Neema says to the man.

The patients' needs at the clinic manage to take Azita out of her worries and sadness from her friend's death. That is precisely the reason she's working in the clinic.

Once inside the room, Brenda puts the girl on the examination bed, holding her neck and her limbs steady.

Azita circles around Ayana to examine her shoulder. "I am going to push your arm back into place. It will hurt, but you're going to be all right."

The pain is overwhelming her. Ayana is silent for several seconds before gesturing to her arm. She then closes her eyes.

"Brenda, lift her up a little so I can manipulate the bone back into its socket," Azita says, then moves closer to Ayana. "I have to hold you against me."

There is a crunching sound when Azita jams the limb back in place. Ayana whimpers and her head lolls backward and her back arches. Opening her eyes again, she looks at Brenda without saying anything.

"It's not serious enough to require a cast, but you'll be in pain for a while longer. Other than that, you're as good as new," Azita tells her patient.

"Thank you for helping me, Doctor," Ayana says softly.

Forty-five minutes later, the clinic is quiet. There are no patients in the waiting room. The door of Azita's office is wide open. She is slouching behind her desk with a haggard look, her head facing away from the doorway. She stares at her computer screen, but she's not really seeing anything there. The sadness is back. She longs to see Allison Banes again and laugh about something. She feels her heart knocking hard against her chest and her hands beginning to sweat. But soon the moment passes. She rubs her eyes and stares at the ceiling for about a minute.

Everything slows down then. She can't remember the exact moment she realizes; it just occurs to her. She gets out of her chair, grabbing her handbag off the hook behind the door, reaches inside and pulls out Allison's field notebook. Now seems a good time to check it out.

Azita drops back into her chair, reading, going over every page. An extraterrestrial that is part-human and part-feline? It all seems so unbelievable. Seeing the words before her eyes in plain English, she needs to consider their legitimacy.

She closes the notebook with a sigh. There's only one thing she wants to do. Find that alien!

Chapter 34

SINCE FIRST OPENING ITS DOORS in 2002 by a British missionary woman, the St. Mary's Primary School provides free education to the children of poor and working parents in Arusha. They rightly pride themselves on the fact that education has to be for the many, and not for the few. The teaching is of high quality, providing the best possible education for all. The reason is simple: Tanzania needs the labor of the next generation for its survival.

Sitting behind her desk, Cassidy looks at the clock on the wall above the teacher's head. Ten seconds left. Five. She fidgets in her chair. The bell rings. When the teacher gets up from his desk and dismisses the class, a buzz of conversations burst from the children who happily get up and leave the room. She stuffs all her books and notebooks from her desk into her backpack in scarcely a minute. Leaning back in her chair, she waits patiently for Laila.

The teacher leaves the room, but there are three boys standing around a desk laughing, evidently talking, and joking. One of them just so happens to be Jason Farquar, who nudges the smaller boy, and they start whispering to each other as if they're planning something. Then they go back to chatting and begin ogling Cassidy. And she can feel them looking at her.

The smaller boy taps Jason on the shoulder and says, "You just have to. It will be so funny."

"Yeah, I'll do it," Jason says, grinning from ear to ear.

That's when it happens. Jason and his two friends start to move toward Cassidy and start poking fun at her.

"There she is," says Jason.

Cassidy makes a point of not looking at him.

"Who?" the pudgy boy asks, sounding tense, like he's about to burst out laughing.

"The girl who cries wolf. No, no. She's the girl who cries cat person," Jason can't help but joke.

All of the boys laugh, with Jason laughing the hardest, while his body bobs back and forth.

Cassidy still won't look at him. She can't. The joke doesn't settle well with her. But she doesn't bolt out the door. She slumps into her seat, like a turtle retreating into its shell. Toby Diwani is a terrible gossip. She knows he's responsible for this. She assumes Jason will probably tease her, at least for the next few days.

"Where is your imaginary friend now — the cat person?" asks Jason, pushing out his lips and making loud kissing noises.

The boys laugh again.

Patience is imperative. Allow some time to pass, for memories to fade. Cassidy tells herself this, as she bites her lip. She wants to react, but she doesn't.

Laila stands there, in the doorway of the classroom, recoiling at the sight of Jason. She puts her hands on top of her head. She sometimes does that when she's nervous.

Jason starts meowing right in her face. Cassidy folds her arms on her desk and puts her head down to hide her tears, her whole body trembling.

Watching in silent disgust, Laila can't stay quiet anymore. She walks into the classroom and glares at Jason, who shrugs, like it's no big deal.

Laila can't be any madder. "Jason Farquar. If you don't leave her alone, I'm going to tell the teacher that you've been skipping school with your friends to spend the day in the basement of your house playing video games on a PlayStation you've been hiding there. My brother Toby says your parents don't know about it either. You better apologize — or else!"

"Yeah, I'm sorry," Jason says quickly and looks around from side to side as if to check that no one's listening, as the other boys look at each other in shock.

After lifting her head back up, Cassidy takes a breath in and out.

"You're not going to tell on me, are you?" Jason retorts.

Jason ignores Cassidy, talking directly to Laila. That is fine with Cassidy, because it gives her a chance to wipe her eyes and compose herself.

"I won't say anything," says Laila.

"Come on, or we'll miss the bus," Jason says to his buddies.

The boys run out of the classroom, down the hallway and out the front doors of the school where the buses are waiting.

"It's really good of you to stand up for me," Cassidy says, perking up.

"It's nothing. After all, what are friends for?"

Cassidy sniffles, and Laila raises her arms in a friendly gesture. She hops out of her chair and walks into her embrace. Laila gives her a warm, earnest hug. Moments later, they pull apart.

"Jason will forget about it soon enough. You wait till I get my hands on Toby, then he'll be sorry. My brother has a big mouth. May I apologize on his behalf?"

She slings her backpack over one shoulder. "There's no need to apologize. It's all just water off a duck's back. Anyhoo, we better hurry up. We don't want to miss our bus."

Sometime after three o'clock, the school bus drops Cassidy and Laila at the corner of the road. Cassidy won't let it go. Days later, she still can't stop talking about it. There's no need to keep on about it, but she does.

"It's real, I tell you. I don't usually see things, like, see things, you know? I don't know how to explain it, but I know it's the alien."

After listening to her talk about it on the bus, Laila isn't in the mood for this. "Forget about the alien. There's no need for you to concern yourself anymore. It's now in the hands of the Chagga. You won't be seeing it again."

Don't bet on that, Cassidy thinks to herself. She's going to find it, but she doesn't let on. That's her own little secret.

"Maybe you're right, Laila."

Thankfully, Cassidy drops the subject. With a smile and a cheery wave goodbye, Laila turns around and walks the other direction.

At the front door of her house, Cassidy pulls out a set of keys from a pocket in her backpack. She jiggles the key in the lock and swings the door open into the living room. In a carefree manner, she quickly steps inside and closes the door behind her.

Chapter 35

LATER ON, THAT EVENING, Kitty is standing under a tree watching the sun starting to set in the sky. Looking out at the fading daylight, she marvels over the streaks of rose and orange that layer the horizon, branching outward into the darkening blue. It's quite a spectacular sight to her. But then, she's an alien, and anything going on in the sky fascinates her.

With the coming darkness, she's feeling the urge for a snack. With her tail wagging, she walks through the forest, searching for something edible. Over the course of these past days, her fears are subsiding, and she is managing very well, living in the wild. Strolling toward the large-leaf plum trees, she admires the plants and listens to the sounds of the insects and birds which is like music to her ears.

After taking a few steps forward, she extends her hands gingerly, reaching up to pluck a wild plum from the tree.

Hungrily, she bites into the large ripe plum, the juice running down her chin until she wipes it away with the back of her hand.

About to take another bite, she pauses, not quite sure what she's going to do next. She feels her heart thump when she hears a sudden noise of cracking twigs and crunching leaves. Knowing there's someone nearby, a kind of desperation takes hold of her, and the plum slips from her hand to the ground. In a desperate scramble, she drops onto all fours and takes cover in the bushes as fast as she can.

The man, walking with a slight limp, angling around behind trees and bushes is Thobias Miranda, the Chagga elder. His lower-leg injury is from his recent encounter with the Evil Shadowy Figure. A scuffle that almost cost him his life. After dusting off his shirtsleeve and the knees of his brown trousers, ridding them of random tree debris, he takes a few steps, stops, peeks behind a tree. What Kitty doesn't know is that Thobias is looking for her.

"Where's that darn cat person?" he growls.

While it does nothing to improve his prospects of finding the alien, complaining to himself vents some of his frustration, so he keeps going with it as he continues on his way around the forest.

Peeking through the bushes, her eyes peer at Thobias curiously. Anticipation keeps her tense. When he turns his back and walks away, she steps from her cover in the bushes and finds a tree to scale. Presently she's trying to avoid the humans in her midst. She remembers Allison Banes warning her to not let anyone see her. Will she ever trust any human being again?

Before long, she is high up in the tree, positioning herself in the V between the trunk and a thick branch. Far above anything that can harm her. Far above Thobias.

She's watching him while he walks off to a cluster of shrubs beside Lake Duluti and steps carefully into the shrubs. It looks like he's searching for something. How odd, she thinks. The six-foot-tall African man with broad shoulders and a black muzzle of a beard moves his head from side to side. A sudden look of pain crosses his face. He puts his hand to his sore neck and massages, easing the painful kinks in his muscles. Another reminder of his clash with the Evil Shadowy Figure.

Kitty is sitting for what seems like an hour in the tree while Thobias circles around the Duluti Circuit Trail. Now it's fully dark with the sliver of the last-quarter Moon shining dully in the sky. That he is not enjoying the search is too apparent from the frown of irritation on his face as he makes one more pass around, moving through the shadows of the trees, then disappears from view.

There's a glimpse of a spider's web in the tree, with a large black spider with black hairy legs and a round body sitting in the middle. Kitty doesn't notice it, but the spider sees her. Curiosity gets the best of it. It glides down the web and edges halfway out onto a heavy limb and sets itself in the middle of it.

It looks toward her, its eyes rolling about in its head, and making a chittering sound. The chittering noise rises to such a high pitch that Kitty hears it. Moving her head in the direction of the sound, she glances at the spider with her glaring green eyes. Scrutinizing it intently, she fascinates by its furry, almost four inches long body, and each of its eight legs, which are easily six inches long.

Despite its peculiarity, she's not afraid of it. Slowly, so as not to scare the spider away, Kitty moves her hand toward it with the intention of touching it. Remaining motionless and making no audible sound, the spider seems afraid of her, a questioning look in its eyes. This baffles Kitty. So, she retracts her hand, deciding not to go any closer. It doesn't make any difference. Out of fear, the spider scrambles quickly up the thick branches toward the top of the tree, eventually disappearing in the darkness.

Now that the man is no longer around, Kitty rises, her arms and legs feeling stiff. She climbs down the tree slowly. Once she reaches the ground, she feels thirsty. She strolls over to Lake Duluti, drinks her fill of water, then retreats back to the forest.

Still feeling stiff, she feels the need to get down on the ground and stretch her body. And for what seems like a long time, she stretches her legs out in front of her. Soon her muscles feel less tense. Her body is warm and loose. Basking in the light of the Moon, she rolls on her back and gazes up at the stars overhead. It is a clear night, no clouds. Comfortably on the ground, she keeps her gaze on the sky and reaches to leisurely groom her tail.

After a yawn and a stretch, she gets up and sits down beneath her favorite tree. Scooting closer to the trunk, she nestles in and curls up into a tight ball. Feeling all cozy and comfortable, she closes her eyes, ready for a long sleep.

Chapter 36

IT'S NEW YEAR'S EVE at the Diwani house, and Laila is in her room getting ready. Later she will be going to a glorious Chagga ceremony on the southern slopes of Mount Kilimanjaro. If there is one thing, she knows for sure in her eleven years of life, it is that she doesn't want to be a Chagga forever. Sometimes she thinks the ceremonies and rituals are a waste of time. While she loves her parents, she doesn't like their way of living. Simply put, she thinks differently.

Standing in front of the mirror of her dresser, Laila is twisting her hair back into a tight bun at the base of her skull. Not long afterward, the sound of the front door opening, and closing shake the daydreams out of her head. She hears her father's voice, and she relaxes.

A fraction of a second later, Esther Diwani comes to stand in the doorway of Laila's bedroom, watching her. She is wearing a kitenge skirt, and a chartreuse blouse, which contrasts with the bright colors of her skirt.

"Are you almost ready?" her mom asks.

"Just adjusting my dress. It's feeling loose, you see," she answers, looking at her in the dresser mirror.

"Where's that smile of yours, Laila? This is a night of celebration."

Always the dutiful daughter, Laila casts an appeasing smile over her shoulder. "Mom, you're right."

"You look so lovely in that dress. I enjoy watching you sing. That's part of the joy of tonight's ceremony. You have such a beautiful voice. You make me so proud."

"Thank you, mother. I'll do my best," she assures her, tucking in her dress.

"I know you will, baby."

Just then, her father strolls down the hallway, and stops beside Esther.

"Hi, Daddy. I'm almost ready to go."

"Just waiting around for you. Laila, your brother and I are ready."

"How is it you are always ready when we are not?" Esther asks playfully.

"Maybe it's a man thing," he shoots right back.

She kisses him on the cheek, and adds, "Maybe it is."

He arches an eyebrow. "What's that for?"

"An early New Year's present."

"I'm so grateful," Karl winks at her and runs his fingers through her curly black hair, making it stick up even more than usual.

Laila's eyes roll in her head. Her parents are too lovey-dovey for her. Trying her best to ignore them, she slips on her sandals.

"Take it somewhere else," Laila says mockingly.

"She's right, honey. Not in front of the child," Esther reproves him.

"Go out to the living room and wait. We'll go to the car together," her father says before walking off, Esther in tow behind.

"Hurry up, slowpoke!" Toby says, poking his head into the room.

"Scram," she hisses at him.

Toby scurries off without another word. He really gets on her nerves. She's still mad at him for telling Jason about Cassidy's cat person sighting.

In those few minutes, she wonders whether the Chief will ever find the alien and if the curse of the Evil Shadowy Figure will end. She hopes so. That makes her smile. She is sick of the story and doesn't want to repeat it anymore.

Before heading out of the room, she takes one last look in the mirror and fixes a stray hair by her right eye. It's not easy wearing this get-up. She thinks she looks very adult. She looks nothing like herself — not the free-flowing girl who likes to wear T-shirts and jeans.

Later, in the SUV, Laila sits as far away from Toby as possible in the backseat, thinking about meeting some other kids her age, even though she only sees the children of the Chagga settlement on Mount Kilimanjaro once a year. Maybe she'll meet a boy. She dares to think. Her parents are too strict. They don't even let her watch television. Her mother keeps telling her, maybe when she's older. Yes, maybe then. At least they let her go to a regular school and listen to the radio. Unusually progressive for tribal people.

Two hours pass with nothing but road noise and the whistle of the wind through the crack of an open window. Toby is fast asleep. Esther Diwani points toward Mount Kilimanjaro in the distance, the dazzling cone rising against the sky.

"We're almost there," her mother announces, turning to look into the backseat.

"Dinner under the stars and a drum circle. Does it get any better than that?" her father asks jovially.

"You say that every year," Laila reminds him.

"You have a little attitude this evening, young lady," Karl Diwani comments.

"Need I tell you the story of the old woman and the calabashes that magically turn into children thanks to the spirit of Mount Kilimanjaro. This story teaches us to be mindful, not ungrateful," her mother says, looking at her in the rearview mirror.

Laila knows the story. It's another Chagga tale. That's really what they are. Stories for children.

Laila's tone is flat. "Yes, Mother, I understand."

"The feast will cheer you up. Mtori is on the menu tonight. Meat, bananas, and carrots stew. So delicious," Karl says, just as he is turning into Mount Kilimanjaro National Park, driving to Machame Gate.

Toby is now awake. "My stomach is already growling."

As darkness falls around them, the sky is filling rapidly with stars, scattering like fairy dust across the horizon. Laila decides to enjoy herself no matter what. She will sing her heart out. That will make her happy. Singing is her refuge. In actuality, singing along to a pop song on the radio instead of singing Chagga traditional songs, is her favorite thing to do. Her parents don't know that of course. Staring out the window at the starry sky, she will make the best of the evening. Like she has another choice.

Chapter 37

ON THE SOUTHERN SLOPE of Mount Kilimanjaro, the Chagga come together to celebrate New Year's Eve. At the foot of the mountain, that straddles the border of Kenya, you'll find the largest congregation of Chagga in Tanzania.

Dark and looming, the snow cap of Kilimanjaro rises high and clear out of the clouds. The meager pale silvery light of a tiny waning crescent Moon little more than a silver arc in the sky barely illuminates the surrounding forest.

There will be no talk about the Evil Shadowy Figure tonight. Rather, they honor their almighty Ruwa, their liberator. This is the important subject Chief Naruma will share with the people. In a tent, he wraps his leopard-skin cloak around his shoulders. Wearing the leopard skin is his way of inhabiting the species, activating its qualities and strength, and gaining its knowledge. The leopard knows things because it sits and watches. He takes a few deep breaths. In some ways he's nervous to be around so many people. Thinking of his speech, he concludes, as much as he wants to share the news about the alien, he doesn't want to get their hopes up in case they don't find it.

When he leaves the tent, he positions himself in front of the crowd and wastes no time getting into it. After mentioning how prosperous he's hoping the next year will be, he smiles at the children, who are in a position off to the side of the adults. They will be singing right after his speech.

While he's talking, Laila's attention drifts to the low rumble and crackle of a low-burning campfire in the near distance, the heat of it making her hair move. Her eyes lock on it as if in a trance. She almost jumps as she sees a figure move into view. Now standing next to the campfire is a woman in a multi-color kitenge wraparound dress that reaches to her knees. Oddly enough, there are streaks of black soot on her arms, legs, and bare feet. Something about her feels familiar, but Laila can't see her face because she's standing sideways. The woman mumbles something she can't hear, calling to her. Laila has to blink twice as she sees a powerful vacuumlike force pull the woman's body back into the burning campfire. It all happens so fast that she thinks she's imagining things. A moment or two after that, Laila turns to look at the Chief just in time to hear the tail end of his speech.

"Now let the celebrating begin," Chief Naruma says, finishing his little speech with a grin on his face.

Laila Diwani steps forward to sing a song of praise to Ruwa. She alone begins to sing, and goose bumps rise on her mother's arms. Her voice is pure and sweet. After she sings a couple of verses, the other children join in the chorus. Their treble voices carry around her and invite the wind to complement the singing in a deep, rumbling undertone. Behind the children are three African men sitting on wooden stools, who start beating on round wooden drums with their hands in sync with their singing.

The adults start dancing in a circle. It's an iringi, a celebratory dance. Still singing, Laila stands in the inner circle. The other children stand outside the circle, singing and swinging their arms. The women and men move in rhythm linking to one another with their arms around the shoulders.

After the song and dance, everyone starts clapping, some whistle and stomp their feet. Standing together, the elders, including Rhoda Kisanga and Thobias Miranda, speak Kiswahili, calling out the names of their ancestors. Chief Naruma asks Ruwa for a blessing on the food, and invites everyone to dig in. For the next couple of hours, they feast on mtori stew and other delicacies, juice for the kids and mbege brew for the adults.

At midnight, there is a sudden burst of commotion — whistles and the sharp crack of fireworks. With only a few clouds in the sky, nothing can stop the magical appearance of the fireworks coming from Uhuru Peak, the top of Kilimanjaro, the highest point on Kibo's crater rim. Seeing it brings a joyous feeling to the Chagga, making it an ideal way to end the evening.

Lots of people are leaving while Chief Naruma's brow furrows as he stares off into the distance, like his mind is a million miles away. As his eyes take in the beauty of the Mawenzi Peak shimmering in the moonlight, the second highest peak on Kilimanjaro, — his brain buzzes with questions about the alien until Rhoda's voice comes from behind him. He then slips out of his trancelike state.

"Can you repeat that?"

"I trust everything is to your satisfaction this evening?" she asks him.

"Very fine indeed."

"It's hard to believe that somewhere out there, there's an alien that can help end the curse."

"That is weighing heavily on my mind," he says, his voice dead serious.

"I can just tell that my niece Paulina knows about the spaceship. She doesn't talk about it at all. Her job doesn't allow that. But she seems to know nothing about the alien."

"Yes, I have to agree with you on that. It is pointless to question her further. Otherwise, she'll be suspicious. You can't have her knowing about the alien. We have to do this our way, the Chagga way, amongst ourselves and without outside interference."

"As discreetly as possible, the elders, including myself, will maintain a low profile while keeping a watch for any sign of the alien."

"I believe in you, and I have every confidence that you will succeed. This seems a good moment to make our departure."

Chief Naruma leads the way, walking with a sense of purpose, with an eager Rhoda hurrying to accompany him. His eyes settle on the little campfire up ahead, still quietly smoking. He considers it a moment, then keeps walking. Malevolent eyes flicker in the depths of the few remaining flames. The Evil Shadowy Figure is stirring, desperate to get a hold of the alien. He has to stop them from carrying out the ritual to end the curse. He isn't the kind of spirit to give up so easily.

Chapter 38

ON A BRIGHT SUNDAY AFTERNOON IN JANUARY, Azita Hussein turns onto a dirt road off a trail to Mount Meru Forest Reserve on the western border of Arusha National Park. If Allison's notebook is right, this is the area of the crash landing of a strange craft.

What she's been reading in the notebook is gnawing at her. So here she is checking it out, to find out what's true and what's not. Wearing hiking boots, and with her hair in a ponytail that makes her look like a college student, she feels so dumb.

Azita takes a quick breath, climbs out of her Audi, and looks around to make sure no one is watching. She begins walking, feeling awkward, and asks herself for the second time in twenty seconds what she is doing here.

She pulls a bottle of water from her handbag and takes a long gulp. It's not long before she sees a ring of yellow barrier tape around an area where some trees are missing from the row and a few trees have branches missing. An aircraft may be responsible for the damage. And the plot thickens.

It won't hurt to take a look at it.

Somewhere behind her a voice yells, "Halt! Don't take another step!"

Something in the voice strikes a memory, some nuance of familiarity in the voice has her stopping in her tracks. She turns around to see Paulina Mongella, donning her park ranger's outfit of black boots, a khaki short-sleeve button-down shirt and matching pants, and a floppy khaki safari hat hanging behind her head by a string. Azita gives her a blank look, glances away, looks back again, her eyes narrowing.

"Surely you remember me, Dr. Hussein? What brings you here?" Paulina asks, and waves her hand in a bandage in the air.

Azita frowns and tries to think of an appropriate response. "Paulina, right?"

"That's my name, don't wear it out."

"What a coincidence to find you here! I'm out exploring on a nature walk. Is that a problem?"

"Is this your first visit to Arusha National Park?"

"It sure is."

"This area of the park is off-limits for a while. There is maintenance work under way," Paulina says officially.

"I'm not sure I understand what you mean," Azita says, even though she understands perfectly.

There is something suspicious about the way Azita glances toward the barrier tape, then away, then back again.

"You want to tell me what you think is happening here, Dr. Hussein?"

Azita must lay it all on the table. "Will you tell me something honestly? I know this may sound like a crazy question, but I have to ask you. Is this a crash site of an alien spaceship?"

Paulina's glistening eyes blink in bewilderment. She takes a step back. Her mind floods with questions. How does the doctor know about it?

She simply asks, "What makes you think that?"

"Apparently you can't tell me what I want to know. I will just have to ask Geoffrey Mkama," Azita says, and turns her body away from hers.

Azita is about to walk away when she says, "Hold on there! First you must tell me something and then I will answer your question."

"What do you want to know?" Azita asks, turning around and looking at her like she's some kind of nuisance.

"What gives you the idea that this is the site of a spaceship crash?"

"I don't suppose you know Allison Banes?"

Paulina shakes her head no.

"You think a white woman studying monkeys in the forest of Arusha National Park is going to stand out."

"Sorta rings a bell, but I don't really remember. The park gets many white women visitors."

"My friend Allison Banes is a witness to an alien spaceship crashing in this area. That's how I know about it. Well, she's dead now. I just want to know if it's true."

It is disturbing to Paulina to know that a witness to the alien spaceship is now dead. How come? She wants to know, but she is not going to ask anything of the sort. She must keep cool and calm and provide as little information as possible.

"Dr. Hussein, what I'm going to tell you is confidential and must stay between you and me. Please don't ever repeat it."

"Who am I going to tell? My only friend is dead."

Paulina steps in closer to her, leans forward and speaks quietly. "I'm sorry about your friend. And yes, it's true that this is the scene of an alien spaceship crash. It's under investigation by the Law Enforcement and Strategic Security Section of TANAPA. And that's all I can say."

"Hearing you say that means a lot. But one more thing. Where is the escape pod?"

"I'm not even going to ask how you know that," Paulina mutters.

"It's quite simple. My late friend, Allison Banes."

"I suspect you are correct," and here she lowers her voice to a quite confidential tone: "You know I can't confirm or deny anything."

"You don't have to say anymore," Azita says warmly.

"Promise me you won't say anything about our conversation to Geoffrey Mkama?"

"Paulina, thank you for being honest with me. This will stay between us. Now if you don't mind, I'll be going now," she says before turning to walk back to her car.

Paulina calls out to her in a loud voice, "Happy New Year, by the way."

"Yeah, whatever," Azita mumbles to herself, without looking at her, as if it means nothing to her.

Chapter 39

ALMOST AN HOUR LATER, Azita pulls into the driveway of Allison Banes' former house on Kigongoni Road. After switching off the engine, she opens her door and exits the car, ready to begin her search for the elusive alien. It may still be around the house somewhere — or in the forest by Lake Duluti, perhaps. According to Allison's notes, the alien likes to explore that area, which is a good thirty-five minute walk from here.

What will she do if she finds the alien?

She's still not sure. The worst part is she's harboring a strong belief in the possibility it may be hostile. It may be the reason Allison's dead. She forces herself to think more positively. Otherwise, she may as well turn around and go home.

The late afternoon sunlight shines down on the Duluti Circuit Trail. The forest is quiet. She walks through the area, where spots of sunlight tunnel down through the branches, pooling patches of light on the soft ground. Azita wastes no time. Peering into the bushes, she really wants to find Kitty, Allison's pet name for her. And this is Allison's story. And what a story it is!

"Kitty, where are you?" she yells out.

A twig cracks, then a sudden heavy breathing cuts through the silence of the forest. She sees something moving amongst the trees. On second look she sees it is undeniably catlike, at least so it appears. She hurries toward it, quick as a fox, and in the process, she trips over the roots in the grass, hits the ground with a smack, grazing both knees.

Wheeling around, struggling to get back up, she yelps as a hyena zooms past her face, scaring the living daylights out of her. A hyena? Now she feels like a fool.

She stands back up and brushes off her clothes. Taking a couple of breaths, inhaling the sweet scent of fig and the alkaline smell of the lake in the distance, she definitely needs a time-out. She decides to take a stroll to the lake.

Approaching Lake Duluti, she sees a shadow to her left, slightly ahead, at the edge of the lake. Maybe, it's the alien. She is about to find out. The closer she gets, the clearer the outline of a man emerges until she can make out that it's Chief Naruma of the Chagga, in a white linen tunic with matching knee-length pants and sandals. He frequently takes sick people to the clinic, but she doesn't really know him. She can feel the Chief staring at her oddly through his glasses with eyes that register his shock of seeing her there. And she's not in the mood to talk to him.

A quick glance at her wristwatch shows that it's after four o'clock. She is finally ready to call it a day.

"Good afternoon, Doctor," the Chief says heartily.

His words carry over to her just as she's turning her head. There is no hope of avoiding him.

"And a good afternoon to you, too," she says turning to face him.

"How nice it is to see the busy doctor here," he says, adjusting his hold on his walking stick.

He really thinks it's strange to see her here. Does she know something about the alien? He ponders that for a moment. Maybe he's just getting paranoid.

"I'm taking advantage of a day off work to just trek around Lake Duluti," she says as she walks over to him.

Azita dare not tell him the real reason she's here, for surely, he'll think she's a quack doctor.

"Forgive me, but your name escapes me."

"Azita Hussein. Chief Naruma, it is a pleasure to finally make your acquaintance, after seeing you bring patients to my clinic."

"Well, Dr. Hussein, I'm enjoying the quiet beauty of the lake. Just because I spend most of my time around Mount Meru. My New Year's resolution is to visit other places in Tanzania."

"See any new and interesting animals around?"

He frowns as if he considers it an odd question. "Maybe a hyena, but I'm not really sure."

"Actually, that hyena is the reason for my fall," she says, pointing to the dirt stains of her olive-green pants.

"Quintessentially, the hyena is a scary animal, wolflike in color but more shaggy and has a mane along the whole of its spine," he says, rather precisely.

"It's nice talking to you, but I need to clean up and change clothes, so I'll be off," she says properly, and in a depressing tone.

"I'm leaving too. Where is your car? Maybe I can give you a lift. My Jeep is close by. I don't mind the company," the Chief says in a calm, insistent tone.

Looking at his eager face, she caves in like a sandcastle. "That is very kind of you to offer, Chief Naruma. I will accept a ride from you. To tell the truth, because of my fall in the forest, I'm in no mood to walk back to my car. It's in the driveway of my late friend Allison Banes' former house on Kigongoni Road, a reasonable distance away."

"I know Kigongoni Road. Let's get a move on, shall we?" he asks, giving her a big denture smile.

After a while sitting in the passenger seat of his Jeep, Azita has yet to say anything. He's very curious about her. Hiking around Tanzania? That's something she never does. Why is she really at Lake Duluti today? Something just doesn't feel right. Perhaps he will ask some questions.

"I'm sorry that your friend is dead. Recently, if I may ask?"

"Eleven days ago, to be precise," Azita answers, taking her gaze from the window.

She stares at him, obviously ready to launch into something more epic.

"I don't understand why. The police think it's a heart attack. After examining her body, I have to agree with the police. But she has no history of heart problems. Seeing the fear in her dead eyes still haunts me."

After hearing that, he starts to wonder. Her death occurs after the alien's arrival. Is it an evil alien? Or is she a victim of the Evil Shadowy Figure? His victims die with their eyes open all the time. In all likelihood the latter, he figures.

"Sometimes there are no answers. But everyone dies. It's a part of life, a natural progression," he says, turning onto Kigongoni Road.

"You may have come in contact with her and not know it, spending most of her time in the Mount Meru Forest Reserve in Arusha National Park, studying primates."

The very forest of the alien's arrival? He's seeing a connection. His mind begins spinning with questions. If Allison Banes knows anything about the alien, he'll never find out. He thinks about it some more. Maybe that is why she's dead. But he can't tell the doctor any of this.

"I don't remember seeing her at all. I'm sorry."

Chief Naruma turns into the driveway of Allison Banes' former house. Azita gets out of the vehicle, and she stands for a moment, staring at him.

"Thank you for driving me here," she says through the open passenger's seat window of the Jeep.

He leans over and says, "Don't be a stranger."

Watching her walk to her car, keys already in her hand, she seems clueless about the alien. But for some reason or another, he's pretty sure she knows more than she's letting on.

Inside her car, she turns the key in the ignition and notices a long tear in the sleeve of her beige cotton blouse. One more disappointment. She releases a sigh as she pulls out of the driveway. In her rearview, she catches Chief Naruma pull onto the road behind her. Further down the road, he turns onto another road, disappearing from her view.

Chapter 40

LE PATIO is a terrific bar and restaurant on Kenyatta Road in Arusha that does local dishes as well as continental French fare. After eight o'clock on a Sunday night, a group of rowdies crowd the dance floor, listening to a local rock band perform cover music. The band is covering the song "Kilimanjaro" by Johnny Clegg & Juluka when Kwami Amutullah and his underling Edwin Joseph push through the entrance doors and head through the talking, drinking crowd at the bar at the end of the lounge, opposite the dance floor, heading to an outdoor table.

"Let's get a couple of beers and some pizza. Now that the Spanish tourists are out of our hair, we finally have the opportunity to really talk about it in great detail," Kwami tells Edwin, trying to keep his voice light.

"I don't know, Kwami. Shall I be honest between the two of us? It's foolish talk. It's probably some kind of goat and it's not worth our time. You know how those Chagga people are."

"Let me try to explain it to you again. Take a seat at the table, Edwin."

After taking their seats, the waitress arrives to take their order. She's tall, wears her curly Afro hair in lots of little braids, and her blue apron is tied up under her bosom. She welcomes them, a corner of her mouth lifting in a demi-smile.

"Miller Lite from the tap, for both of us," Kwami returns, a smile on his thin lips.

"Do you need anything else?"

Kwami waves her off, flipping his hand as if he's flicking off a fly.

Leaning comfortably back in his brown wicker chair with red cushions, Edwin says, "So, run it by me again."

"First of all, Chagga she may be, but Rhoda is solid, and reliable. You mark my words."

While they are talking, heat is blasting from the open fireplace crackling just a few feet away. Sparks from the fire snap up and fade into the dark. Something shifts in the flames that slither around, evil radiates and the eyes of a spirit are taking shape. The Evil Shadowy Figure is lurking. He rolls his fiery black eyes and sets it up for others to do his dirty work. Capture the alien.

When the waitress returns to the table with the beers, Kwami takes the glass and drains half of it in one swallow.

"Now, we need a plan for how to capture it. Have you any suggestions?" Kwami asks eagerly.

Edwin always thinks before he acts and weighs each word before saying it. He takes a sip, smiles, revealing yellow tobacco stains on his teeth and sets his glass on the table.

"I have a few ideas. How hard can it be to find something that's both human and feline?"

"Here, here," Kwami agrees, raising his glass in a toast.

Seeing the waitress buzzing around the tables, Kwami calls her over. On the way back to their table she clears two tables, takes their order for more beer, and returns quickly with two glasses of beer. She sets the glasses on the table and picks up the empty glasses, placing them on a round metal tray.

Kwami moves as close to her face as he can and says to her, "Shame on me for not asking you before. How are you this evening, Alexis?"

Often, with Kwami, there is a fine line between flirting and pursuing someone relentlessly. He has an eye for the ladies, as they do for him. A large number of the tourists who come to Tanzania are women, most under thirty, most of them single and keen to party. On some occasions he makes the acquaintance of a group of single women traveling together, looking for a good time. He constantly reminds himself that he needs a wingman, and it's the only reason he keeps Edwin around.

The twenty-seven-year-old Alexis, an African beauty, responds with a rumbling purr and a gracious movement of her head. "Oh, I'm quite fine, thanks."

Kwami flashes Alexis a tender, almost wistful look of longing in his eyes before moving away from her to take a swig of his beer. He has good reason to feel confident this evening. He's wearing the most adorable outfit — a pair of black khakis, a short-sleeve plaid shirt and a little bow tie and his best boots.

"I'm glad to see you tonight," Edwin says, grinning stupidly at her and leaning halfway across the table.

Edwin's pungent odor of stale cigarettes and abrasive cologne repulses her, yet she smiles demurely, and Edwin melts. Most definitely not as suave as Kwami, he's wearing a simple blue and white button-down shirt, just-off-the-rack Wranglers with creases, and old brown boots.

"I'll be right back with your pizza."

Keeping his expression inscrutable, Kwami nods to her before she goes to the kitchen.

While eating their pizza, the talk around the table turns to money. Trapping animals and selling them on the black market is very profitable. What most people, like Rhoda Kisanga, don't know is that Kwami is the brains behind much of the poaching in Tanzania.

Kwami is drumming his fingers on the glass top of the wicker table. His lip twitches into a smile, showing some teeth. A sound, somewhere between a gasp and a growl, escapes him.

"An exotic animal from the Amazon jungle can fetch five figures nowadays."

Edwin clears his throat and manages a one-word response as he thumps the table with his empty glass. "Yes."

Kwami calmly drains the last of his beer.

"There are no safari tour bookings for the next couple of days. Why don't we start searching now?" Edwin asks him directly.

Leaning forward in his chair, Kwami jabs his index finger at him, stopping just short of poking him sharply in the chest.

Kwami starts to raise his voice and almost spit out the words. "Don't get greedy now. Reload your tranquilizer rifle as soon as you get a chance. That's all you need to do right now."

"No problem, boss, I'll get right on it," he says under his breath, grudgingly.

"We'll start tomorrow afternoon. Sound good to you?"

"It works for me," Edwin says off-handedly.

Something in the fireplace pops, but not loud enough to draw attention. The Evil Shadowy Figure likes what he hears. Orange light dances from the flames as the evil spirit cackles and roars on the way down into the depths of darkness. With the last of the flames fading, he lets out a small, creepy laugh. No one hears a thing. The fire is out, and a thin wisp of smoke rises.

There really is no need to discuss the matter any further. Kwami seems anxious to change the conversation to something else while Edwin is quiet as a corpse, his eyes staring off into space.

"The night is young. You want to shoot some pool?"
"Yeah!" comes the short reply from Edwin.

Chapter 41

TWO-THIRTY is fast approaching with just eight minutes until the bell. Cassidy Mkama is in the third desk closest to the windows. Impatiently, she glances at the wall clock, then out the window of the classroom.

Jason Farquar is flat-out no-apology sleeping, with his head down on the desk. It is almost farcical. The teacher decides to make an example of him. Stepping out from behind his desk, the teacher walks over to stand beside Jason's desk. He raises his stick with a brass claw on the end of it, that looks like a backscratcher, and lightly taps him on the head, waking him up instantly.

"Rise and shine, sleepy-head," the teacher says dryly.

A few of the boys laugh and start drumming on their desks with their pencils.

"Be silent at once!" the teacher barks, rapping his stick on Jason's desk.

Jason looks around and tries his best not to look foolish as he sits up straight at his desk. "I'm sorry, Mr. Dominic."

"Don't let it happen again."

Mr. Dominic turns his back to the class and busies himself with erasing the chalkboard and blowing his nose into a tissue for an impressive five full seconds. Cassidy stares down at her math worksheet on the desk, glances at the numbers, picks up her pencil, then writes down the answer as quickly as she can seconds before the end-of-the-school-day bell rings.

Before dismissing the class, Mr. Dominic stands in front of the room and clasps his hands together. "One thing I want to mention before you all leave for the day. Make sure your names are on your papers when you put them on my desk tomorrow."

Cassidy slides out of her seat, puts the worksheet into her backpack and slings it over one shoulder. She joins the crowd of eleven-year-olds spilling out the door, pushing and chiding one another as they fill the hallway. She's not going to wait in the classroom for Laila. Well, not for a while.

Almost instantly she gazes between people and sees Laila a little farther down the hall. She lets out an audible sigh of relief and hurries her step to catch up to her.

"Let's go to the bus," she says, linking her arm through Laila's and tugging her down the hall and out of the crowd.

"What's the rush? The bus doesn't leave for another ten minutes."

"I want to get a good seat up front."

"That's where the special ed kids sit."

"It's just for today."

"Well, if you say so."

Once on the bus, Cassidy slumps in her seat, anxiously waiting for the bus to leave. Sitting by the window, almost every minute, she can't stop herself from looking outside to peering over the seat at the bus driver.

"I don't understand. Why doesn't he leave already?" Cassidy asks in frustration.

"Don't stress about it. He'll be leaving soon," Laila tells her while looking at her in a questioning way.

"I'm just wondering, that's all."

Clearly, she's not very good at playing it cool, because Laila picks up a distinct anxiety vibe. The driver starts up the engine and swings the lever that closes the bus door. Looking in the rearview mirror, the cranky bus driver orders the children to be quiet and they immediately fall silent.

Despite the jerky stop-and-go rhythm of the bright yellow bus, Cassidy does her homework the whole time the bus is moving. Eventually the bus creaks to a stop on the corner of Tengeru Road and throws open its doors to discharge the girls.

Cassidy scrambles out of the seat, steps into the aisle on the black-rubber floor mat, and nudges past Laila to exit the bus first. Laila notices, but doesn't say anything. Within a minute Laila comes bounding out of the bus after her.

Laila opens her mouth but before she can say anything, Cassidy whirls on her and says, "I have to leave now."

"Why are you in such a hurry to go home?"

"I'm not going home just yet. I have to go somewhere, and you may have to cover for me."

"Can I go with you?"

Cassidy is shaking her head. "Sorry bestie. Not this time. In case my Dad calls your house, try not to let your parents answer the phone. Tell him I'm on my way back home after working with you on a school science project."

A look of confusion passes over Laila's face, as though she can't figure out what she's saying or how to form a response.

She lets long moments pass in silence, studying Cassidy before speaking. "We are?"

"No, we are not. But I want my dad to think we are. So, I need you to back up my story."

Laila gets the feeling she's lying because she knows something, but she doesn't know what about. She keeps catching a certain evasive expression in her eyes that says she is keeping a secret from her. Moments like this make her want to shake the truth out of her.

"What does that mean?"

"I'll explain everything to you later, Laila. My Dad won't be home till around six o'clock. If I'm lucky, I'll be back by then. So, he won't call you. And you won't have to tell him anything," Cassidy says, and starts walking away from the bus stop.

"There is so much you're not telling me, so much I don't understand like where you're going — why you won't tell me," she says pleadingly, following after her like a puppy dog.

She stops a good ten feet away. "I can't explain now, Laila."

And with that, Cassidy spins around and runs off. Laila has an ache to go after her, to run behind her, but she lets her go. There's just no catching up to her. Calmly, only a little breathless, she stops walking. She watches her run until she disappears. Her mouth opens as if she wants to speak, a light bulb moment shining from her brown eyes as the answer for her suddenly illuminates in her mind.

"Does this have to do with that alien?"

Chapter 42

THE SUN sparkles over the forest by Lake Duluti in the afternoon hours. Moving down the Duluti Circuit Trail, Kitty pauses beside a tree when she feels something crawl up her leg and bite her. It is an ant. Her blunt feline nose twitches as if sniffing a scent in the air. She flicks the ant like a paper football, then squashes it into the ground with her heel. A little smile permeates her face as she sits down on a log on the ground.

For the second time in the span of less than thirty minutes, Cassidy finds herself standing in the same spot she remembers seeing the cat person the day before Christmas. But she's not there now. *Where is she?* she wonders. She momentarily considers the possibility that the cat person is just a hallucination. On top of it all, her backpack is weighing her down. The straps of her backpack are digging in and her shoulders are getting sore. On the plus side, if she doesn't find the alien, she won't mention today's little adventure in the forest to Laila.

Turning in another direction, she hears a twig snapping. She turns her face in the direction of the sound. What a delightful surprise it is to see the cat person sitting on a log near the trail, moving around, swatting, and flicking off bugs. After wiping her brow in relief, Cassidy moves closer to the alien, staring with happiness at the sight of her.

When she is barely twelve paces away, she whistles out loud, her head swiveling as she cups her hands to her mouth. "Hello. Remember me?"

As a matter of fact, Kitty does. She detects a certain excitement in her voice. She glances from Cassidy's eyes to her feet, then back up again, as if taking an inventory of her features, then with a smile she meows softly.

For a long, quiet moment, they just stare at each other. Cassidy can feel the warmth coming from her. Her gut instinct tells her she's a good alien.

She walks right up to her, a giddy expression on her face. "I'm really glad you're here."

It's the way the human looks at her — and the way she talks to her, it shows that she has good intentions. Kitty flashes her a humble Cheshire cat grin. She has that look of a happy camper, nervously twitching her tail. Has she come to rescue her? Take her back to her planet? Clearly wishful thinking, because she knows that she's on this planet for good. And right now, she is just about desperate. She needs an ally now more than ever, someone who can watch her back and be useful to her.

"I have something for you."

Cassidy pulls out a red apple from her backpack and holds it out to her. Kitty reaches out slowly and plucks it out of her hand, her fingers slightly brushing against hers. She nods a thank-you and gobbles down the apple, crunching the core between her teeth, eating hungrily, without restraint or embarrassment.

"My, my, you are hungry, aren't you?"

As a way of showing her gratitude, Kitty jumps up from the log and begins to show off her acrobatic skills, taking a running start for a cartwheel. She turns a cartwheel and executes two and a half consecutive backflips and a forward roll into a handstand, wagging her tail in the air. With a combination of flamboyance and utter precision, she walks on her hands. Then, in a hot move, she flips out of the handstand and sits on the ground with her knees bent and her head between them. Cassidy watches her tumble over and over. Lastly, she runs up a tree and backflips, but instead of landing in a handstand she comes to a standing position.

Cassidy laughs like crazy; a full-body laugh while Kitty stomps her feet excitedly.

Blinking into the bright sun, Kitty squints at her tiredly and shakes her head. Needing a breather, Kitty waddles over to a nearby tree, sits down with her back against it. Cassidy lowers her backpack to the ground, leaning it against the tree trunk. She hunkers down next to Kitty, reaches into her backpack and pulls out a history book. She opens to a page showing a map of the world. Africa is a tiny smudge.

"There," she says indicating a page in the book. "This is where you are. Let me welcome you to Tanzania. It's a nice place to live. I hope you like it here."

Kitty's eyebrows raise several inches in surprise, then her eyes sharpen on the map of the planet she is on. She is so nervous that she almost forgets the little English she knows from reading magazines, thanks to Allison Banes. A dozen words surge to her lips, but she can't bring herself to speak any of them.

Closing the book, she puts it back inside her backpack. "My father knows about you. His employer has your escape pod. Don't you need it? How else will you transport back to your homeworld?"

Cassidy waggles her hand like a spaceship a few inches above her head and swoops down to the ground. After some thinking on that, Kitty shakes her head no.

"Exactly what are you saying no to? Don't you want to go to your home planet?"

Kitty nods a yes, sails her hand like a spaceship a little above her head. Frown lines crease her forehead, and shakes her head no again.

"I get it. That escape pod isn't capable of traveling to your planet. Can your people come here on a ship and get you?"

Kitty shrugs and shakes her head no.

"Your people have no idea that you are here."

Kitty nods in agreement.

"I'm sorry I can't help you. Without a ship, there doesn't seem to be any way. But if I think of anything, you'll be the first to know. It'll be all right. I'm your friend now."

Kitty nestles closer to Cassidy, who takes her hand in hers, linking their fingers and squeezing gently. She holds her hand as Cassidy closes her eyes and whispers a short prayer in her mind.

"Dear Lord, Thank you for this gift of an extraordinary friend. Amen."

Simultaneously, they both drop into a nap.

Chapter 43

CASSIDY'S EYES fly open as she remembers that she may be in trouble if she isn't home before her father comes in. She springs to her feet and stands looking at Kitty.

"Wake up," she nudges her.

Her eyes peel open wide as a dull meow comes from her, and she bows her head. Cassidy raises her hand and rubs the top of her head as an act of friendship.

"It's getting late, I must be getting back. And you're coming with me. I'll explain more on the way."

After some careful thinking, she doesn't want to say anything to Laila. She wants to know more about the ritual to end the curse of the Evil Shadowy Figure. What if it's a ritual involving animal sacrifice, or rather alien sacrifice? She needs to know for certain that the alien won't be hurt.

Once they're walking, Cassidy gets right into it, babbling away. "I can't tell my father or Laila about you. I don't know yet what they will do with you."

She treats her like a friend and Kitty appreciates the girl in more ways than she can imagine.

"You have to stick with me. And don't let anybody see you up close. You never know how people will react because you're different."

"Meow?" Kitty says in a questioning tone.

"You're probably wondering where we are going. I have a place you can stay. The shed behind my grandmother's house. It will have to do for now, until I can think of something better. No one will think to look for you there."

As they are coming out of the forest, Cassidy feels a sense of responsibility to her. She doesn't know how to protect her. What more can she do? She's only a child. She needs someone to confide in, someone other than her father or Laila, someone to help her make the right decision, an outside opinion.

It takes about twenty minutes for them to reach Nyerere Road. Cassidy wants to stop for a break under the shade of a tree up ahead.

****

The sky is bright blue, almost blinding Azita Hussein with its intensity as she briefly looks up while exiting the Nambala Pharmacy, just off Nyerere Road, on the way to her car. Around five-thirty, like every first Monday of every month, she's carrying a shopping bag full of medical supplies for the clinic and prescriptions for her patients.

Being in the vicinity of Lake Duluti makes her think of Kitty, the extraterrestrial. She feels down in the dumps, still trying to come to terms with Allison's death, thinking she may never know the actual truth about the circumstances surrounding her death.

She sets the shopping bag in the trunk of her Audi. After closing the trunk, she heads around to the driver's side of the car and catches a glimpse of a little girl and a strange-looking animal with bushy hair and a black tail, catlike in her movements, tagging along behind her on Nyerere Road, halfway down the road from her. For some odd reason, the little girl seems familiar. Stopping to look, she recognizes it's the daughter of Geoffrey Mkama.

Standing beside her car, she watches Cassidy, who is now standing near a tree, conversing with this strange-looking animal. Is it an animal? Is it human? From where she is standing, she can see how odd it looks. Is she the only one who notices? She can only assume that nobody pays them any mind because it's not uncommon to see beautiful, strange animals in Africa. Can it be the alien? On a hunch, she slips the car keys into the pocket of her white lab coat that she's still wearing and starts walking toward Cassidy.

Unexpectedly, a look of dread overtakes Kitty, and she falls to all fours. Sensing someone approaching, Cassidy doesn't bother looking, trying to think where Kitty can hide.

"Duck! Get behind the tree and stay there. Better yet, climb up the tree," Cassidy whispers, her heart thrumming.

Kitty moves behind the tree and plants her feet on the trunk. Without Azita noticing, she quietly climbs up the tree and settles herself comfortably in the crook of the leafy bough.

Cassidy turns and leans her back against the tree, like she's waiting for someone to appear, holding her breath, hoping whoever it is will turn around and leave.

Azita walks nonchalantly toward Cassidy, who's not looking at her. "Excuse me. Cassidy, is it? Can we talk? I promise I won't take much of your time."

After hearing her name Cassidy looks at her with a puzzling gleam in her eyes. After recognizing the doctor, she turns her face away from her quickly as if angry about something.

"What do you want?"

"Where's that animal?"

Cassidy glares at the nosy doctor. "I don't know what you mean."

"I know how cut up you are about losing your mother to West Nile virus. That you hold me responsible. And I sympathize. But I can assure you that there's no way that her death is my fault."

Cassidy hesitates before saying, "My father blames you for not trying hard enough."

Azita has a strange feeling that the alien is close by. Call it woman's intuition.

"I assure you that isn't the case," Azita says then changes the subject. "Look I need your help. I'm trying to find this hybrid species, part human and part feline. She is a discovery of my friend Allison Banes, who is now dead."

As Cassidy steps forward from the tree, the look on her face tells Azita all she needs to know. Azita gets the feeling she wants to hear something else from her.

Azita flashes a trustworthy smile. "Talk to me. I can help you."

Cassidy doesn't answer, just nods her head in silence.

When that doesn't work, Azita decides to up the ante. "Kitty, where are you?"

When Kitty hears that, her brows come together in bewilderment and a meow slips from her lips. She inches out on a big branch, making herself visible. Azita glances up in the direction of the meow and sees Kitty. Then, for the next thirty seconds or so, Azita freezes in place, staring with wide eyes at Kitty.

"There you are at last," Azita says, relief in her tone.

A long, thin smile lengthens across the doctor's face. The creature fits the description in Allison's notebook to the letter. As hard as it is to admit, Azita is certain she's an alien from another galaxy.

She turns back to Cassidy. "She is fantastical, obviously not from around here. Why don't I give you a ride home before someone sees her?"

"Okay, Doctor," she agrees, reluctantly.

"You can just call me Azita."

"I want you to stay here and wait for me. Just give me a few minutes and I'll be back with my car."

After a short interval, Azita pulls her car up alongside Cassidy. Leaving the motor running, she reaches over to unbuckle her seat belt, gets out of the driver's side, and opens the back door for them.

"It's okay. You can come down from there," Cassidy assures Kitty.

Kitty climbs down from the tree and crawls into the backseat of Azita's car. Cassidy climbs in after her, clicking her seat belt in, and then turns to face her.

"Don't worry. She already knows about you."

After closing the back door, Azita hops into the driver's seat. Glancing in the rearview mirror, she thinks the alien looks so harmless, even with a look of pure radiance emanating from her. There's something inside of her on an unconscious level, telling her that the alien has nothing to do with Allison's death. Foremost she is wondering how the girl fits into all of this.

"Where am I taking you?" Azita finally asks.

"To my house a little further down Nyerere Road."

It's actually her grandmother's house, but she doesn't want Azita to know, after all, she still doesn't completely trust her.

Chapter 44

SHE'S ONLY MINUTES into the drive when Cassidy tells her to stop the car. As Azita comes to a stop on the side of the road, there are a host of questions queuing up in her mind begging for an answer. In a subtle way, she needs to have a serious talk with Cassidy.

"Before you leave, may I ask you some questions?"

"Yeah, okay, but make it quick."

"You two seem to get along so well together. Are you able communicate with her?" Azita asks nonchalantly, before turning off the ignition.

"Somehow, we manage to understand each other."

"Do you know where she really comes from?"

"No, I don't know where she's from, only that she lives in the forest."

Cassidy is fibbing, of course. She can't bring herself to share what she knows. She won't believe her and may try to take the alien away from her.

"I may be able to help you with that."

"Meow," Kitty murmurs to herself, meeting Azita's eyes in the rearview mirror.

"You can?" Cassidy asks with a little surprise in her voice.

After asking that, Cassidy does a double take on her comment. What can Azita possibly know?

Azita shifts to face the backseat. "Brace yourself because the truth may surprise you. Surely, you are a girl with an imagination, so you may believe me when I tell you."

"Go ahead, tell me," she says with confidence, just like she has no idea what she's going to say, but she feels dreadfully nervous inside.

"She comes from a distant planet in another galaxy – a faraway world I don't know."

Kitty straightens herself a little, managing to get more comfortable so she can watch and listen to them talk to each other.

"A being from outer space? How do you know that?" Cassidy asks, her eyes practically doing cartoon spirals.

Much to her delight that Azita knows, a part of Cassidy wonders if she wants to lock the alien away and study her. Azita is a medical doctor, and she doesn't trust doctors.

Azita pulls out Allison's field notebook from inside her handbag on the passenger seat and holds it up for a moment to show her. "This notebook of Allison Banes contains page after page of descriptions of her. She even calls her Kitty."

"Kitty is a nice name. Since she's staying here on Earth because there's no way for her to return to her world, I'm going to have to come up with a better name for her."

Her jaw twitches aware that she let something slip out and Azita can tell she's holding back something.

"What makes you say that? Cassidy, is there something you're not telling me?"

"Okay, okay, I already know she's an alien. A couple of days before Christmas my father learns about the wreckage of a spaceship and an escape pod in the forest in Arusha National Park from Paulina, then he tells me about it. Days later, I see her in the forest around Lake Duluti and I figure she comes from that escape pod."

"Cassidy, I understand your hesitation to not tell me everything from the beginning. It's a lot to deal with. Where do you plan to keep her?"

"I'm in a dilemma and I'm not sure how to deal with it. The Chagga want her to participate in a ritual that will break the curse of the Evil Shadowy Figure on them. What if they plan to sacrifice her to Ruwa? I don't want any harm to come to her."

"Allison's right. They do believe in some curse," Azita remarks, remembering her last conversation with Allison. "Tell me more about this Evil Shadowy Figure."

"All I know is from Laila, my very good friend who is also a Chagga. The Evil Shadowy Figure is an underworld spirit that dwells in the fire and holds captive the souls of their ancestors."

"Dwells in the fire?" she asks alarmingly, then asks the question slowly. "Do you think the Evil Shadowy Figure is looking for the alien?"

"Yes, because the alien can help the Chagga put an end to him. If he knows where she is, he'll come for her and eliminate anyone who gets in his way. I hope for both our sakes the Evil Shadowy Figure doesn't find us."

Azita suddenly goes quiet. It takes a moment for her words to sink in. The significance of them. She thinks back to Allison keeping the alien in her house. Tears come to her eyes as she realizes that Allison Banes is a victim of the Evil Shadowy Figure. Deep down, she knows it. The thing about being Muslim is that she has an open mind. It's silly to believe in evil spirits and curses, but seeing as aliens really do exist, she can believe that anything is possible. Not wanting to scare Cassidy half to death, she wants to keep this bit of information to herself.

"Cassidy, this is all so fascinating. But you must be very careful. I know Kitty, the extraterrestrial, is going to be in good hands with you. Find out from your friend Laila what the ritual to end the Evil Shadowy Figure actually involves, and then make your decision."

"First I must tell my father," she says with conviction.

"That's a wise decision."

"Oh, that reminds me. What time is it?"

"A minute after six," Azita says, looking at her wristwatch.

"I have to go now. I'm already late."

Azita holds out her hand for the rigid formality of a handshake. "Farewell, my friend."

Cassidy pauses, not sure what to do. After a beat, she takes Azita's hand in hers and shakes it firmly.

Reaching inside her handbag, she pulls out a card. "Here's my business card with my cell phone number on the back. If you run into trouble or need help, Cassidy, call me."

She takes the card and slips it into her backpack. "I will. And thanks for talking to me."

Cassidy leaves the car with Kitty trailing behind her. Azita watches them until they disappear between two houses.

Before driving away, she thinks for a minute. The earlier revelation that Allison is a victim of the Evil Shadowy Figure, really upsets her. This time the tears don't come. Her eyes seem full of anger. Now she wants revenge. If that's even possible.

Chapter 45

AS AZITA HUSSEIN'S AUDI moves down the road, Cassidy emerges from behind an empty house. The house Azita thinks is hers. She crosses the street toward her grandmother's house. Kitty loiters behind her.

Thinking about her talk with Azita, she realizes that she can trust the doctor. Her past feelings concerning the loss of her mother, she is quickly recognizing, are those of an immature young girl. Despite this she considers it best to not be completely honest with Azita. For one thing, she doesn't need to know exactly where she lives. Secondly, by walking to the empty house across her grandmother's house, it gives the impression that she lives there. And, last of all, with utmost caution, she most definitely doesn't want Azita to know that she's going to hide the alien in a shed for the night. Though it's probably the safest place.

"Shhh," Cassidy whispers as they quietly creep up to the side of her grandmother's house for a look through the window.

She sees her grandmother walk through the living room to the kitchen. Her grandmother is busy preparing dinner. Kitty sniffs at the complex aroma in the air, a rich beef stew and spices. Her mouth waters. The smell of meat cooking catches Cassidy's nose and drags her along as surely as any rope. It reminds her how hungry she is and how she has to prepare dinner the instant she gets home. Her father is probably already home and wondering where she is.

It's a good chance her grandmother won't hear anything happening outside the house. If she gets wind of her lurking outside her house, knowing she has no reason to be there — or sees the alien — she'll have some serious explaining to do. On the off chance that her grandmother finds the alien in the shed, she hopes the sight of the alien doesn't scare her, though it probably will. And she suspects that her grandmother will shoo her away. Then she'll have to go out and find the alien again. Of course, when her grandmother later asks why the alien is in her shed, she will know nothing.

With no more time to lose, she moves as quietly as she can, heading toward the back of the house with Kitty close behind. Stepping up to the shed, she pulls the door open as quietly as possibly, but can't avoid a few creaking noises. With an instant shock of horror, the smell coming from inside overwhelms her and she feels a little sick. It is bad, some odors unpleasant — the stench of some dead animal.

She waves her hand in front of her nose in a desperate attempt to fan away the smell.

"Pee you," she says, dropping her voice and clasping her hand over her nose. "Sorry about the smell. Hope it isn't too much for you."

Kitty's feeling a little antsy and won't step inside.

"Get in there. Come on, I haven't got all night. You have to go inside. You can't come with me," Cassidy urges then points to the brown blanket on the floor. "Do you see the blanket? You're going to be just fine. Go ahead and make yourself comfortable."

The moment prolongs. Cassidy's patience is running thin. She stands there with growing horror and folds her arms in front of her chest, waiting for some response from Kitty.

Nodding her head, softly, Kitty unhappily complies. She enters the shed, and, in a flash, she stands in the midst of darkness. Cobwebs cling to her face and neck as she walks forward. The pungent smell of decay fills her nostrils, turns her stomach. The shed feels tinier than the amount of air she needs to breathe.

Cassidy fishes a red apple out of her backpack and holds it out to the alien. "Here's another apple."

Kitty grabs the apple and brings it to her mouth. She takes a loud bite, a spray of juice squirting out.

"Don't eat it all at once. It's all you are getting until tomorrow afternoon."

With sad glowing green eyes, Kitty turns to her, earnestly searching every inch of her face. For what? Understanding?

"Never mind. Enjoy the apple."

Kitty wants to go with her. But that's not happening. Knowing that, she whimpers and wiggles around a little until she is sitting just right on the blanket on the floor. She is staring hard at nothing, her expression vacant as her green eyes scan the room around her, seeing but not seeing, then her eyes settle on Cassidy. Her facial muscles relax, and her lips open slightly, giving her mouth a pouting expression, obviously wearing her feelings on her sleeve. Quite simply, she is no longer a happy camper.

"Don't look so sad. It's for your safety."

Kitty lowers her head and complains with a soft meow.

"Nighty-night. I promise I'll come back tomorrow after school with food and water," she says, and closes the door, firmly, but doesn't lock it.

Cassidy is already hurrying down Nyerere Road. After turning left onto Tengeru Road, she breathes a sigh of relief of satisfaction, realizing she's almost home. Still, she has a bad feeling inside. She trusts that the alien will not leave the shed, but she's not at all sure. What's worse is knowing that the Evil Shadowy Figure is out there somewhere, trying to get to the alien. It's all too much for her to absorb. It's times like these that she needs to shut off her brain.

At twenty-five after six she's finally walking toward the front door of her house. Her father's Land Rover is in the driveway off to the side of the house. The moment of truth is at hand. Whilst she is anxious to have her father's help, in order to get it she has to tell him everything. It's not going to do her any good to say she's just returning from Laila's house after working with her on a very important school science project. She can't return to her original plan.

Walking to the door, Cassidy lowers her head, worrying and deeply afraid about what her father will say when she tells him all of it.

Chapter 46

AT THE LAST POSSIBLE SECOND, as Cassidy's hand touches the door knob, Laila moves toward her, coming from the side of the house and taking her by surprise. The expression on Laila's face is not good. It seems that something is bothering her.

Cassidy leans back against the door and looks at her. "What are you doing here?"

"What am I doing here?" Laila asks with a note of sarcasm.

"Am I missing something?"

"You know good and well that the Chagga need that alien to break the curse of the Evil Shadowy Figure," Laila says, looking at her with wild eyes.

"Yeah, so what?"

"Where's the alien?"

"What makes you think I know?"

"Cassidy, I'm not dumb. This is your best friend you're talking to. I know when you are hiding something from me. It has to be that you know where the alien is."

"I'm trying to decide what to do."

"Well, you need to decide quick."

"Cassidy is that you I hear out there?" shouts her father from somewhere inside the house loudly, as if he is standing right beside her.

She just barely manages to keep from flinching when she hears his voice calling her name. "Yes, I'm talking to Laila."

He opens the front door to find Cassidy and Laila there. "Greetings, Laila. Cassidy, my dear, I've been pacing back and forth in the living room for the past twenty-five minutes, stealing glances out the window and wondering where you are."

"She's coming from my house after working on a school science project. Isn't that right, Cassidy?" Laila asks, covering for her.

Cassidy can't tell if he believes that lie. It's days like this that she's not happy that Laila lives less than a block away, practically a stone's throw away.

"Well, um, yes. The assignment is complete. Ready to hand in tomorrow."

"That's great, but Laila, you need to be heading back to your house. It's starting to get dark. I don't want your parents worrying about you."

"I'm just about to leave."

"Cassidy, you need to come inside."

"In a minute, Daddy."

He closes the door and returns to some place inside the house.

Laila starts up again. "This is serious. This involves the Chagga. This involves the Evil Shadowy Figure. If you know where the alien is, I advise you bring her to the Chagga tomorrow. I'm counting on you, so you have to do it."

"What if the ritual involves sacrifice? I don't want the alien to die."

"I don't know what takes place in the ritual."

"Can you find out?"

Laila takes a second to ponder it. "How about we take the alien to Chief Naruma. I'm sure he can answer any questions about the ritual. He'll explain the ritual to us. How does that sound?"

"I will agree to that on the condition that if the ritual will cause the alien harm, she doesn't have to participate."

"I guess that's fair. I'll get my mother to call Chief Naruma and tell him to come over to my house because you're bringing the alien," Laila says, hurrying off down the lawn.

Cassidy slips inside the house and heads straight toward her bedroom to drop her backpack on the bed and change out of her school uniform. After putting on a floral-print short-sleeve shirt, comfy jeans, and flip-flops, she makes a quick trip to the bathroom. After a moment's pause, she goes to the kitchen.

"I'll have dinner ready in a jiffy," she says to her father as he comes to the room.

With everything she has to contend with, so much weighing on her mind, she manages to have dinner ready a half hour later. She sets out a plate of rice, beans, tomatoes, and cuts of meat for each of them on the table. With a self-conscious smile, she quickly fills two glasses with lemonade and places them on the table, taking a chair next to her father. Once he starts eating, she feels, perhaps, now is a good time to talk.

"I have to tell you something," she says, wanting to get it all out quickly.

"What is it, my princess?"

"Do you remember me telling you about the alien in the forest around Lake Duluti?"

"Of course, I remember. I can't forget that Christmas Eve," he says after taking a bite.

"It is the alien from the escape pod. I'm keeping her in the shed behind grandmother's house," she says coolly.

Geoffrey, still chewing, bolts from the chair. His eyes are wide with alarm. Many questions are running through his mind.

"How do you know it's the alien from the escape pod?" he asks, after swallowing.

Cassidy takes a sip of her lemonade. "You can tell just by looking at her. And Azita tells me it is an alien."

"Who exactly is Azita?"

"The doctor from Selian Lutheran Hospital. She's working at a clinic now. I have her business card. She has her friend Allison's notebook. But Allison is dead now. The notebook contains her research notes about the alien that she calls Kitty. That's how come Azita knows all about the alien."

"Dr. Hussein? Now I need to sit down."

"She's a nice lady, too. And it's not her fault that Mom is dead."

"Don't bring your mother into this. Even if the doctor is not responsible for your mother's death, don't change the subject."

"I won't bring mother up again."

"Does this mean there's no school science project?" he asks, before taking another bite.

"No. There's no science project. Laila is just covering for me, saying I'm with her when in fact I'm with the alien and Azita."

"The doctor again?" Geoffrey pauses and seems to be carefully thinking through what he will say next. "Why don't you bring the alien here?"

Cassidy hastily swallows the last bite on her plate. "I don't want a member of the Chagga to see her. They will try to take her for their ritual to break the curse of the Evil Shadowy Figure. I'm afraid it may be a ritual of sacrifice. And now Laila wants me to take the alien to her house to meet with Chief Naruma and find out what kind of ritual it is."

"In my opinion, the Evil Shadowy Figure is a myth of the Chagga. No one outside the tribe knows whether the curse is real or not. Then again, you do seem to believe it," he says, glancing up from his plate.

Cassidy stands up and brings her plate to the sink. "I'm a mess about it. What do I do, Daddy?"

"Ah, well, let's hope Dottie doesn't find the alien in her shed. We'll keep that to ourselves. We don't want to send your grandmother into shock, right?"

"No, I don't want that."

"If she does find the alien, tell her that you're hiding her there until you can take her to Laila's house. Exactly what I want you to do. Honestly, I don't know how to handle this alien thing. And tomorrow I won't be able to take time off work. I have some pressing matters which I must attend to, which means I will be working a little late at the office. Since the Chagga have a plan, let's give it a try. After school tomorrow I want you and Laila to go to Dottie's house and retrieve the alien from the shed. Then the two of you will take the alien to Laila's house and find out what the ritual entails from Chief Naruma. If it sounds good to you, go for it. If not, you come back here with the alien and I'll come up with something. Sound good?"

Cassidy returns to the table, grabs her glass of lemonade and drinks it down. "Yes, it does actually."

"That's my girl."

After clearing the table with brisk efficiency, Cassidy retreats to her bedroom to prepare for bed. Once she is in her pajamas, she tumbles onto the bed. As she drifts off to sleep, she thinks about the alien. Will she still be there tomorrow?

Chapter 47

AT HALF PAST EIGHT in the evening, Kitty wakes from a nap and slowly gets to her feet. In one fluid motion she spins around with a questioning look on her face. The look she has is not because of the foul odor in the air that's nagging away at her a little. The look on her face is not only because of the staleness of the air in the shed, but there is a sort of continual moaning sound coming from outside. It seems to be calling to her. Strangely, there is no wind to explain that strange moaning sound, so the sound must be coming from somebody.

To satisfy her curiosity, she creeps to the door, lifts the latch, and pushes it open a crack so she can peek out. By adjusting her head and squinting through the crack, she sees a young African woman, wearing a multi-color kitenge wraparound dress that reaches to her knees, standing at an angle to the house in the middle of the yard. Kitty doesn't stir, obviously not wanting to attract her attention.

Kitty tilts her face up to stare at the pale gray wedge of a waning crescent Moon. Then returns her gaze to the woman in the yard. Opening the door wider, she sticks her head out for a better look.

When the barefoot woman swings around, she isn't moaning anymore, but her deep breathing punctures the stillness of the night. She looks at Kitty with a rather desperate expression on her face. Tears streak through the black soot on her face.

"He is coming for you," she warns Kitty.

Somewhat bafflingly, Kitty responds with little purr-meows in her throat. When the woman starts to walk toward her, a powerful vacuumlike force begins pulling her body backward. Her arms reach up for Kitty, at the same time she's trying to shake herself loose from the force.

"Leave now before he finds you," the woman murmurs in a pleading way.

To no avail. The strength of the suction is too strong, and instead, the woman's body flies backward, rapidly vanishing into the darkness like an apparition, silent and invisible. Kitty can't fathom why the woman is no longer anywhere in sight. She blinks hard, half afraid she is seeing things until something inside her shrugs "oh well," whereupon she draws a deep breath, thinking nothing more of it.

Suddenly feeling thirsty, she can't remember the inside of her mouth ever feeling as dry as it does right at this moment. She creaks open the door. In two steps she is outside, breathing in the fresh night air. She immediately stretches her whole body to its full length, readying every muscle, tendon, and ligament. She's going to snoop around, hoping to find some water. She won't stray away too far or too long, knowing the little girl will return, and she wants to be there when she does.

She's relishing the crispness of the air, enjoying the chance to stretch her legs after a short confinement in the backyard storage shed. Already she's moving across the yard, her tail wagging happily behind her, but after a few strides she turns to see some lights on in the house in front of the shed but can't see any movement inside. She pauses for a moment to admire the bands of light from the waning crescent Moon quiver over the house, along with patterns of darkness. When her thirst comes roaring back, she loses interest quickly and returns her attention to the task at hand — finding water.

No sooner does Kitty leave, an angry mass of dark clouds accumulate and pulse with a flickering glow, swirling in slow motion, morphing into shapes, covering the sky above the house with their turbulence. There is electricity in the air. The Evil Shadowy Figure is slowly materializing in the backyard of the house.

When he manifests as physical matter, he takes the shape of like an Egyptian god of evil. Bearing a head in the shape of a lion's mane, stands for bravery, of which he has no fear of anyone or anything. Like the country of Kenya, the evil spirit uses the lion as its emblem. He embodies all of the traits and characteristics of a fierce, untamable lion. Except he is not king of the jungle, he is the dark king of the netherworld, the world between life and death.

Sensing the alien's presence, the Evil Shadowy Figure turns so that he is facing the shed. Good thing for Kitty she isn't there right now. Seeing that the door is wide open, he slithers to the front of the shed. With his own penetrating vision, his dark, fiery eyes pierce through the dull surroundings inside the shed to find nothing. There is no sign of the alien. He steps back and turns his head in all directions as if appraising the situation, wondering why the alien is no longer there. This does not go over well with the Evil Shadowy Figure.

Groaning in disappointment, he turns his attention on the dim golden light pouring from the window of the grandmother's house. The light, like a flame, attracts him. The evil entity twists out in the darkness, moving toward the house. Perhaps he thinks he will find the alien there.

Peeking through the window, the Evil Shadowy Figure cannot see or sense the alien. He does not see anyone, but he hears someone moving about the house. From the bedroom comes a voice, a single voice of a woman singing an African lullaby in a throaty hum. Despite the pleasant sound of the grandmother's voice, the Evil Shadowy Figure is not happy to hear it. Briefly an exotic mix of tongues and dialects rise out of his mouth mimicking her tones, as if mocking her. Nothing will please him more than to find the alien. But not finding the alien fuels his anger!

The fire in his eyes rages believing she's protecting the alien, keeping it safe from him. A wicked expression comes into his fiery black eyes. Now he wants to snuff out the old woman. And this he will do. His face twists in delight, and he can sense the anticipation: in the tension inside him, in the stillness of the dark clouds that swell overhead.

Chapter 48

DOTTIE MKAMA exits the bedroom wearing a pink chiffon nightgown, a white terry robe over it, and slippers. She enters the kitchen to pour herself a glass of lemonade for which she carries the full glass into the living room and sets it down on a dark-wood side table by her deep royal blue suede armchair. She takes a seat in the armchair for a few moments of rest to drink her lemonade and to think of something calming to do before turning in for the night.

Not more than a couple of minutes later, she feels like reading something. She gets up from her armchair and dashes off to her bedroom to grab her wire-rim reading glasses from the top of the dresser and slips them on. Then she walks back to the living room to peruse the walnut bookshelf in the corner. After selecting a book to read, she returns to her armchair and begins reading the book in the dim light of the baby blue porcelain lamp on the dark-wood side table.

In one fell swoop a burst of air rushes over her startling her out of her concentration. What happens next is the light bulb in the lamp goes out. Needless to say, this doesn't go over well with her, either. She turns the switch on the lamp, and nothing happens. That means the electricity is out.

Squinting through her glasses, she looks about the room and asks to nobody in particular, "What in the world is going on in here?"

Is it possible that there is just a power outage in the area? Possible, yes, but she can find out for certain once she goes to the basement to turn the main switch at the top of the breaker box off and then back on.

Something feels off. She feels a cold chill dance up her spine. Is someone in the house with her?

And then she sees him, a dark shadow materializing in the corner of the room. One minute there is nothing, and then he is there. She sinks back a little in her chair, her eyes still on the shadow. In utter disbelief, she blinks her eyes twice watching him move closer. Is he what she thinks it is? Yes, it is! What is the Evil Shadowy Figure doing in her living room?

Now it makes sense. She knows that the Evil Shadowy Figure lives in the fire and wherever he appears, he absorbs electricity, feeds from it. The fire and electricity provide him with energy to maintain his physical presence.

Standing before her, he emits a distinctive, sickly odor, like that of rotting flowers, burning flesh and sulfur. Then, he lets out a deafening screech that makes her flesh prickle as if to announce his presence.

A feeling of the most enormous dread has come over her. Biting her upper lip, she is thinking over her options.

Snapping her book shut with a clap, she rises from the chair with a wince to face him head on. In the process, the book slips out of her hands and falls to the floor with a thump. The fear inside of her burrows its way deep into her heart. Nevertheless, she is in her mid-sixties, and she is ready to meet her maker, if it comes down to it. She opens her mind to feel Jesus Christ's presence, hoping for guidance. But she is alone, and not even prayer can drive the evil back to the underworld.

She speaks directly to him, "Evil Shadowy Figure, why have you come here? There is nothing here for you!"

He stops moving, a strange glitter in his sinister eyes, and responds with a loud war whoop. After a moment of glaring at her with real menace, he moves even closer until they are almost face-to-face. He's looking at her real close, their faces only a couple of inches apart. His eyes are raging with fury, hovering in front of her, cackling with a demonic laugh.

What does he want? What is he looking for? Uncertain what to do next, she can't beat back the cold hard fear growing in her chest. That is, until the fizz of adrenaline shoots through her veins. Moving carefully in the dark, she walks straight to the kitchen and grabs the broom standing up against the wall. She will chase him out of here or die trying. At the present moment she can't see any other way.

Coming back into the living room, without thinking she holds the broom in front of her, pointing the bristles at his chest. Dottie Mkama is a courageous woman, resorting to this behavior against the Evil Shadowy Figure.

"You go on and get out of here!"

This is her turf, and she doesn't take any bull from anyone, especially from a dark and disturbing spirit like the Evil Shadowy Figure. Her expression is cold like a blizzard in January, knowing he's here to harm her.

The Evil Shadowy Figure doesn't budge, and she looks straight into his fiery black eyes. "I'm telling you, there's nothing here for you."

His mouth opens like he's going to say something. But what she hears are the voices of the souls in his possession. The ones that will be free upon his demise. Many conflicting voices, melding into one and chattering all at once at different levels, echoing, and ringing around the room.

"Don't start speaking in tongues," she says defiantly.

With a clench of her jaw, Dottie holds her ground, tightening her grip on the broom handle and looking at him harder. No doubt she is afraid. She must admit she is. She is shaking with nervousness, pulse echoing in wrists and the pit of her stomach, limbs quivering. But she won't back down. Not tonight.

"Don't make me repeat myself," she says with some exasperation.

His mouth closes and all the voices cease. When he moves closer to the threatening woman, she shoves the bristles of the broom toward her opponent, giving him a jab in the side. His fiery black eyes flare with uncontrollable rage. Sulfurous yellow smoke rises from his rib cage, desiring to unleash it on her out of sheer anger.

Her blood pressure is up, she's short of breath and needs rest. She's squinting and she can't bear it any longer. Her heart gives an almighty, chest-breaking thump. A horrible screech is the last thing she hears before her legs go out from under her as she sags onto the hardwood floor.

The Evil Shadowy figure stares at the grandmother, who is motionless, lying flat on the floor, his black eyes wide with silent condemnation. He touches the old crone on the side of her head, just above her ear. Disappointingly, it feels like she's still alive, but weak. But he clearly has no wish to waste any further time here. When he disappears in a wisp of smoke, a hint of his presence remains in the air. But not something to see, just a sickening odor.

Chapter 49

AT A QUARTER PAST TEN, skulking across the lawn of someone's backyard, Kitty steps in a small puddle of water. She looks down and swipes the rubber hose from the ground at her feet. When she opens the rusting water spigot, the hose stiffens, and water spurts erratically from the nozzle. While drinking water from the hose, she catches a boy in his pajamas looking at her from the window of the house. He smiles and waves hello. She waves back and turns off the hose. Now she is ready to return to the shed.

Evening shadows finger across the backyard of Dottie Mkama's house. Kitty approaches the shed with a lack of enthusiasm, knowing she has nowhere else to go. She stares into the strange darkness that surrounds the house. This seems odd. She remembers seeing lights on in the house earlier.

Just for the sake of it, she drops to all fours and crawls to the front of the house. She goes to the window nearest the door, slowly raises herself into a standing position, and peers into the living room.

That's when she sees her! No way, not again! It's too much of a coincidence. Is she alive? Does she need help?

It is a déjà vu moment, reminding her of that dreadful night finding Allison Banes lying on the floor, dead. This time. It's someone else lying on the floor.

She moves along the side of the house, looking for a way in. At the far corner of the house, she sees a window open a few inches. She lifts the window up and climbs in.

The house is dark, the lights out. Making her way from the old woman's bedroom to the living room, her footsteps send vibrations through the hardwood floor. She squats next to the old woman on the floor, listening to her breathing, watching her face by the thin silver light of the waning crescent Moon shining in through the window. She's not dead!

Before leaving, she sees a half-full glass of lemonade on a side table. She grabs the glass, drinks the last of the lemonade and wipes her mouth with the back of her hand. Like a bolt from the blue, the lamp turns on and the room floods with golden light. Putting the empty glass down with a sigh, she notices the old woman stirring.

Dottie's eyes aren't open, but she's already talking, "Don't think I don't know you're here. I can smell the death on you. You smell exactly like the dead Indian house crows I keep finding in my shed."

Kitty listens to everything she says, watching her with intensity. Then to her surprise, Grandmother Mkama opens her eyes and screams at the sight of her. Kitty falls on her hands to a position on all fours, backs away a few steps and sits down, staring at the woman in shock. For a brief spell they both stare at each other in silence.

When Dottie has something to say, she is quiet at first. Then she talks a lot, sometimes for hours.

"Ignore my screaming. I'm not afraid of you. If I can face the Evil Shadowy Figure, I can face anyone. Let me get to my feet, and take a good look at you," she says in a trembling voice, after getting her breath back.

The grandmother wiggles around and slowly starts to pull herself off the floor. She's not all there after fainting from pulmonary hypertension due to the stress of taking on the Evil Shadowy Figure. She rights herself slowly and blinks hard, trying to clear the last wisps of fog from her brain. Then she snatches her reading glasses from the floor and sets them on the side table.

"Come over here, closer. Let me get a better look at you. My eyes don't work so good these days," says Dottie, straightening her robe, moving her arms with a little effort.

Kitty scoots a little closer and looks at her, a question in her eyes.

"You are a magical sight. What are you? Some kind of alien?"

Dottie Mkama is right about that. The words jump out of her mouth as if of their own accord.

After thinking carefully for a moment, she wonders if this creature in her living room, is what the Evil Shadowy Figure is after. She sure hopes the evil spirit doesn't come back.

She puts her hands on her hips and glares at Kitty. "Despite your looks, you seem harmless enough. Tell me what brings you to my home? I know by the smell on you that you have been staying in my shed. Why? You don't look like a squatter."

Kitty sighs and gazes at her with sympathetic eyes.

"Uh-huh. I think the cat has your tongue."

Dottie carefully retrieves her book from the floor and returns it to the bookshelf in the corner of the room. Thinking things over, she paces to and fro in front of Kitty. Clearly, she must inform her son. If the park rangers find stray animals inside Arusha National Park, they take care of them, help them, or so she believes.

She stops pacing and asks, "Do you have a place to sleep tonight?"

Kitty shakes her head no.

"You can't stay in my shed. But I'm not going to put you out. You can sleep on the sofa. Then in the morning, I'll call my son. I'm sure he'll be able to help you."

She looks Kitty over and gets a whiff of her again. "You need a wash. I won't have you stinking up the place. I'll just be a minute, I promise. One minute."

The grandmother exits into the hallway at a slow pace and then disappears into the bathroom. When she returns to the living room, she stands in the doorway looking at Kitty, and raises her hand in an ushering motion.

"Come right this way," she says, giving her a smile.

Kitty steps into the bathroom. She notices wisps of steam rising from the water that is at a level close to the brim of the tub. She watches the soap bubbles rise up and pop against the ceiling. Tweaking her nose, she notices the sweet-smelling water is similar to the smell of the flowers in Allison Banes' house.

"Come on, let's go clean up. Let's get you in the tub for your bath," she commands sharply.

Kitty's jaw goes hard at that comment.

Chapter 50

JUST LIKE any other morning, Grandmother Mkama is sipping chai tea in the kitchen, the light from the window casting dramatic shadows across her face. The remains of her toast are still in evidence on a plate. She sets down her teacup with a clink of cup to saucer. Thereafter, she drags a last corner of toast through a smear of jam.

She goes to the living room, ostensibly to check on her houseguest still sleeping and snoring on the blue fabric sofa. Periodically, she walks back and forth, between the kitchen and the living room, watching with great interest, wariness and maybe a touch of fear.

Lying on her side facing the back of the sofa, Kitty wakes up with bells on. Literally. When she moves her tail, she can hear the jingle of two little silver bells that are hanging on a white string from around her tail.

Now for the reason of her being awake.

There is a strong smell of some kind of food beside her head. She jerks her head around to find the grandmother holding a cast-iron frying pan in her right hand.

"My, you are awake. I know you're wondering about those bells on your tail. Why? So, I can hear you coming. Don't want you sneaking up on me. At any rate, do you eat eggs?"

Kitty's eyebrows snap together, and she stares at her with an irate expression. She groans and turns her head away from the smell, although by the tilt of her head, Dottie guesses she's still listening.

"Forget the eggs. I have some fresh salmon steaks. When you're ready, come to the kitchen," she says and leaves the room.

Kitty shifts against the sofa cushions, rolling over to curl her body around one of the pillows. Two deep breaths and she resumes her low snore without missing a beat.

Some hours later, Kitty joins her in the kitchen, ready to eat. She sits down on the floor next to the table and the grandmother sets down a plate of salmon steaks in front of her.

"I know now for certain that you are an alien of uncertain origin. I know from talking to my son, Geoffrey, on the phone earlier. Get yourself together, because when Cassidy gets here, you're heading out."

"Meow," Kitty says between bites.

After washing her hands in the sink, wiping her hands on her flowery apron, and removing it, Dottie sits down at the table. She sets the apron on the table next to her.

"But I don't mind you being here at all. Just knowing that the Evil Shadowy Figure may be after you is a sign that there is something special about you."

Later that day, Kitty is sitting on the sofa, reading a magazine while Dottie Mkama is sitting in her armchair at the end of the living room in the house when a knock comes on the door. Her face breaks into a smile.

"That will be Lil Cassie."

She opens the door to find Cassidy and her friend Laila, out of their school uniforms, both wearing T-shirts, jeans, and tennis shoes.

Before Cassidy can say a word, her testy grandmother holds up her left hand. "You have some explaining to do, young lady."

"I know, I know," Cassidy says immediately.

The girls proceed to walk inside the living room. Kitty rises to her feet and tosses the magazine on the sofa, anxious to see the little girl again.

"Don't you look all sparkly!" Cassidy says, noting Kitty's appearance.

"A real alien, born on another planet! She is stunning!" Laila says, unable to keep the shock from her voice.

"But the bells need to go," Cassidy adds quickly.

"Just next time check with me before you sneak her into my shed. I know this now for certain from speaking to your father on the telephone early this morning," Grandmother Mkama says, standing defiantly on the other side of the room.

"Please hear me out, Grandma," Cassidy says after a sigh.

"Go on, I'm all ears," the grandmother says sternly.

"She's a helpless alien. If nothing else, this is a safe place for her to be. Can she stay one more night? Please," Cassidy asks, a pleading note in her voice.

"You are kidding me, right?" the grandmother asks in disbelief.

"Chief Naruma of the Chagga needs to see her, but he can't come over today because his Jeep is in the shop until tomorrow. There are mechanical problems with his Jeep. He lives near Mount Meru. It's too far to walk," Laila explains to her.

Dottie Mkama changes her tune quicker than a flash. "Guess I'll be driving you. The alien can't stay here another minute. Just let me freshen up and change."

Cassidy and Laila stare at one another with quizzical expressions on their faces.

Heart slamming, the grandmother bolts from the room in a way that appears she's come through yesterday's ordeal all right, what seems like a full recovery. For the next dozen minutes, the girls and Kitty sit close together on the sofa, waiting feverishly for the grandma. While waiting Cassidy and Laila barely speak to each other, whereas Kitty is purring with glee.

At ten till four, the grandmother comes back into the living room wearing a neat dark blue dress, satin dress sandals, and a cream cashmere cardigan. The dress slithers down her body, skimming the skin just below the knees.

"Well, we're off," the grandmother announces joyfully.

"Thanks for helping us out, grandma," Cassidy says, then hugs and kisses her cheek.

After grabbing her purse and keys, the grandmother opens the door to leave. Everyone steps outside, and Dottie locks the front door. She opens the back door of her Volkswagen SUV and the girls, along with Kitty file into the backseat. Cassidy unties the string around Kitty's tail, sending the bells to the floor of the backseat. Dottie opens the door, gets into the driver's seat, careful not to mess her hair. Adjusting the rearview mirror to check her appearance, the grandmother double-checks that her hair is tidy.

Placing her key into the ignition, she turns it. "Don't forget to buckle up, kiddies. Laila, you know where he lives, don't you?"

"His house is near Saddle Hut. Once we're near Mount Meru, I can direct you there," Laila affirms, somewhat proudly.

"Just point the way," the grandmother says frivolously.

Chapter 51

"PARK HERE," Laila points to a spot just off the trail near Chief Naruma's house.

They all come climbing out of the grandmother's SUV, looking enthusiastic. Cassidy and Laila move quickly toward the door. The grandma and Kitty, who is repeatedly squinting her eyes against the bright sun, are walking side by side. Overall, they get along well enough.

The front door opens before Cassidy has a chance to knock, as if he is waiting by the door expecting them to show up on his doorstep. His blank expression turns to surprise as he stares at the alien.

"The Gotham alien is here. She's a beautiful, magical creature," he says, smiling graciously. "Dottie, what a nice surprise."

And just like that, with one look at his face, Dottie is breathless yet again. What a strange man he is, she reflects.

So cool in some ways, so pensive, yet he's capable of such incredibly sweet gestures.

A slight hesitation before Dottie says, "Always a pleasure to see you, Anton. I'm just the transportation. Don't let me get in the way."

"Gotham alien? She's actually a cat person," Laila states, correcting him.

"I know the prophecy says it's a Gotham alien," he says, his voice rising with affirmation.

Cassidy stands there watching their conversation silently, turning her head back and forth like a tennis match, from him to Laila, looking at one, then the other.

"The prophecy isn't exact. She's not goat-like. She is catlike," Laila clarifies.

"You have a point, my dear," Chief Naruma concludes.

"Gotham Kitty. That's what I'll call her," Cassidy adds decisively.

"Sounds good to me," Laila responds.

Dottie looks at him, at his brown eyes behind his glasses. "Fine by me."

"Gotham Kitty it is. It's a great name," the Chief says after thinking on it for a few seconds. "All of you, come inside."

The instant they step inside, Chief Naruma closes the door behind them, but not before looking around from left to right and all around, even though there is nothing to see. They file into the tiny living room, look about and he offers them seats.

Standing in the center of the room, he gets right down to business. "First and foremost, Cassidy, you want to know about the ritual?"

"I just want to know that Gotham Kitty is not going to be hurt," Cassidy says, somewhat nervously.

He only smiles — that knowing grandfather's smile of reassurance. "Gotham Kitty is not going to be a sacrifice. She is essential to our future. There's so much we can learn from her. This alien lifeform proves to humanity that we are not alone in the universe. With the discovery of alien civilizations in star systems we don't even know about, we find ourselves in a new era."

The sound of his warm voice makes Cassidy relax. With an expression of confidence in his eyes, he doesn't even flinch as he looks at her, almost as if he's saying, "Trust me." And why not?

The Chagga Chief starts to pace hither and thither in the small space. "The Chagga believe you can kill a man by plunging a spear into his shadow. Ah, but the Evil Shadowy Figure is not a man, nor human. Being a spirit, he has no shadow. However, as seemingly physical he appears, he has no physicality in and of itself. Hence, only the ritual can destroy the evil spirit."

He stops his pacing and looks from face to face to make sure that he's being clear.

"Anton, please continue," Dottie says, leaning forward in the white Moroccan leather wing chair.

His grandfatherly voice strengthens, echoes throughout the room. "Unity between the extraterrestrial and the descendant of a victim of the long-ago volcanic fires of Mount Meru is necessary to carry out the ritual."

Startlingly, Laila rises from the white leather loveseat. "I am a direct descendant of Sayida Jaquier, a victim of the volcanic fires. She is my six times great-grand-aunt."

"The alien is at your side. This is the sign to you from Ruwa. As it turns out you're the child who has a special destiny. And in your heart, you know it's true."

I am the one who can end the curse! Laila thinks to herself as she sits back down.

He starts explaining the ritual to her. "During the ritual, Gotham Kitty is your protector. Your unity is your strength. Together, the Evil Shadowy Figure can't harm you. You must always remember this. Since early times, fire is a symbol of the Divinity throughout all civilizations and religions of the world. In this case, the fire flame represents the inner light that burns in the Evil Shadowy Figure. You will stand together by the fire. You will say a prayer for the souls of the victims from the long-ago volcanic fires of Mount Meru who are all under the dominance of the Evil Shadowy Figure. When the Evil Shadowy Figure begins to materialize out of the fire, you will throw a lock of your hair into the fire. The hair will disintegrate in the heat of the fire and will reach the soul of Sayida Jaquier, delivering her from damnation. Once her soul is free, the other souls will be free, too. That will lift the curse from the Chagga, extinguishing the Evil Shadowy Figure's presence in our world. The entity will permanently vanquish to the netherworld. Last of all, the Chagga members will sing a song of praise to Ruwa and take turns tossing a handful of dirt into the campfire to put out the last glowing embers."

"Sounds pretty easy! We're in, right?" Cassidy asks, nudging Laila's right shoulder with her left elbow.

Everyone looks at Laila, who shrugs and says, "Let's do it."

The girls look over at Gotham Kitty, who is no longer sitting on the loveseat. She is smelling the rose incense rising from a small brass incense burner on a dark wooden side table in the corner of the room. Feeling all eyes on her, she turns away from the incense burner and looks at the girls. Chief Naruma folds his arms across his chest, waiting patiently for a response.

"Meow," Gotham Kitty says with a shrug of confusion.

Cassidy, Laila, and Dottie laugh in unison. The Chief unfolds his arms and lets them hang at his sides.

"Time is of the essence. The Evil Shadowy Figure senses what is about to take place and, is in anguish. He wants to prevent Gotham Kitty from participating in the ritual. But he knows that time is running out and fast. As a substitute, in the evenings around the campfire, the Chagga will soon tell tales about Gotham Kitty," he proclaims with a sincere smile.

The Chief gives them further instructions. That they must go to the southwestern slope of Mount Meru. He will meet them at eight o'clock that evening to guide them through the ritual.

"Do you know the way from here, Laila?" the Chief asks, peering at her over his glasses like a schoolmaster.

"I definitely do, Chief Naruma."

"So be off with you!" he says in a commanding voice.

Outside the door, Chief Naruma and Dottie watch them walk off at a leisurely pace, with Laila leading the way.

Dottie waits until they are out of earshot before saying what is on her mind. "Before I go, there's something I have to tell you."

Standing in the doorway, leaning on his walking stick, Chief Naruma turns his still, intent face in her direction. "Yes, Dottie?"

She tells him every detail about her encounter the night before with the Evil Shadowy Figure.

"I don't want the children to know."

"I understand completely. In light of this information, I must telephone Rhoda Kisanga immediately. It's rather last minute, but she will gather as many Chagga as she can for tonight's ritual."

They briefly hug and say their farewells. Watching her drive away, he's thinking about the way she looks at him, his stomach fluttering. After a last, sweeping gaze, Chief Naruma hurries into the house, clicking the door shut behind him.

Chapter 52

ON A SCENIC ROUTE up a path to Mount Meru, comes a Toyota Land Cruiser, with the logo of Africa Quest on the doors. Kwami Amutullah is behind the wheel, driving about twenty miles per hour. And Edwin Joseph is riding shotgun like he always does, fiddling with a matchbox and his cigarette pack, shaking the matchbox, rolling an unlit cigarette back and forth between his fingers. By some twist of fate, the girls and Gotham Kitty come into view as he rounds a corner.

"Maybe today is our lucky day. Edwin, tell me you see what I'm seeing?"

"Is that what I think it is?" Edwin asks, just to be sure.

Kwami's chest muscles clench as he chuckles. "Half-human, half-feline. It certainly fits the description. That Rhoda is solid."

"It's exactly the creature we're looking for."

"This is going to be a piece of cake. Looks too easy. Real easy," Kwami says with a big grin on his face.

"What about those girls?"

"Don't worry about them. We can easily take the creature from those children," Kwami says, stopping the SUV about thirty feet from them.

The sound of the SUV stopping causes Laila to twist her head over her shoulder. When she sees the men inside, she whips her head back around, not thinking anything of it and assuming the men are on safari. She just keeps walking beside Cassidy and Gotham Kitty, thinking, there's no reason to worry. Just for the moment.

Staring intensely at the creature, Kwami turns off the Land Cruiser's rumbling engine. "Five figures for sure!"

"Gee, I don't know. There are two children, that's not right," Edwin starts to object, but Kwami persists. "Don't worry about those kids. You'll do as I tell you to do! I'll scare the girls off while you shoot the tranquilizer darts into the creature."

Edwin Joseph complies reluctantly. "Fine, I'll get the tranquilizer gun."

"We need to get going before they get too far ahead of us," Kwami says with emphasis on the going.

Kwami steps out of the Land Cruiser, a throw net in his hand, and slams the door shut behind him. Edwin shuts the trunk with an apprehensive frown, then leans his body against the trunk, squinting while inspecting the barrel of his rifle.

Acting on impulse, Laila looks back again and sees the men coming toward them.

Things can change quickly.

"This doesn't look good, Cassidy," she says out of the corner of her mouth.

"What's wrong?" she asks, turning her head and seeing the men.

Out loud Kwami asks in a cool voice. "Hello, girls. May I have a word with you?"

"No can do. We're in a hurry," Laila says briskly, trying to sound as tough as nails.

"We just want to look at that creature," Kwami says, moving closer to them.

Cassidy stops walking and regards them warily. Then Laila and Gotham Kitty stop walking. They all look at the men at the same time in a confusing sort of way. Neither of them answers. Edwin cocks the tranquilizer gun, making a clacking sound that startles Gotham Kitty into lowering to all fours and dropping back an inch or two.

"Run, everybody! Run!" is all Cassidy has time to say, as she grabs Laila's hand, and the two girls sprint forward.

"That means you too, Gotham Kitty!" Laila exclaims as she runs, turns, and begins to run through the trees. "We'll just detour this way."

"Try to take aim at the creature," Kwami tells him before running after them.

Edwin raises the tranquilizer gun and steadies himself. He presses his cheek against the rifle, looking through the scope. He fires but the dart misses its mark. He reaches for another dart, inserts it into the chamber, and pulls the trigger again. Again, the dart misses its mark. He lifts the rifle and looks through the scope at the two girls.

Edwin hollers to him. "I'm sorry, Kwami. The girls are in the way."

With urgency Edwin begins running and rips a hole in the side of his dark blue jeans.

"You better hurry up, they're getting away," Kwami yells back to him.

Somewhere in the foothills of Mount Meru, Cassidy, Laila, and Gotham Kitty are still running. That the men are nowhere nearby gives them hope, but then, Cassidy worries about getting lost.

"Are you sure you know where you are going?" Cassidy asks, almost out of breath as she tries keeping up with Laila.

"Trust me, I know this area pretty well. Don't give up just yet. It isn't far now. We're really close," Laila says, nearly out of breath.

At 5:30 in the evening, the men are somewhere in the lush greenery surrounding the foothills of Mount Meru. After losing sight of the girls and Gotham Kitty some minutes ago after a turn or two around some trees, they're no longer running and beside themselves with frustration. Out of sheer boredom Edwin is fingering the hole in the side of his jeans. Bending over at the waist, Kwami braces his hands on his knees, taking deep breaths.

"They run fast. Do you see them anywhere?" Kwami asks, breathing heavily.

"No, I don't see them. And once it gets dark, we'll never find them," Edwin says, his eyes scanning the area.

"You must try to be more optimistic."

"Kwami, I'm getting a bad feeling about this one. I don't think we're going to get it."

"Don't even think about leaving. You best believe that we're going to find them."

"I'm just venting," Edwin says, as he slides a dart in the chamber of the gun.

Kwami moves toward a tree, a tall one, with long leafy branches dipping toward the ground. He puts his hand on it and looks further abroad.

"The trail is up ahead. They're probably going there. Let's take a look."

Stepping away from the tree, Kwami detects something in the air. It is distinct, a familiar smell. Strange in an unpleasant sort of way. He sniffs at the air and his nose fills with the acrid smell of body odor from the baboons on the tree's branches high above his head. He looks up briefly and gives them a cold stare. The baboons don't pay any mind to him, not even a look of curiosity. Out of anger, a low, fierce growl comes out of his throat in an attempt to scare off the baboon on the branch closest to him. The baboon squeals with fright and tries to raise itself to another branch, but not before Edwin shoots a dart between the baboon's shoulder blades. They watch in awe as the baboon slides down the tree trunk to the ground, keels over and goes to sleep like a baby.

"Don't waste another dart on those baboons. We need them for the creature," Kwami snaps at him.

"Just a little target practice," Edwin says and laughs a tiny laugh.

"Let's go get that creature."

"Can we just walk? I just can't run anymore?"

"Just hurry it up," Kwami says and begins walking.

Edwin slings his rifle over his shoulder. He looks at the baboon out cold on the ground, smiles and starts walking after him.

Chapter 53

"WHERE TO NOW?" Cassidy asks, catching her breath.

"Let me get my breath back first. And I'll tell you which way to go," Laila says, sounding out of breath.

In the middle of nothing but a dense forest surrounding them, they're standing beside a dirt path leading steeply up toward the slopes of Mount Meru. Nearby, somewhere behind them, Gotham Kitty hears a vehicle's engine slowly increasing in intensity. She turns to see a white GMC pickup truck approaching. In two shakes of a lamb's tail, she takes a fearful step back, taking cover behind Laila, sheltering herself.

Cassidy recognizes the truck and is already standing in the path of the truck. By the oddest coincidence it is Paulina Mongella. She needs Paulina's help.

"Stop, please!" Cassidy shouts, waving her arms in the air.

The pickup slows and comes to a stop in the middle of the dirt path. Paulina can't imagine what the daughter of Geoffrey Mkama is up to. She's also wondering what that strange-looking creature, hiding behind that girl, is doing with them.

Paulina yells out her window, "Hello, Cassidy Mkama. What's the problem?"

As she steps from the pickup, Cassidy runs up to her, blows out a burst of breath, and says, "It's just awful. Some men are chasing us!"

Laila and Gotham Kitty walk over to join Cassidy.

"What men? Where are they?" Paulina asks, looking around.

"They are probably somewhere in that direction. We're ahead of them. Any second now, they'll find us," Laila says, pointing toward some trees.

Cassidy is hysterical. "One of them has a rifle! He's been shooting darts at us."

"Is that right?" she asks absently, knowing better, and then opens the back door of her truck. "We'll see about that. You girls, and whatever you are, get inside and keep your heads down. And I mean keep your heads down. I'll handle this."

"She's not whatever. Her name is Gotham Kitty," Laila informs her.

"She's the alien from the escape pod," Cassidy says, climbing into the backseat.

"I believe it, too," Paulina declares.

"Hurry up, because we have to go to a Chagga gathering for an important ritual," Laila says from inside the truck.

"This won't take long," Paulina says firmly.

After closing the back door of her GMC Sierra, she circles to the passenger's side to get her walkie-talkie and AK-47 rifle. While she's doing that, Kwami and Edwin step out from behind some trees. When she goes to stand beside her pickup, rifle in hand, they come into her field of vision.

"Well, well, if it isn't Kwami and Edwin! What are you boys up to?" Paulina asks, her displeasure evident by the flat tone of her query.

Edwin glares at her as she takes a couple of steps forward. Paulina glares back at him. She is a good glarer, too.

"That's none of your business," Kwami says sharply.

Kwami's face is red with rage. The veins in his forehead are bulging out threateningly as if they may explode at any minute.

Paulina acts in a reasonable manner. "Considering you are chasing a couple of kids with a tranquilizer gun. It is my business."

"We are not chasing after kids. We are chasing a game animal," Kwami says, dusting off his blue cargo pants.

Sitting on the floor of the backseat, Cassidy and Laila are barely visible, peeking out the window every few minutes, counting the seconds until Paulina returns. Gotham Kitty is lying in a fetal position on the backseat, unable to see anything.

She glares at Kwami. "There's no game animal around here. If that's why you're here, you may as well turn around and go back home."

"And what if we don't?" Kwami responds, a hint of attitude in his voice.

Kwami is inching closer to her and getting angry. The growling, guttural voice sounds like that of a man whose short fuse is about to blow. On the contrary, Edwin keeps calm and backs up a little to thwart any altercations.

"I may file charges against the two of you. Shooting darts containing etorphine hydrochloride at two little girls. Shame on you. Not even to mention your lack of respect to the Fauna Conservation Ordinance, which protects many of the animals you call game," Paulina says, raising her AK-47 rifle.

Kwami stops his approach, but the impression remains.

Edwin's neck turns red with anger. "Spare us your park ranger spiel about laws on protecting wildlife."

"Don't bother yourself about it," Kwami says, holding up a hand to stop him from speaking any further.

Edwin looks away while Paulina glares at him.

"My apologies. I'm afraid the heat is getting to me. I'm not thinking too clearly. We'll continue our search elsewhere, while we still have a little light."

"I'm glad to see you finally coming around to the right way of thinking," she replies with a frown, lowering the rifle to her side.

"We'll be on our way. We can't afford to lose any more time," Kwami says, walking away.

Before turning to follow him, Edwin waits a moment, spits on the ground, and grinds it in with the heel of his sneaker.

Paulina exhales, retreats a step, her heart racing. Just for good measure, Paulina waits two minutes. She wants to make sure the men are on their way out of the vicinity. Then she grabs the walkie-talkie from the belt of her khaki pants and calls Geoffrey Mkama.

"Geoffrey? You still in the office?"

"Just walking out the door. I've been working a little late in the office, taking care of some urgent paperwork. Is there some emergency that needs my immediate attention?"

"Well, yes, to an extent. Your daughter, Cassidy, and some of her friends are in my truck up here in the foothills of Mount Meru. To make a long story short, Kwami Amutullah and Edwin Joseph are after the alien that's with them. So, they end up here on the road I'm driving after running from them. I'm assuming you know about the alien?"

"Kwami and Edwin? Well, I'll be. Yes, I know about the alien."

"I'll explain more later. But not now. They're eager to get to the Chagga campsite. Do you want me to drive them there?"

"No. I'll drive them. Paulina, stay where you are. I'll be there in about forty-five minutes. Over and out."

After glancing around to make sure the men are not around, she pulls on the handle of the driver's door and climbs in.

She leans to look in the backseat of the truck's cab. "How's everybody doing back there? By the way, you can stop hiding."

"Thank you for helping us," Laila says, raising herself up.

Cassidy lifts her head up. "We're so grateful for your help."

"It's all part of the job," says Paulina.

Gotham Kitty swings up to a sitting position to look at her and Paulina startles a bit.

"What a lovely alien you are!" Paulina exclaims straight away.

"Are you driving us to the Chagga campsite?" Cassidy asks, eagerly.

"Cassidy, your father will be here soon to take you there. You can all sit back and relax for a while," Paulina casually informs them, then unconsciously, she starts fidgeting with the bandage on her left hand.

Chapter 54

AT A QUARTER TO SEVEN, the sun is setting orange and red over the enormous sky. The darkness gathers around Kwami and Edwin as they walk to the SUV. There's a look of frustration on their faces as they enter the vehicle. The engine starts with a roar as Kwami guns it, sending his Land Cruiser speeding down the dirt road, seeming to know exactly where he is going despite the darkness of dusk.

For what seems like the longest time, there's complete silence. With one limp wrist on the wheel, Kwami is feeling reckless and daring, driving fast. Edwin pushes up from his slump position in the passenger's seat, turns his eyes out the window, twisting to view the path behind them as the vehicle skitters around a curve.

"We need to get that creature," Kwami finally says, breaking the silence.

"How are we going to do that? We don't even know where the creature is," Edwin speaks to the window.

"I'll tell you where it is. Paulina is hiding the creature in her truck. I just know it."

"Then you can forget about getting your hands on it."

"I call the shots, Edwin. I want that creature."

"I do, too, Kwami. But there's no way to get it. You need to think rationally."

Silence, for an eternal second. Edwin's hands begin to tremble with frustration. Struggling to calm himself, he rolls the sleeves of his plaid flannel shirt up to his elbows, rolls down the window and takes out a cigarette.

"I'm not one to back down. How about I turn this car around and drive all the way back to where Paulina is?" Kwami suggests.

Edwin is smoking, sucking on the cigarette in short nervous puffs. "And then what?"

"We take the creature from her truck," Kwami says with a wicked grin.

"That'll get us into some serious trouble," hisses Edwin.

"So, what? I can deal with it."

"What if the creature isn't in her truck?"

"Do you have a better idea?"

They continue arguing in the SUV. Kwami turns the wheel, and the Land Cruiser begins to bounce on some rougher dirt path. Just above them the sky is filling with low, billowy clouds. Their volatile conversation seems to match the chaos in the sky.

"What about the two little girls?"

"What about them?" Kwami asks, shifting his eyes to Edwin.

When Kwami turns his eyes back to the road, his attention shifts to the dark shape materializing out of thin air directly in his path. His breath catches on the fear in his throat when the shape becomes clear and he realizes that what he's seeing is a young African woman, wearing a multi-color kitenge wraparound dress that reaches to her knees, standing with her back to him.

"Watch out!" Edwin warns.

As the woman turns to look directly at Kwami, he turns the steering wheel, taking a sharp swerve to the left at high speed, to avoid hitting her.

"You let him down," the woman remarks.

As if in a slow-motion sequence in an action movie, Kwami looks at the smudge of black soot on her face, losing control of the Land Cruiser due to excessive speed. Next comes a loud yell from the woman when a powerful vacuumlike force pulls her body backward into the darkness, disappearing to God knows where. In the span of it all, as the SUV begins to skid off the dirt path, Kwami instinctively grips the steering wheel tighter attempting to control the vehicle just before it crashes into one of the trunks of Fig Tree Arch.

On impact, Edwin's head slams hard into the windshield in front of him just before the airbag deploys, exploding against his chest, sending an acrid smell and a white powdery dust into the air. He is out cold. Whereby Kwami's body propels forward and, just as quickly, back when the airbag deploys, hitting his head against the headrest of his seat and covering his hair and face with white powder. He remains conscious and closes his eyes to still the swirling sensation.

The smell of fumes from the Land Cruiser's exhaust lingers in the air, while smoke and bright sparks from the engine are coming from under the hood. Slowly Kwami opens his eyes. He nudges Edwin and gets no response. His face is severely cut from the windshield glass and blood is streaming down his cheeks to his neck. Peering out the windshield, Kwami can see the headlights illuminating the brush and the smoke, casting shadows around the vehicle.

In that very moment, the headlights cut off. Something supernatural is afoot. Kwami isn't the only one upset by his failure to capture the creature. The most unfortunate thing is coming his way. And this thing can't accept failure as an option.

Kwami reaches inside the dashboard cup holder where he keeps his cell phone. It's not there. He fumbles under the front of the seat until he finds the adjuster and carefully edges the seat back until he feels less like a sardine and catches a glimpse of the cell phone on the floor below the steering wheel.

A strange screeching sound cuts through the air. Then comes a bunch of voices. There seems to be a chorus of voices speaking to him. Kwami can feel a torrent of power in the center of those voices growing louder and louder. And he has to raise nearly all the strength inside of him to keep from sinking into it.

Frantic, he presses his hands over his ears. "Shut up! I can't think."

The voices abruptly stop.

What is happening? he thinks as he unfastens his seat belt, pushes the airbag to the side, and grabs his cell phone to call for help. In his current state of mind, he fails to notice a fire burning in the engine, until he starts to dial a number. A faint image is materializing within the smoke and flames, and the smoke is building, filling the air around him with a foul odor. His eyes water from the awful stench. The call connects, making the panic subside until the cell phone goes dead.

Everything is dark. All he can see is a figure taking shape in the flames. Is he dreaming? Is he dead? It's as if reality is bending around him somehow.

The face of the Evil Shadowy Figure looks at him head-on with dark, fiery eyes. He shakes his head and wonders if he is having some late-appearing shock from the accident. Kwami doesn't have any idea what he's dealing with. He seems to think he's imagining it.

Time is running short. He needs to get out of the vehicle. In a matter of seconds, he puts his hand on the door handle and the engine explodes with a sharp bang.

Kwami is out cold. A mushroom cloud of thick black smoke billows into the sky from the Land Cruiser. The gas tank blows, another explosion sounds, and flames engulf the vehicle, which is crackling and popping as the fire consumes it.

Kwami Amutullah and Edwin Joseph are dead.

An odd cackling sound splits the air just as the Evil Shadowy Figure disappears into the flames.

By some miracle, the fire doesn't spread. Nothing in the surroundings change. The fire burns out just as the clouds dissipate above, and there are gaps in the clouds where you can see a Moon and bright stars.

Chapter 55

AFTER PUTTING HIS leopard-skin cloak around his shoulders, Chief Naruma can't be any happier looking in the mirror in the hallway of his house. That's the final touch to his outfit, which consists of a dark brown long-sleeve tunic with matching three-quarter-length pants, and brown leather sandals.

At a quarter past seven, turbulent clouds churn above the house, releasing an occasional glimmer of the Moon, like a spotlight behind curtains. Through the rush of the wind and the rustle of the trees outside, Chief Naruma hears an eerie, moaning sound. The sound seems to call to him, whispering in his mind, bringing wordless feelings of disorientation and dread.

Through the window of his living room, he can see a young African woman standing outside the house, facing him, looking in at him. Even in the darkness, he can see the smudge of black soot across her face, and streaks of black soot on her arms, legs, and bare feet. Their eyes meet. A chill creeps into every part of his body and burrows under his skin as her eyes delve into him. And he realizes she's the woman from his dream just a little over two weeks ago. But he's not dreaming now.

She moves closer to the window, not even a nose length from the glass. Her stare pierces like needles, eyes as still as death. She doesn't speak. Her eyebrows raise, giving him a warning look just before a powerful vacuumlike force starts pulling her body backward. Though she struggles to shake herself free, the force won't let go, and her body sweeps backward, vanishing in the dark.

It is a strange occurrence to the Chief — somehow peculiar — but there is no time to dwell on it. Like it or not, the time is at hand for him to leave. He must conduct a ritual. As Chief Naruma turns around and walks toward the closet in the hallway by the front door to grab his walking stick, the hall lights go out. The house is pitch-black.

"How can this be?" he asks himself.

There comes a sound. He catches his breath as his shoulders slump, terrified, when he hears a growl, almost like that of an animal. He feels a sudden breeze all over his body. Then, the swell of noise, of too many voices speaking at once, reverberates like a shock wave through the house, so awful it makes the hair on his back spike. And Chief Naruma recognizes it dead on.

"This is not good," he says to the empty hallway.

He looks around, trying to see where the Evil Shadowy Figure is, but it is too dark to discover him.

The voices stop, and then, silence follows. Is the Chief imagining it? The sooner he's out of here the better, he tells himself. He turns toward the front door but at the last minute some strange force pulls him backward. His body hurtles through the air with the force of a bomb shooting out of cannon.

"Killing me isn't going to stop the ritual," Chief Naruma yells as his body hits the wall at the other end of the hallway.

A terrible, horrible screeching sound blasts through the air. The Evil Shadowy Figure shows himself, blocking the front door, watching Chief Naruma's body slide to the floor. The spirit wants to kill him. Yes. Will it make a difference? No. Still, the Evil Shadowy Figure is in his house, for that very purpose.

With his fiery black eyes, the Evil Shadowy Figure looks at Chief Naruma, who is now sitting on the floor with his back against the wall. With a gasp the Chief forces himself to meet his cold stare. A hard, calculating, all-knowing stare. Need he ask? He is the master of ceremonies who will lead the descendant and the extraterrestrial through the ritual to end the long-standing curse. And the Evil Shadowy Figure foresees this.

Chief Naruma swallows hard and says, "I demand that you leave here at once!"

As he speaks, he realizes there's no injury to any part of his body. Not yet anyhow. His hands are shaking, and he needs to get out of the house. His life depends on it.

"Evil Shadowy Figure you can't win. Your time is at and end," the Chief chastises the spirit.

That's not a very smart thing to do. The Evil Shadowy Figure is angrier and starting to approach him. The spirit cackles again and again, getting closer and closer. Chief Naruma must defend himself somehow. But the only object near him is a wooden side table with a marble lamp on top. That's it, he thinks to himself.

Something inside him snaps. As fast as his old bones can carry him, he rises to his feet. From the nearby table, he jerks up the heavy marble lamp, pulls the cord clean out of the socket and throws it at the Evil Shadowy Figure with enough force to spin it in the air.

No luck. Despite catching the spirit by surprise, the Evil Shadowy Figure deflects the lamp straight into the wall and it smashes into a dozen dark glittering pieces with a most satisfying crash. The pieces fly in all directions, scattering over the floor. The evil spirit continues toward him.

Within the span of a few minutes, Chief Naruma's luck improves tenfold. When the spirit crosses over the cord of the lamp on the floor a tremendous electrical charge occurs causing a small explosion. Even better is when a fire miraculously appears from the explosion. The timing can't be any better.

The Evil Shadowy Figure stops to look at the fire, staring into the flames. Just the distraction he needs, the

Chief takes the opportunity to slip away. Panicking, he runs down another hallway leading to the kitchen. He is running for the back door.

The fire is spreading quickly throughout the small house. He doesn't slow down, and he doesn't look back. The Evil Shadowy Figure is in hot pursuit and not far behind him. He can hear eerie, raw and animalistic chittering, cackling sounds, closing in on him.

As his hand reaches for the handle of the back door, he feels a very powerful force pulling him back. He seems to stagger back. With all his might, he pushes forward, grabbing the door handle and opening the door just as an explosion happens in the house forcing him out the door, landing on the ground three feet from the burning house.

Angrily, the Evil Shadowy Figure releases a horrible screech from the core of his being before disappearing into the flames. On a positive note, the flames are not high, or fierce and the fire is containing within the house, not spreading to the surrounding foliage.

As he lies on the ground, watching his house go up in flames, he's upset to lose his belongings. His eyes, behind his glasses, sting with the scents of sulfur and ash floating in the air. Still, Chief Naruma thanks his lucky stars that he's alive. Other than a few scratches, he's in surprisingly good shape, considering.

Overhead, dark clouds scatter as though an invisible hand is parting them, revealing a Moon and a starry sky. There is a little breeze, and the thick smoke from the fire, which is already beginning to die down, billows up straight into the night.

Before getting to his feet, a great big smile comes to his face. "To a ritual, I must go."

Chapter 56

IT'S NEARING eight o'clock in the evening. Geoffrey Mkama, still wearing his work clothes of a khaki button-down shirt, matching khaki pants, and black boots, waves goodbye to Paulina Mongella as she starts her GMC pickup and drives away. He starts walking toward his Land Rover just as Cassidy, Laila and Gotham Kitty enter through the back door.

After sliding into the driver's seat and closing the door, Geoffrey's jaw slackens just a little, and he says to them, "I'm sorry to keep you waiting, but I want to be the one who takes you to the Chagga campsite, and especially after this business with those men chasing you all. I'm upset by it."

"I know you're just being Daddy. But thanks to Paulina, we're all right!" Cassidy answers him.

He glances at Cassidy in the rearview mirror. "Yes, thanks to Paulina. Is there a specific time you have to be there?"

"We're already going to be late as it is," Cassidy says, looking morose.

"We need to get to the campsite on the southwestern slope of Mount Meru for the ritual to end the curse of the Evil Shadowy Figure now, eight o'clock," Laila adds.

After catching a glimpse of Gotham Kitty in the rearview mirror, Geoffrey twists to face the backseat. "So, you're really from outer space? I still can't get over seeing the escape pod. You really are magical-looking, I admit. I can see why poachers want to get a hold of you."

Cassidy casts a wild look at her father, who is gawking at Gotham Kitty.

"She goes by the name of Gotham Kitty," Laila informs him.

Staring keenly at Gotham Kitty, he smiles and says, "That's a lovely name."

Cassidy and Laila are looking at him with anticipation, wanting to leave. Even if the conversation is very brief, they are in a hurry.

Gotham Kitty leans forward in the backseat, the shade of her eyes shifting from chestnut brown to gleaming green. He notices the change and does a double take. His mouth opens in astonishment, giving her a peculiar look.

"Daddy! Stop ogling Gotham Kitty," Cassidy says to get his attention.

Cassidy's words are like a dash of cold water, and he snaps out of his trancelike state.

"The Chagga campsite, right?"

"Yes, Daddy. The Chagga are counting on us to be there," Cassidy implores him.

"Remember, you have school tomorrow. Is this going to interfere with your schoolwork and chores?" he asks in a fatherly tone.

Cassidy looks at him hard, shaking her head no. "I promise it won't."

"Well, in that case, I won't ask any more questions. Onward and forward," Geoffrey says, whips his head around and turns the ignition.

"Yeah!" Laila shouts excitedly.

"And step on it!" Cassidy says in a demanding voice.

He makes a face at Cassidy in the rearview mirror but says nothing.

"Please," Cassidy says in an even tone, no lift in her voice to suggest a question.

For most of the way, everyone in the vehicle is silent especially Geoffrey who is reflecting on everything. Nearly fifteen minutes later, Geoffrey's Land Rover approaches the southwestern slope of Mount Meru where campfires burn with soft glows, and only the movement of shadows is visible.

He pulls his SUV to a stop. After cutting off the engine, he shifts to face the backseat, looking at them, reluctant to say something, but feels as a responsible parent, he must.

"Be careful with this ritual. Just remember, you can pull out any time. The bottom line is that you can count on me for assistance as well, if you need it," he cautions in an anxious voice.

"Daddy, we'll be careful. Chief Naruma is there to watch over us," Cassidy says in a reassuring tone.

"Chief Naruma is up in years, and while he is wise to such matters regarding this Evil Shadowy Figure, I still have to question."

"Can we go now, please?" Cassidy asks hurriedly.

"By all means. Let me get the door for you."

He jumps out of the driver's side and opens the back door for the girls and Gotham Kitty, who spill out eagerly.

Before he can close the door behind them, Cassidy, Laila, and Gotham Kitty start walking away at a fast pace toward the gathering of Chagga.

"I may as well just wait inside the car," he says in a loud tone, then grimaces at his decision and starts to follow after them. "I'll just watch from the sidelines with the other parents, readily available to help if need be. I'm rather curious about this ritual."

Cassidy stops walking and turns to address her father. "Chief Naruma says it may be dangerous, but don't worry. We can handle it."

"Dangerous?" he questions to himself.

From the shadows Rhoda Kisanga emerges wearing an orange and brown pattern head covering and a matching kitenge dress that reaches to her ankles, and sandals. She greets them with a bubbly smile here, a pat on the back there. She's always effortlessly vivacious, but now she's even more so.

"Come along now, all of you. You mustn't keep Chief Naruma waiting. And Laila, a T-shirt, and jeans is not the kind of attire for an important ritual. For crying out loud, you're a key player in this ceremony."

Rhoda rushes them along, all the while staring oddly at Gotham Kitty.

Chapter 57

DESPITE THE SHORT NOTICE, there is a significant crowd of Chagga on the southwestern slope of Mount Meru for tonight's event. At half past eight, the feeling among the crowd is as though the hour of judgement is at hand, the ritual to permanently remove the curse of the Evil Shadowy Figure on the Chagga. Even Laila's parents and brother are there. Knowing her daughter is playing an important role in the ritual, the prideful look on Esther Diwani's face speaks a thousand words.

"The cat person is real," Toby Diwani says, admiring the alien.

"Shhh," Rhoda Kisanga says as Chief Naruma steps forward to the center of the gathering.

Chief Naruma speaks, and everyone listens, not even daring to cough. "I am proud to say the alien is among us. Let me introduce you to Gotham Kitty."

After seeing her, the air fills with oohs and ahhs and gasps of wonder. To the Chagga she is a magical vision, one of hope and intrigue. After giving the crowd a glowing smile, Gotham Kitty gives a soft meow before taking a few steps back.

"For too long, the Evil Shadowy Figure has been a black cloud over the Chagga, a reminder of our unfortunate past that Ruwa doesn't want us to forget. But all things must end to fulfill their beginnings. Which brings us to the purpose of this gathering. I say the time of the future is upon us. It is with great pleasure that I undertake the ritual to stop the curse of the Evil Shadowy Figure. Everyone, take your places," Chief Naruma proudly declares.

Thobias Miranda and another African man sit on dark wooden stools and begin to softly beat on round wooden drums with their hands. The two men have on long-sleeve orange kitenge shirts with red patterns, dark brown trousers, and sandals.

Chief Naruma gestures to Laila and Gotham Kitty to take their place by the campfire. Seeing the look of anticipation on everyone's face, as Gotham Kitty steps forward, she senses something important is going to happen. Every feature of Laila's sweet face illuminates, giving her an otherworldly glow as she stands there, holding the hand of Gotham Kitty with her right hand, curling a lock of hair in the fingers of her left hand. To her relief, Laila catches sight of Cassidy and her father among the crowd.

Cassidy looks at Laila, grimaces, and mouths the words: "You're not afraid, are you?"

Laila mouths the words: "Not in the least."

"Brace yourselves for the Evil Shadowy Figure. I can sense the spirit manifesting his presence among us," Chief Naruma shouts over the drums and the crackling of the flames.

A blink later, dark clouds gather in clumps above, changing the pressure in the air. The wind makes the fire burn wildly. The clouds catch the orange light from the fire, making the sky glow.

As Laila speaks a prayer for the souls of the victims of the long-ago volcanic fires of Mount Meru, the crowd watches with anticipation. The tension around the campfire is as sharp as the cutting edge of a steak knife.

A harsh cackling sound is coming from the fire. From the sound of it, the Evil Shadowy Figure is raging mad.

"Look, he's coming," Cassidy yells and points to the fire.

After looking at the evil spirit's image in the flames, Laila looks at Cassidy and mouths the words aloud: "Well, maybe a little afraid."

To everyone's surprise, the ground shakes slightly with an angry burp. The shuddering vibration is almost like an earthquake. The drums stop beating. There is a little pause. Everyone starts to wonder, anxiously staring at Chief Naruma. Is Mount Meru going to erupt?

No. Nothing happens.

With a quick gesture of the hand, Chief Naruma urges the ritual to continue. He suspects the Evil Shadowy Figure is sending a vibration through the fire, causing the ground to tremble as though from an earthquake. Almost certainly, the evil spirit is unleashing a storm of fury to try to scare them into quitting.

The drums start beating harder and faster.

Almost imperceptibly, the Evil Shadowy Figure is beginning to fully materialize. The minute his fiery black eyes latch on to the alien, he starts to babble in what sounds like many voices chattering at once. A murmur of fear ripples through the crowd.

Laila stands before the fire, her eyes cast down, assuring herself she can do this. She wants to end this. Right here. Now.

"I cast you out. Evil Shadowy Figure. Back to the abyss. Fall into nothingness for all eternity. Set the soul of my ancestor, Sayida Jaquiar, free from your possession!" Laila says in Kiswahili.

Just at the moment Laila is about to cast the lock of hair into the midst of the fire, the Evil Shadowy Figure comes out of the flames, charging toward her full tilt, exasperation darkens his fiery black eyes to the color of fire. Unsettling murmuring ripples through the crowd.

"Nooo!" Gotham Kitty screams.

With lightning speed, Gotham Kitty leaps at the Evil Shadowy Figure, her green eyes rolling wildly. She swipes the back of her hand across his head. A look of the most ludicrous surprise crosses the Evil Shadowy Figure's face as he falls back into the flames.

After Laila tosses the hair into the fire, eardrum-piercing screeches fill the air as the Evil Shadowy Figure is disintegrating. The flames grow and yellowish smoke billows out as the Evil Shadowy Figure vanishes.

The crowd watches in awe, and the drumming stops.

"Yeah!" Cassidy says, leaping up.

A succession of souls rise above the leaping flames of the campfire, shooting up into the sky like stars to their new lives. One of them is slower to rise out of the heart of the blaze and is strangely familiar to Laila. The soul is the image of a young woman in a multi-color kitenge wraparound dress that reaches to her knees. Chief Naruma looks at her more closely and recognizes her as the woman from his dream, and earlier, outside his house. With the same classic features. The same dark hair and eyes and smudge of black soot across her face. The Chief can't help noticing that Laila recognizes her, too.

"Laila, do you know who she is?" Chief Naruma asks in a whisper that Laila has to strain to hear.

"It's Sayida Jaquier, my six times great-grand-aunt," she says, with an emotional look in her eyes.

Sayida's soul is free from damnation. As she locks her eyes with Laila, a small smile graces her face. With a nod of thanks, heat swells behind her eyes and when she blinks, a tear slips out as she mouths the word: "Goodbye." Sayida's spirit rises into a cloud-free sky, leaving Laila to feel a sense of pride.

"I'm so proud of you, Laila, for having the courage to stand up to the Evil Shadowy Figure," Chief Naruma says, congratulating her.

Laila smiles shyly. "Thank you, Chief."

Cassidy screams Gotham Kitty's name, and when she gets to her, she almost knocks Gotham Kitty off her feet with a bear-hug. "I'm so grateful to you, Gotham Kitty."

Gotham Kitty purrs with content. With one fluid movement, she flows into a cartwheel and turns another cartwheel and then runs forward and does a backflip.

The days of the Evil Shadowy Figure are over, and the time for celebration is at hand. And the Chagga have every right to. It all starts with little Toby Diwani, who begins to sing a song of praise to Ruwa in Kiswahili, surprising his sister Laila and just about everyone else. In a gesture of sisterly love, Laila takes his hand and sings with him. Their parents move to stand behind them. Which prompts Cassidy and her father to walk over and join them. And soon everyone is singing along — some definitely louder than others, a few slightly off-key but making up for it with enthusiasm.

After they finish singing, some embrace one another, and others clap their hands. Some of the Chagga toss dirt on the campfire to extinguish it, closing the portal to the netherworld for good. When things subside, Geoffrey Mkama cocks his head, and looks at his daughter giving the impression they have to go. Cassidy and Laila say their goodbyes.

Whereupon Cassidy turns to Gotham Kitty and says, "Come on, we're going home."

Chapter 58

THE CELEBRATION continues that coming Saturday. A party for Gotham Kitty and her closest friends at Dottie Mkama's house. That's the least they can do for her, the alien responsible for restoring peace to the Chagga.

Standing in the doorway to the backyard, Dottie is all smiles as she watches all the people sitting at the wooden picnic table eating, the delicious meal of meat stew with rice, spinach and ugali, a firm cornmeal porridge. For the special occasion, she has her hair just right, and is wearing a short-sleeve lilac lace dress reaching past her knees, and ivory sandals.

Geoffrey Mkama rises from the bench and wanders over to where his mother is to thank her for everything. "Mother, you really know how to throw a party. Even the ugali is fresher than usual. How do you do it?"

"It has something to do with age. The longer you live, the better you cook," she states simply.

"I'll keep that in mind," he says with a grin, then turns and walks back to the table.

As soon as he sits on the bench, he slips easily into the conversation already in progress, sipping lemonade and being his effervescent self.

"The sad thing is that all they can find is very little remains of their Land Cruiser. Their bodies are beyond recognition. On a good note, Gotham Kitty doesn't have to worry about poachers trying to get her," Paulina Mongella informs them.

"I don't like to speak ill of the dead, but I'm not too keen on Kwami and Edwin chasing my daughter with a tranquilizer gun," Geoffrey says with a raise of an eyebrow.

"I'm going to miss that Kwami Amutullah," Rhoda Kisanga says sadly.

"Auntie, you never cease to surprise me, " Paulina says, shaking her head.

Paulina, who is wearing a pale peach lace knee-length dress with short sleeves that looks weirdly like a doily, is sitting next to Rhoda Kisanga, who is wearing a colorful silk head scarf and a beige dress with embroidery all over the bodice and a full skirt with a wide flounce that reaches just past her knees, and Chief Naruma is sitting next to her. On the bench on the other side of the table is Geoffrey Mkama, who is sitting next to Cassidy, who is sitting next to Gotham Kitty, who is sitting next to Laila, who is sitting next to Toby, who is sitting next to Azita Hussein, whose hair is wildly loose all around her shoulders. Minus her white lab coat, Azita appears comfortable with everyone and is even wearing jeans and trying to look less serious by unbuttoning the top fake-pearl button of her multi-floral blouse with three-quarter sleeves. It's a display of an entourage of people, who see Gotham Kitty as a friend and perhaps their savior.

Later in the afternoon, the table is full of empty plates and empty glasses. Paulina and Rhoda are the first to leave, excusing themselves politely and exiting via the back door, through the kitchen and the narrow hallway and toward the front door.

"It's been a wonderful time with all of you. Now, if you'll please excuse me," Chief Naruma says, getting up from the bench like he's ready to leave.

Azita quickly walks up to him and says, "Thank you for explaining that whole curse thing."

"No problem at all. I'm sorry about Allison Banes. I truly admire her for rescuing and protecting Gotham Kitty," he answers in kind.

"Thanks for mentioning it."

"Perhaps I will see you around Arusha National Park or Lake Duluti."

"You most certainly will. A little more lately than before, I want to see the beauty of Africa from outside the walls of GoHealth Walk-In Urgent Care," Azita explains to him.

"Until we meet again," he says, and walks away.

Azita sits down on the bench and digs inside her pink raffia handbag and pulls out Allison Banes' field notebook. "Look, Cassidy, here, this is for you to keep."

"Thank you. This is great," Cassidy says, flipping through the pages.

"It's in the right hands now."

As Azita looks at Cassidy with the notebook in her hands, she thinks of Allison Banes, and how far she's come. The shock of Allison's death is fading. In short order, she has put aside the awfulness of Allison's death and cherishes the memories of the good times with her late friend.

After excusing herself, Geoffrey catches up to Azita before she makes it to the back door. "Don't trouble yourself about my wife's death anymore. I don't blame you."

"That puts my mind at ease."

He leans in and pats her on the back. "You come and visit Cassidy and Gotham Kitty anytime. They'll be happy to see you."

"Now that you mention it, I'll need to do a physical exam of Gotham Kitty at least once a year," she agrees, smiling and steps away.

Azita walks through the kitchen, where Dottie and Chief Naruma are talking. He is smiling, a warm gentle smile, stroking his goatee, and digesting all that Dottie tells him. There is something in the Chief's eyes that gives the impression he's more than fond of her.

"I'm just settling into the new house. Again, thanks to the administration of Saddle Hut," the Chief explains with a carefree smile.

"Here's a plate of ugali. Consider this a housewarming gift. And something to remind you of me," she says, smiling broadly in a gracious manner.

He peeks under the tin foil covering the plate she hands him. "Why, thank you, Dottie."

"Anton, it is my pleasure. Step this way. I'll walk you out," she says and walks out into the hallway.

Following behind her, Chief Naruma seems so much a part of her already. As he maneuvers through the hallway with his black walking stick with a brass knob for a head and a small steel cap on the tip, she feels his caring nature settle over her.

"I like the new walking stick. It suits you well."

"Glad you like it."

"You come by anytime," she says, opening the front door.

"I will be happy to," he says with a wink and walks off.

Dottie watches him walk toward his Jeep. He turns to see if she's standing there, and, of course, she is. She waves to him, winking her right eye. Despite the distance, he catches it and smiles.

"Is there something going on that I don't know about?" Geoffrey asks, surprising her by coming quietly up from behind her.

Dottie gives him an innocent grin. "Not at all. That three-piece charcoal suit is very becoming on you."

"Don't even try to change the subject. You just make sure to tell me if something develops between you two."

"Why do you say that?"

"I see that look in your eye."

"And what look is that?" she asks, closing the door.

"Just keep me in the know."

"Don't worry, son. You'll be the first I tell," she tells him as they head toward the kitchen.

They come to a stop at the open doorway to the backyard and stare at Gotham Kitty.

"Let me ask you a question. Do you think she'll be happy here on Earth with us?" Dottie asks her son.

"She seems to be adapting very well. But who can say for sure? I suppose only time will tell."

"Cassidy just adores her," she says gleefully.

"She sure does. I know she will do everything she can to make her friend happy. But still, you have to wonder. Will it be enough?"

"It will have to, son. We are all she has."

Cassidy runs from the table with Gotham Kitty chasing her. "Catch me if you can!"

Laila and Toby sit on the bench, watching and laughing as Gotham Kitty turns a cartwheel. With a toe pivot, her cartwheel turns into a walkover, her back and thighs curve with hidden strength to pull her up again. That's how Gotham Kitty plays. Like a child. She seems to be having the time of her life.

Chapter 59

ON SATURDAY, JANUARY 15, 2011, there's a surprise coming to Gotham Kitty. One that everyone knows she'll like. After placing a soft silk blindfold over Gotham Kitty's eyes, Cassidy leads her by the hand through the kitchen and out the door to the backyard of her house. Following behind them are her father, Laila, and Toby. All the kids are in their play clothes, T-shirts, and jeans.

Reaching the middle of the yard, Cassidy brushes the blindfold off her eyes, and everyone shouts, "Surprise!"

One of Gotham Kitty's bushy eyebrows raise when she sees an elaborate wooden treehouse about twelve feet from the ground, sitting securely between two limbs of the tree, accessible by a wooden ladder, complete with a rope handrail. That will be her home. And it is something she needs more than anything being that she can never return to her homeworld.

"Cassidy, Laila and Toby are the one's responsible for this," Geoffrey says sincerely.

Gotham Kitty understands mostly everything that they tell her. She even understands some things that they don't say. But despite that, she resorts to using the language of her own people of her homeworld, which sounds like feline vocalizations to Earthlings.

"Meow!" Gotham Kitty exclaims with surprise, striving for a tone that lets them know how much she appreciates it.

"I can come out here to play with you every day," Cassidy tells her with a smile.

Cassidy believes it's the best present to give Gotham Kitty, who is going to spend the rest of her life on Earth. And she comes to the realization that as much as she wants her to have happiness in her new life, a part of her wonders whether Gotham Kitty is truly happy being on Earth. For as much as she tries to make her feel at home on this planet, she doesn't have the scope to fully comprehend Gotham Kitty's prior life or where she comes from.

"That treehouse is amazing," Geoffrey states.

"Anything is possible if you believe in it enough," Laila says with sincerity.

"I agree with you completely," Geoffrey adds, then says to all of them. "You kids enjoy. I'll be inside the house if you need me."

"I have a present for you, too. This is a slingshot you can use to protect yourself against pesky spiders, mosquitos or other bugs, any creepy crawlies that may bother you. Being that you're living in a treehouse. It's really easy to use, and you can practice for fun. You fit a rock or other small object in the slingshot pouch and draw back the band, ready to strike," Toby explains to Gotham Kitty.

Gotham Kitty offers her most pleasant smile and accepts the slingshot with cool acquiescence. Then all three of the kids gather around Gotham Kitty giving her a warm embrace. Afterward, they jump up and down around Gotham Kitty like pigeons around a picnicker, laughing and giggling. Their gracious acceptance overwhelms Gotham Kitty, filling her with a sense of belonging.

Looking at Cassidy for a quite affectionate moment, Gotham Kitty hugs her. Cassidy aims a delightfully exhilarating smile her way and breaks into a fit of giggles. It feels to her like it's her destiny to be part of Gotham Kitty's life. Beaming, Cassidy returns the hug, giving her an extra affectionate squeeze.

"Go check out your house. But if you need us, come back down, we'll just be playing around here till it gets dark," Cassidy says encouragingly.

Laila smiles in a reassuring manner. "It's your own place to do as you like. But we'll visit you up there from time to time."

"I can't wait to see you again, Gotham Kitty. Don't forget to watch out for all those creepy-crawlers," Toby says with a wave.

Gotham Kitty nods compliantly and turns toward her majestic treehouse, ten or twelve feet away from the long wire clothesline, where Cassidy hangs clothes for drying. She carefully crawls up the sturdy wooden ladder, not knowing what to expect. Only knowing that it will be something special.

Stepping inside, she can stand comfortably in the eight foot high space. The woodsy smell of the cedar lining wafts all around her, instantly calming. Her eyes sparkle with delight as she glances at the small living room. In the far corner, to the left, there's a mini fridge and a cot-size bed in the other corner. In the rear corner, to the right, there's a window seat, looking out over the backyard. The thick trunk of the tree runs through the center of the house, and out through the roof.

What stands out the most is an area with a table and a small bookshelf. She puts the slingshot on the table and her eyes skip over the items. On the table there are pencils, markers and drawing paper, which will serve well for sketching her planet and its solar system. The bookshelf contains a heavy encyclopedia, some books mostly on the history of the world, and a stack of magazines.

She becomes aware of being thirsty. Very thirsty. Now she wants to check out the fridge. Before doing so, she stops next to the fridge and quickly glances at the wooden stool and small raw-wood table with a white ceramic bowl atop the table. That is where she will sit and have her meals. Opening the fridge door, she finds it chock-full of all kinds of goodies, including bottles of water and milk, and ten cans of sardines and ten cans of tuna with easy-open tops. Her mouth waters at the sight of it all.

After helping herself to a glass of milk, she strolls over to the window seat to check on her friends in the backyard.

It will be good for her to sit a spell and watch the kids. Not a minute after, Cassidy sees her at the window and waves hello to her. Gotham Kitty happily waves back.

Chapter 60

THE HOURS pass very quickly. Still at the window seat, Gotham Kitty is sitting in a relaxing state. Smiling to herself, she watches the kids playing in the backyard. It's already getting dark, and things are winding down. Laila says something in a low voice to Cassidy, that she doesn't quite catch, before walking to stand by the door of the house. For a minute, she stares oddly at Toby, who is running around the yard, with a red long-sleeve shirt around his neck like a cape.

Laila calls out to him in a loud voice, "It's time to go, Toby."

"Okay, sis. I'm coming."

Toby stops running, removes the shirt from around his neck, and pegs it up properly on the long wire clothesline. Then he hurries over to stand next to Laila just as she's turning her head to look at the treehouse. As she waves at Gotham Kitty, Toby waves too.

"Bye-bye, for now, Gotham Kitty. I'll come back and visit every chance I get," Laila says loudly.

"Bye. I'll come, too," says Toby.

Gotham Kitty nods, beaming a smile at them before they turn around and leave. Her eyes turn to Cassidy who is standing, looking around the yard.

Geoffrey Mkama comes into the doorway. "Cassidy, my dear, you need to come in and wash up. It's almost time to start dinner."

"I will, Daddy. Just give me a minute," she answers politely.

Before dashing off into the house, Cassidy lifts a hand to wave goodbye to Gotham Kitty. "Until tomorrow, my friend."

Gotham Kitty smiles and gives a soft meow. Truly, she's looking forward to seeing Cassidy tomorrow and the next day and the day after that, and so on. Obviously, her true name isn't Gotham Kitty, but she accepts it for her new life on Earth. She longs to tell Cassidy her real name, and about her planet, and about all the different planets and the many beings in her galaxy. Once again, flashes of memories play through her mind.

Her bond with Cassidy has been strong from the outset, but different than the one with the late Allison Banes, who she sometimes misses, remembering her kindness to her. Generally, most of the people on Earth are very kind to her, yet understandably, she misses her people.

The time seems to move faster on Earth than on her home planet of Corsettia. Well, it feels like that to her as she watches the sun do its nightly disappearing act, slipping completely off the horizon. It is peaceful and very pleasing to the eye. Hypnotic in a way that she loses herself in the sight. Her mind drifts back to almost a month ago when on an exploratory mission on Malterra, the Brozians, a malicious insectoid race, catch her by surprise. And she feels regret about taking her ship out. She appreciates the Earthlings' kindness, but she prefers to go back in time, back to the moment she decides to go on the mission to Malterra and squelch the whole plan of going. But it's not possible. How the Brozians' spaceship ends up in this galaxy is a mystery to her. When she thinks back to the intense turbulence on the spaceship, she can only speculate that only an extreme gravitational anomaly or wormhole can toss the Brozians' ship, unfortunately with her aboard, into this far distant galaxy.

Darkness has come quickly, and a waxing gibbous Moon is already hanging in the sky. Her sharp green eyes study the sparkling stars that speckle the velvet black sky. Is there no end of wonders about this planet she's on? How does she fit in? Maybe she doesn't. What does the future have in store for her? Her nose starts twitching as too many concerns swirl around in her mind for her to process all at once.

While in that frame of mind, she turns her head away from the window and looks around the tidy treehouse. Her eyes move to the cot-size bed in the corner of the room, an indication that she is ready to go to sleep. In particular, a catnap is exactly what she needs.

Leaving the window seat, she makes her way directly to the bed. After lying down, her hand reaches for a small pink blanket, just her size, at the foot of the bed. After unfolding it, she drapes it over her body. She begins writhing around the bed attempting to get comfortable. At long last, willing her body to relax, she comes to a resting position, cuddling with a floral throw pillow that she finds rather cozy.

Moonlight seeps in everywhere and on to her face, coming from the direction of the house's only window. She turns on her right side, crosses her hands on her stomach and curls up in a ball. It's no more comfortable than her left, just that the moonlight is off her face.

Before letting herself fall asleep, she reminds herself of one vital thing. Little by little, she has to start speaking the language of the Earthlings. She already understands some words from hearing people talk and reading magazines. As with everything else in a good relationship with people, communication is essential. She has so much to teach, so much to share with the Earthlings. This is her purpose. If she has any aspirations at all, it is to educate Cassidy and others about her species, and what undeniably sets them apart from other species, and about her homeworld, and the many planets and species in the galaxy she's from. What's more, she hopes one day in the future there will be a safe way to cross the barrier, with no limit to how far a spaceship can travel from one galaxy to another.

Thinking about these things puts a pleasant expression on her face. She lies there, thumping her tail and starts purring. But it's still too much thinking. Her eyelids grow heavier and heavier until they close, and her tail comes to a rest as she slips into a deep and peaceful slumber almost at once.

Chapter 61

IN THE FAR reaches beyond the Earth's solar system, in another galaxy far far away, incomprehensible to Earthlings is where you'll find the Brozians, the Catusapiens and many other species. Not quite four weeks since Gotham Kitty's capture by the Brozians, somewhere in her galaxy a Brozian deep-range exploratory vessel is soaring through space. The Captain of the ship is on a search-and rescue-mission to find the missing cargo spaceship.

The lights are dim, as they are all over the Brozian vessel. The Captain at the helm turns his attention to the forward viewscreen and sees the planet Malterra. He steps to a console, taps carefully, and glances the monitor where the tracking information, coordinates and systems status are on display.

"These are the correct coordinates. Take us down there!" the Captain says, not taking his eyes off the monitor.

The two long antennae atop his second-in-command's head wriggles as he nods, "Yes, Captain."

The Brozian vessel, in a position at the dark rim of the planet, begins a sharp arc around the planet. The vessel is a massive silhouette descending through the atmosphere of the warm, moss-green planet. The second-in-command has to strain to see through the white clouds churning through the atmosphere.

"There is no trace of the cargo spaceship, or debris, but scanners are picking up an object near the ship's last coordinates," the Captain's second-in-command says in a neutral voice.

The Captain checks his sensors and jerks his head up at the information. His eyes observe the wreckage of another ship through the viewscreen.

"Send a crew out to inspect the wreckage for identifying markings to determine who the ship belongs to. See if there's anything about it — either the weapons residue or anything else — that may tell us who is responsible for destroying that ship," the Captain says, his greenish-brown exoskeleton shining in the light.

The landing struts deploy automatically. The Brozian ship settles onto its steel legs, with a hard thump, kicking up dust and powdery stones, wobbling slightly. Not the best landing.

The landing party analyze the weapons residue on the remains of the ship. It is clear that a Brozian spaceship is responsible. Furthermore, preliminary readings suggest that the little spaceship is a Catusapien reconnaissance vessel, approximately two years old, and with a crew complement of roughly one to three.

The Brozian vessel rises from the planet's surface, flies up through the atmosphere and into space. The vessel moves along the same trajectory as before, continuing at standard orbit speed. The big question the Captain isn't able to answer remains — where is the missing crew, and the cargo spaceship? The Captain strides purposefully across the room from the communications system to the helm, stooping to watch the piloting monitor.

"Now that I think about it, the Catusapien may be to blame for this. Don't underestimate their capabilities," the Captain states.

"I agree, Captain. Where to now?" his second-in-command asks.

After thinking for a minute, the Captain says, "Set a course for the Vlar Station trading port, warp speed now. We'll stop there for maintenance and begin a thorough search for the crew members of the cargo spaceship. See if we can find some answers there."

"Yes, Sir," his second-in-command responds.

As the Brozian vessel continues searching for the missing crew of the cargo spaceship what about Gotham Kitty's family? Are they searching for her? Naturally, they already have. And they've come up dry in all directions. There's nothing more they can do. There are no clues to her whereabouts. There isn't going to be. Gotham Kitty's arrival on Earth is all by chance and no one in her galaxy is aware of the Milky Way Galaxy or of any planets there.

Somewhere in this sector of the galaxy lies the planet Corsettia that has a sufficiently complex biological system. From space, the planet looks like a jewel. When you come out of the reddish-orange layer of clouds, you look up and see a beautiful rose-gold hue sky.

On the outskirts of the city Vanitis, the oldest settlement on the planet's northern continent, are dome huts, one of them belonging to the family of Gotham Kitty. Her name is actually Merlee. Weeks later, Merlee's parents have come to suspect the worst. Lying in their bed, there's a look of distress creasing their brows. They're starting to grudgingly accept the possibility of never seeing their daughter again. She may be dead by now or worse, in captivity by some alien race. The possibilities run through their minds, as they have difficulty falling asleep. They will heal in time. But that is a long time from now.

A young female Catusapien walks by her parents' room, heading down a corridor toward a small bedroom. She's the spitting image of her older sister, Merlee. No question, though she's shorter and not as vibrant.

When she enters the room, she first goes to the window. It's another melancholy evening for her as she stares up at the three small moons hovering in the dark sky, wondering about her sibling's disappearance.

Whiskers twitching, she lets out a piercing long meow, which translates as: "Good night, my sister, wherever you are."

The little Catusapien tries to maintain hope. In her mind she tries to convince herself that there is a slight chance Merlee will return.

Turning away from the window, she crawls into bed, looking at the moons' light coming in through the window. She pulls the dark charcoal blanket up over her shoulders and curls her legs against her chest. Just as she closes her green glowing eyes to sleep, a tear meanders down her cheek.

Epilogue

2061. Tanzania, Africa

FIFTY YEARS LATER, Cassidy Mkama, who is now Cassidy Mshuma, is in her early sixties. A grandmother to two little girls, since her father's passing and ten years since her divorce, she's living in her childhood two-bedroom home on Tengeru Road in Arusha. She's sitting in a hardwood rocking chair on the low porch facing the backyard where her grandkids are playing. She's wearing a long-sleeve, sky blue blouse, long gray tweed skirt and sandals. In her lap is Allison Banes' field notebook.

Cassidy touches the armrest and leans back to rock the chair slowly. Her gaze follows a flock of birds winging their way across the slowly darkening sky across which a crescent of Moon floats. And she wonders about the galaxy beyond our own system. Interstellar travel is still not possible, for some time to come at least, to be nothing more than science fiction. But science fiction often becomes science fact, such as the existence of life in other galaxies, such as Gotham Kitty, an extraterrestrial. She smiles to herself, thinking that.

Laila Diwani, who is now Laila Tarimo, and just as old as Cassidy, is standing under the treehouse. She has two adult children and one grandchild. Her husband is no longer alive and there are times this makes her sad.

"Darius, come down from there," Laila calls loudly.

Seven-year-old Darius sticks his head out the window of the treehouse. "Oh, Grandma. can't I stay a little longer?"

"Come and listen to Ole Cassie. She has a story to tell you."

"About Gotham Kitty?"

"Yes! But first you have to clean up in the bathroom. So, get down here."

"Yeah, I'm coming!" he says excitedly and leaves the window.

Dusk is Cassidy's favorite time of the day. Happy that the glaring heat is over, she watches the sky, remembering those early days, hoping Gotham Kitty will find a way back to her homeworld, but it never happens. As of thirteen years ago, the impressionable alien is dead. Tearfully, Gotham Kitty is merely a memory in her heart.

In the direct path of the moonlight, Cassidy wipes tears from her face with a napkin, unable to stop the emotions. Thinking of her late friend affects her very deeply. It's just that easy for a woman of her age to have sentiments.

A little girl walks up her, holding a glass of lemonade in her hands. "Grandma, do you want a glass of lemonade?"

"Tessie, I certainly do. Why, that is mighty kind of you. You can tell your mother, Elisa, how grateful I am for you bringing it to me," she says, taking the glass from her hand.

"I'll go and tell her now."

"And come on back. I want to tell you a story," she says, then takes a sip of her lemonade.

"Okay, Grandma," Tessie responds, managing a small smile before running into the house.

It's just Gotham Kitty's luck that the governmental authorities don't know anything about her. After months and months of rigorous tests and analysis, government officials and executives of TANAPA determine the escape pod belongs to an insectoid species from another galaxy. A search for an insectoid alien carries on for some months in East Africa. Nothing turns up. The head of the TANAPA's Law Enforcement and Strategic Security Section comes to some conclusions. It is his opinion that more than likely a technical malfunction is the cause of an empty escape pod ejecting from the spaceship just before the explosion. Another possibility is that soon after the insectoid alien leaves the escape pod it dies from lack of nourishment or from an attack by a lion, cheetah, or some other animal. It is a complete mystery to TANAPA executives who end up closing the case.

In the years since her death, Gotham Kitty's arrival on Earth is now the big, exciting story the Chagga tell at night around the campfire. No more singing about the Evil

Shadowy Figure, a mere myth now, according to Laila, who is still a Chagga. Her participation in the ritual that ends the curse of the Evil Shadowy Figure, to this day remains a pivotal moment in her life restoring her faith in being a member of the Chagga.

More than the Chagga, Cassidy enjoys telling the children about Gotham Kitty. And the children don't mind her retelling the story again and again. Kids love fantasy and other-world adventures. When it comes to Gotham Kitty, her story has those qualities. Every chance she gets, she'll show them her 5x7 photos of the alien with herself that she keeps in Allison Banes' field notebook, along with the best of Gotham Kitty's sketches and drawings of her home planet, and other species and planets in the galaxy she comes from. There's even a double photo frame of Gotham Kitty on the side table by the nubby blue sofa in her living room.

Darius comes out of the back door with Laila following slowly behind him. He goes to sit on the porch in front of Cassidy. Laila takes a seat in an identical hardwood rocking chair opposite Cassidy, waiting for her to say something.

"There, there, old girl. You comfortable?" Cassidy asks, looking over at her.

"Somewhat comfortable, Ole Cassie," Laila says with a lift of her shoulders.

Smiling warmly, Cassidy stares at the three children sitting on the porch in front of her. Elisa, her only daughter, turns on the porch light and goes to stand on the left side of her rocking chair.

"Now listen closely to Ole Cassie," Laila says, with a quick nod towards Cassidy.

"Who can tell me about Gotham Kitty?" Cassidy asks them, but not to anyone specific.

Cassidy drinks the rest of her lemonade in one giant gulp, then hands the empty glass to Elisa. She lets her eyes move slowly around. Something of her bright personality comes across in her expression. Staring at the children, she waits. Complete silence.

Nine-year old Tessie raises her hand. She can't wait to tell all that she knows. This is her favorite story, and she tells it many times in substantially the same words.

"Tessie, please enlighten us all," Cassidy says.

"Gotham Kitty is an extraterrestrial, an intelligent being from outer space. A Catusapien to be precise, from the planet Corsettia, which is in another galaxy," Tessie says, smiling widely.

It is something you can expect from Tessie. The girl can recite the story of Gotham Kitty word for word. She is Cassidy's eldest granddaughter. Her five-year old sister, Frances, who is sitting next to her on her left, doesn't fully grasp the story, but she will one day.

"You're right. A magical alien, so kind, and acrobatic, turning a cartwheel and making you laugh," Cassidy says, holding up Allison Banes field notebook with her right hand.

That makes the kids laugh. Cassidy knows she has their full attention. Her energy is infectious. On some level the kids are in awe of her, listening to her every word as if they are under a fairy's spell. Even Laila and Elisa lean in closer to her, listening and watching.

"That's good, Tessie. What else?" Cassidy asks in a gentle way.

Listening quietly, Cassidy smiles again remembering, her late friend Gotham Kitty. Trying to suppress her tears, she looks up at the Moon, then looks down at Tessie, who is still talking enthusiastically about Gotham Kitty. Lastly, she lowers Allison Banes' field notebook to her lap.

ACKNOWLEDGMENTS

The author wishes to thank Vivian Davis, Tutoring Art; Alexis Miller, Purple Shelf Club; and Jesse Otazo for their help in making this work of fiction ring true.

ABOUT THE AUTHOR

ANN GREYSON is the author of the novels *The Lonely Vampire,* a Recommended Read in the 2021 Author Shout Reader Ready Awards and First Place Paranormal in the 2021 Speak Up Talk Radio Firebird Book Awards, and *Never-DEAD* which has the Third Place General Fiction in the 2020 TCK Publishing Reader's Choice Awards. Other writing credits include book reviews for *Goodreads* website, poetry for *The Muse* literary & arts magazine, and theatre reviews for *Talent Magazine.*

She has a passion for creating fictional characters for television, acting in the programs: *i Citizen, SpaceWoman Light-years Apart, Birdwatcher, The Out World, The Lonely Vampire,* and *Never-DEAD*. Ann portrays Allison Banes in *puRR* the story of Gotham Kitty, short television program broadcast on Manhattan Neighborhood Network's Culture Channel 4 in 2018. She is the producer of

Pompilia broadcast on Anne Arundel Community Television, *The Watchers*, a nominee for a VOLLIE Award for Best Local Documentary, and *Gotham Kitty,* a nominee for a VOLLIE Award for Best Arts/Entertainment Program, from Community Media Center TV of Westminster in 2014.

With many dancing credits on stage, she also sings and acts in the music videos: *Shine, O Christmas Tree, House of the Rising Sun, Motherless Child,* and *Buffalo Gals.*

Ann Greyson has an Associate of Arts degree in English from Howard Community College. She is a member of Actors' Equity Association, SAG-AFTRA and the Alpha Alpha Sigma chapter of Phi Theta Kappa. She has the honor of receiving the Albert Nelson Marquis Lifetime Achievement Award from Marquis Who's Who in 2017.

www.ingramcontent.com/pod-product-compliance
Lightning Source LLC
Chambersburg PA
CBHW020918110726
47900CB00001B/194